Belle Canadienne
Canadian Historical Brides - Quebec

Juliet Waldron and Jay Lang

Print ISBNs
Amazon print 9780228632788
Ingram Spark 9780228632795
Barnes & Noble 9780228632801
BWL Print 9780228632818

Copyright 2024 by Juliet Waldron
Editor Victoria Chatham
Cover artist Michelle Lee

Dedication

Books We Love Ltd. dedicates the Canadian Historical Brides series to the immigrants, male and female, who left their homes and families, crossed oceans, and endured unimaginable hardships in order to settle the Canadian wilderness and build new lives in a rough and untamed country.

Acknowledgement

BWL Publishing acknowledges the Government of Canada and the Canada Book Fund for its financial support in creating the Historical Brides of Canada collection.

BWL Publishing acknowledges the Province of Alberta for their ongoing support through the Alberta Publisher's Cultural Industry Operating Grant.

Alberta
Government

Table of Contents

Chapter 1

Jeanne reached the top of the stairs. Her day had begun early. She felt sundown weary as she hefted the basket of fish she'd been bargaining for along the quay. She ought to hurry on to the market, already bustling on the street above, but instead she stepped to one side, set down her basket, and turned into the breeze.

There it was, the cruel, blue-gray sea!

Gulls tumbled through the air above her head. Bolder ones landed nearby, shrieking and quarreling. Thieving beggars. A few edged close to her basket. She knew it was risky to stop. These fish had cost more than expected and she didn't want to lose any of them to these feathered freeloaders. Still, she gazed out at the swells, coming in so steadily now, some tossing frothy manes.

Five years ago, Pierre Dube, her young husband, had signed onto a ship that sailed to the great northern fishing grounds that lay ever so far away to the west across the dark Atlantic. Her father's words had proved prophetic; events had unfolded as he had warned when Jeanne chose a poor sailor instead of one of those *Saintonge* cousins who kept their feet on the ground working the salt marshes.

On his first voyage to the New World, Pierre's ship had been blown off course into a labyrinth of fog and icebergs. According to another, luckier vessel in that same fleet, neither his ship nor the men aboard were ever seen again.

Hard to believe that almost eight years had gone by since Jeanne had left her home in Brouage and come to live with Pierre's family in La Rochelle, the port city that had once seemed so full of excitement and promise. For a few busy, bright years, she'd been a wife and a mother, but now she was neither, just another young widow in a noisy, hard-scrabble town.

As if losing her husband had not been sufficient cruelty, her lovely, active little Michel had died last autumn. He'd followed older boys out onto the rocks and had been taken by a rogue wave. Later, his broken body had been found just a few miles down the coast, during a lull in the autumn gales.

Jeanne felt the familiar hollow pain in her chest, the terrible ache that would never go away. She managed to stifle a painful sob but was unable to hold back the hot tears now coursing down her cheeks. Not wanting anyone to see her, she wiped them away fiercely.

"Jeanne! Wake up!"

Startled, Jeanne spun around to discover that the boldest of the gulls had snatched one of her fish. If it hadn't been for her sister-in-law, Sylvine, who'd come along just in time, the gull would have had his prize. Fortunately for Jeanne, he'd chosen such a heavy fish that he couldn't easily fly off with it.

"Get! You dirty thieves!"

Wielding a stick, Sylvine struck the bird as it stumbled along the boards knocking free his prize. The fish tumbled onto the deck, quivering.

"You greedy bastards!"

Arms wide, Jeanne joined in, stamping and yelling, scattering the feathered pirates, who arose in shrieking protest, leaving a splatter of excrement behind.

Her sister-in-law's face spoke volumes.

There is nothing for you to see among those waves. Trust me, sister, I know.

The Dube's were sick and tired of Jeanne's grief.

Time to get to work again, find a new man, or go back to your rich father in Brouage!

"I've been at our stall for a good half an hour, and here I have to come down, looking for you! Where have you been?"

Sylvine was four years older than Jeanne, and she too had lost a husband to the sea. She'd joined the Dube household when she'd married a second time, now to the oldest of the Dube brothers, Guy.

"Maman is impatient! I hope you found something decent during all that time!"

Sylvine stooped, reclaiming the fallen fish. After dropping it into Jeanne's basket, she signaled Jeanne to hurry. Without a word, she turned and began to haul herself and the baby on her hip up the steps. Jeanne, cursing inwardly, gathered the basket quickly, wiped away her tears on her apron and trudged after her.

Halfway, she paused to toss her shawl around her for the wind was brisk. The gulls, still frustrated, were swirling, fighting, and swooping over her head. White splatter landed on her dress. Laughter from a pair of lay-abouts below who were watching the fracas didn't improve her mood.

"So, you found her!"

Maman Dube looked up, cross as usual, when Jeanne arrived. Jeanne, avoiding her, carried her basket to the far end of the stall and took up a fish knife.

Best to just start cutting mackerel. Anything she said now would just lead to more nasty remarks.

It was a precaution taken in vain. Ten minutes later, after finishing a brief chat with one of the regulars, Madam Dube's shadow fell upon her.

"Henri Bouquat's boat was down there. You weren't wasting your time buying from that old fool again, I hope. "

Yes, Jeanne had seen Perè Bouquat sail in, but she'd already filled her basket and had only spoken to him in passing on her way back. He'd told her before she'd asked, that once again there was no reply to the letter he'd delivered to her perè. "No, my dear," he'd said, and then told her, once again, (at great length!) about his final voyage to New France as a pilot on a cod-fishing vessel. She didn't mind much because he was a friendly face along the pier, a native of the Saintonge like herself.

Jeanne knew that from this spot overlooking the boats her mother-in-law realized full well that the fishermen had arrived with only a small catch today, and everyone looking to purchase had been rushing between boats to buy enough to stock their own stalls.

"The catch was poor today, Madam. Getting the basket full took time. "

A snort was the reply, but--*Bless the Holy Mary*--one of the old witch's best customers summoned her away.

It didn't take long today for the stall to be emptied. Jeanne kept her head down, stayed at the far end, sometimes gutting and cleaning fish to order and, at the same time, looking out for passersby with nimble fingers who might steal something. She dropped a few bits and pieces to the stray cats who slunk by. She'd been scolded for that too a few days ago although the scraps she'd dropped were not fit even for the poorest beggar's pot.

The cats all know me because these days I'm a stray cat too.

She and her mother-in-law had never been close, but since Michel's death, quickly followed by Jeanne's long illness, one that had found her during that winter of incapacitating grief, the woman had grown impatient.

Certainly, Madam Dube had her own troubles. Her husband had once been a fisherman himself, but during the last few years, he'd fallen into debt, and in the end, he'd had to sell his boat to save his home. In his old age, old man Dube was reduced to crewing for others--that is, when he was not down at the inn drinking. The women all had to scramble to pay the bills with their fish trade.

The sun was high now, and already everything worth buying had been sold. It was time to return to the house and begin laundry, childcare, cooking, scullery, whatever task offered itself. Sylvine had already packed up her baby and departed.

"Clean up here, Jeanne, and remember, no charity or those lazy beggars will worry us to death every day. "

Much to Jeanne's relief, after issuing orders, Maman Dube had marched away, back to the crowded house they all shared. Jeanne took a deep breath, straightened, then put her knuckles into her back and stretched. A bucket of salt water tossed over the boards of the stall and a scrape of the boards with an old blade would do the trick for clean-up.

She'd use a broom to push the remaining gut and bone into the gutter. The offal she'd dump at the end of the street, down onto the rocks. Birds and other scavengers--already gathering in anticipation--would clear most of it.

Not much later, Jeanne took a bucket and walked down the steps once again. She needed another bucket of salt water to finish up. She went down the steps and then out across the rocks among the tide pools, for the ocean ran low.

Jeanne walked farther than she really needed to, but she wanted time alone, and she wanted some distance between her and the urchins splashing nearby. Hearing their clamor, she was reminded of her childhood near the Bay of Saintonge, which lay to the south of La Rochelle in the military city of Brouage.

In those days, she'd explored that world between the tides and the salt ponds with siblings and cousins. When they didn't have tasks, they rowed and sailed, fished, and gathered shellfish.

Jeanne was now 23, but today she felt twice as old. It had been months since she'd written to ask her perè to forgive her, to ask if she could come home, but there was still no answer.

The lack of response seemed to signal "no," and now she didn't know what to do. Only one thing was certain, she must soon leave her mother-in-law's house. Feeling desperate, she continued walking along the shore.

These days if her mother-in-law saw her crying, she would accuse Jeanne of "upsetting everyone. " There had been so many tears after her little boy--the last creature she had truly loved--was swept away!

For a time, in the howling winds of winter, while a dark sea pounded the shore, Jeanne was bed-bound, sick with fevers and plagued by nightmares. It was not long after Michel's death M. Dube had gambled away his boat, landing them in deep financial difficulty.

Around Christmas, Madame Dube began to accuse her of malingering, of being a drain on the family. She had lectured Jeanne to "get up and go to Mass, pray for his soul and that of your husband, and then get to work again. In the life everlasting, we will all be together if we are free from sin. Bear your losses as did the Holy Mother. As I myself have done, losing three children of my own. As Sylvine has done when her own husband was lost at sea. Who told you that this is other than a vale of tears?"

Jeanne had heard reoccurring variations over the last six months. Still her tears flowed all too easily although she had learned to hide them as best she could from anyone else.

There was little help in the church either. The priest had said much the same thing. "Are you not a Christian? Have faith, bless God, say your rosary every day and support the Dube's as they are supporting you."

For a time, Jeanne tried swallowing the pain, allowing the smooth beads of the rosary and the circling prayers she recited to calm her.

That rosary of seed and bone!

It had been a gift from her sweet lost Pierre, brought from the Canary Islands—a happy voyage—his first voyage crewing beyond coastal trading. In those days, she had been so happy believing their love, their pleasure in one another would last forever.

Today, she found a deep tide pool, squatted upon the rocks and allowed herself to be drawn into watching the activity in the water. There were sea stars, tiny crabs, ribbons of kelp, and darting fishlings all just below the surface of the wind-ruffled water.

The nearby sea heaved and whispered. She couldn't hear those sounds without a pang of grief as she remembered how Michel had loved playing here among these same rocks. A proper little man, he'd wanted to be a sailor like his father. As small as he was, the changing tides, the ships, sailor's knots, fish—all these things had interested him. Free of any censure, away from everyone, tears came for what else could there be when she remembered her darling boy?

Clouds marched overhead; gulls rode the breeze of the warm June day. For a moment, Jeanne thought she ought to get up and hurry back to the house for afternoon chores.

Then, considering, she wondered why. There was no love in that house for her no matter how helpful she was. The Dube women had always been jealous of her because Jeanne's father was, at least compared to their family, wealthy. The black salt of Brouage was much fancied on noblemen's tables and commanded a high price. Since Pierre had disappeared, and even more after she had fallen into the well of grief and illness last winter, they treated her like an undeserving servant rather than a dutiful daughter-in-law.

After the loss of the family boat, one of the elder daughters, Louise, had moved back to her parents' house with her little ones because her husband had abandoned her. Their little home became even more chaotic. Madam Dube no longer hid her desire that Jeanne return to her family in Brouage.

After all, what was there to keep her in La Rochelle? The grandson had been a fine little fellow, had kept Jeanne anchored in the family, but he was gone now, and Jeanne had never fit in.

"Thinks she's better than us because her papa owns salt ponds. . . "

Jeanne had overheard it more than once. Yes, she'd grown up with more than the Dube's, had learned to read and figure, but after her mother had died, her father had surprised them by taking a new wife, a critical, haughty young widow barely ten years older than Jeanne.

That had made it easier for her to run away with handsome Pierre although both of them were far too young to start a family. Her father had been terribly angry when she'd left, so for a long time, she'd feared to throw herself on his mercy. She'd only done so this spring when it seemed her only course of action. With no message from Brouage, however, it appeared she had nowhere to go.

Right now, she felt too downtrodden even for worry. She said a brief prayer to Mother Mary and then lost herself once more in the little world of the tide pool. So many busy lives going on there—quarrels, flights—as the tiny fish flicked their tails and fled from one another!

"There you are!"

Surprised, Jeanne turned her head. Here was a slender young man coming across rocks, waving, apparently searching for her. He grinned and cried out, "Jeannette! Is that you? It's me, Aubin!"

Could it be? The skinny fellow now saluting her only slightly reminded her of her brother. He had been the tail end of the family, her younger by a scant three years.

He'd been just twelve when she'd run away with Pierre.

Today, here he was though it appeared that even his face had lengthened as had his legs, hairy calves sticking out of patched culottes. Dark hair blew around his face, just like hers, but on this day, he was clearly a grown man sporting a patch of stubble.

"Aubin?" Jeanne stood up in a rush.

"Dear sister!"

As he stepped forward, she opened her arms. It was not only good to see him, but hope flooded her heart! Was this the good news she'd been praying for?

Aubin embraced her, warmly, a little awkwardly. It was strange to think of so many years gone by and the changes in both of them.

He smelled of sweat, tar, and salt, but she didn't care. He'd been her baby brother, a chubby fellow she'd cared for and petted when her mother was too busy with the family business. Jeanne realized she herself probably stank of fish after a morning tending the Dube stall.

"I'm taller than you now. "

"And no doubt stronger too. " She smiled up at him, and he beamed. He seemed quite pleased with himself for finding her.

"I've come from our perè," he said. "He's had your letter, but he was not certain how to reply. But when I was about to sail for La Rochelle, he called me to him and asked me to find you. "

She looked up hopefully, but the way his face clouded at her unspoken question made her eyes fill even before his reply. Aubin was quick to forestall her fears.

"Oh, Jeanette, he <u>does</u> want you home, but--but--as you can imagine, Marie-Barbe is not pleased, and they have quarreled about it. He did not write because he was not certain what to say. You have lost so much-- both your husband and your little boy."

Well, well! Jeanne thought. At first, all those years ago, Marie-Barbe had wormed her way into Jeanne's confidence. She'd even encouraged her to run away with Pierre. The new wife had put on a kind face and said, "I will make it right with your father," but with time, Jeanne had come to realize that had been a lie.

When Jeanne had written to her perè after the birth of Michel, she'd received only a note, one written by Marie-Barbe, which had said that "my husband" remained very angry and did not want to hear from his daughter anymore.

Afterward, her only contact with family had been with one of her older brothers, Laurent, who occasionally came through La Rochelle on trade matters. She'd heard that Marie-Barbe, despite her exemplary housewifery and fawning attention to their father, also spent a great deal of energy creating division among his children. Laurent and his wife and children had even moved from the spacious family home to an apartment inside the family's warehouse.

Aubin reached into a pocket and produced a folded piece of paper with the family seal. "This is from Perè. "

The paper was lined and cracked as if it had been crunched into a ball but later smoothed out, refolded, and then sealed. Slowly, filled with dread, Jeanne studied her brother's young face before breaking the wax that sealed the note.

"Marie-Barbe tried to destroy it, but I caught her. " Aubin sighed. "This is how it is at home. When I showed our father that she'd tossed his letter onto the hearth, he was very angry. He now says that now he regrets--regrets--many things he's done in the past. "

Feeling a little braver, Jeanne nodded and slowly unfolded the ill-treated paper.

Ma chère fille, I am saddened that you are now in such straits with a family which once seemed so welcoming. This is a cruel world, my dear child, as now you must know. Le Bon Dieu sends us many trials before we finally come to rest in his arms, but you have had more than your share of misfortune for such a young woman, losing a husband and a son.

Aubin will tell you how things are in our home. I must confess, dear child, that I wronged you when I disowned you. You were very young when you fell in love with

Pierre Dube. Love makes fools of young people easily. In the last few years, however, I have learned that love makes fools of both young and old alike. "Marry in haste and repent at leisure" is an old saying, but I have myself learned that it is sometimes a bitter truth.

You may return home, dear one, for I am still Master here. I have arranged passage for you with my old friend Captain Labonte, with whom your brother Aubin crews. I will never be guilty of abandoning a child born to me and to your Mother of Blessed Memory.

Jeanne, when you left us, you understood all that a woman should know of house and garden, and about the salt, our livelihood. You had even then an understanding of our work, and there is always a place here for those who work for this family.

Come home to us at once, my dear Jeannette . ~~ Henri Joly

A gust of wind came down the shore. In the harbor, ships rose and fell on the glittering ocean. Jeanne inhaled the salt air so deeply she could taste it in the back of her mouth. She felt as if she'd been on a ship stranded at sea waiting for a homeward wind. Now,it was as if the sails of her ship had caught a fresh breeze.

Becalmed no more!

Aubin took her hand.

"Come dear Sister. I will go with you to collect your things. We will sail for home when the tide turns again. "

Sun was slanting low as they went up and into the town. Jeanne thought they were the lightest steps she'd taken in months.

Supper was done when they arrived at the Dube house where the smell of cabbage and sauteed fish hung in the air. The room was in turmoil, as usual. Maman Dube was shouting at the children and at Sylvine. Two little boys were fighting with one another rolling on the floor, but everything stopped when Jeanne came in with skinny Aubin at her back. The little ones stared at her, mouths agape.

Looking around the room, Jeanne saw no sign of M. Dube. No doubt he'd already escaped to one of the wine shops near the docks.

Maman Dube drew herself up and said, "Where have you been Jeanne? Supper is long past." Not giving Jeanne any time to reply, she continued, her voice taking on a strident tone as she looked Aubin up and down.

"We have nothing left for some free-loaders. Who is this fellow?"

"This is my brother, Aubin Joly. He has come to take me home to my father in Brouage. We have come to collect my things. "

As she spoke, Jeanne's lips twisted into a bitter smile for now the old woman's mouth, too, fell open. She'd never dreamed of such a swift turn of events.

Jeanne took advantage of the silence to lead her brother through the kitchen toward the room she shared with Marie-Louise and her children.

They could hear the gabble of voices behind them, but Madam Dube quickly recovered herself and followed, her wooden clogs slapping against the flagstone floor.

"You better not take anything more than you came with."

Quickly, Jeanne rounded on her. "All that I loved that might have been said to also belong to you, Madam, is dead and gone. This house has nothing I want, only what I brought with me."

Amazed at her own outburst and the fire in her chest, she seized Aubin's hand and continued to her room without another word. The last room was against the back wall of the house; Jeanne's room was long and narrow. Marie Louise and her children used the bed where Jeanne and Pierre had slept, and, after, where Jeanne and Michel-- had once cuddled together.

There was a single small window framing the other occupant of the backyard, an old, bent pear tree. Beneath the light the window provided was a sturdy shelf, built there as a workspace for a seamstress who had once cut cloth upon it. Now with a straw mattress and linen, that served as Jeanne's bed, and devilish cold it had been this last winter with no one to keep her warm.

Jeanne felt a pang as she stooped beneath the door to enter for she remembered how perfect this room had seemed when she had first lived here with Pierre.

The few gnarled limbs left on the pear had been in bloom on that May Day when she'd first arrived with her husband, and spring was in the air.

In the space under the shelf was the little box she'd brought with her. Upon it she stacked some folded undergarments, two caps, and two pairs of stockings. Two hooks nearby held most of her clothing: another work shirt, another apron, and her best skirt and apron, the clothes she wore to church.

Aubin, recognizing the box, pulled it out. Though made of wood, it was not large and he could easily carry it. Jeanne removed the linen from the straw mattress.

Madame Dube followed them, bending her head under the low doorsill and then straightening up just inside. Her arms were crossed, her eyes narrowed.

Aubin, on his knees now, opened the trunk. Inside were a well-worn winter shawl, a pair of heavy woolen shirts, and a much-patched shirt. Underneath was a woollen blanket. Jeanne folded her linen quickly and passed it to Aubin who tucked it into the box.

She took the clothes on the hook next. Hands busy, folding and putting away didn't take long. Next, she laid out a rough hemp and wool blanket and stacked what wouldn't go into the trunk upon it. Wordlessly, she and her brother wrapped that up and secured it with a large knot.

Aubin stood up and shouldered the trunk. Madam Dube waited by the door looking as if formulating a final insult, but could not quite do it, especially when one of Marie-Louise's little girls pushed around her, ran up to Jeanne, and embraced her skirts.

"Are you leaving, Tante Jeanne?"

"Yes, Anne-Marie, I am. " Jeanne bent to stroke the little girl's dark curls.

"Will you go far away?"

"To my home in Brouage, to be with my family. "

Anne-Marie seemed puzzled, but Jeanne forestalled any further questions by lifting the child up and kissing her chubby cheeks.

"Good-bye, dear Anne Marie! Be a good girl now and help your Mama. "

She set the child down, for Madame Dube approached, a cross look on her face. She snatched the child up from the floor possessively.

"Give Grandmere a kiss, Anne-Marie!"

Anne made a face and pushed against her grandmother's bosom.

"Anne-Marie! Stop that!"

A smack followed, which, naturally, brought tears.

Jeanne picked up her bundle and without even a glance pushed past Madam Dube and the weeping child. Aubin, trunk on his shoulder, followed.

Away through the rooms they went, passing Marie Louise coming to find out what her daughter was crying about, and past the other children, until, finally, they were standing on the muddy, broken cobbles of the street outside.

Jeanne didn't realize how quickly she was walking until Aubin spoke.

"Slow down, Jeanette. You don't know where we are going, remember?"

Jeanne, breathing hard, came to a stop. She could see his young face in the fading light, his worried smile.

"You were in the same kind of hurry to leave us, I remember. "

"Do not remind me!" Jeanne lifted her chin and shook her head, hoping more of those stupid tears would not come. "So, where are we going then?"

"The ship is moored near where the careenage starts. There are some cook shops there, too, and we can have supper. "

"I have no money, Aubin, and I know full well that you sailors have little. "

"Don't worry. The money is father's. We shall eat and then sail later, with the tide.

The reloading goes on now, but I was excused so that I could fetch you. "

Although it was past supper time, many people still came and went around them. There were traders, sailors, groups of women carrying baskets with vegetables, with bolts of cloth or a few loaves of bread, the remains of the day's trade being toted home as well as passing groups of somber businessmen in black gowns. Scraps of conversation rose around them. Arguments and general chatter hung in the air.

Everyone, Jeanne thought, is engaged in their lives. Some, like us, have not yet had their supper. Hawkers collected the remains of their goods preparing to go home for the night. The light was passing, but slowly as it did in June.

Jeanne was dazed by what was happening, how eight years of her life, a whole chapter -- one which had begun in a wild-bird escape and ended with heartbreaking loss -- were, at this very moment, being left behind.

The stall the Dube's worked lay far behind her as they approached the far end of the stone quay and stepped onto a rough path. Before them, among the flat rocks and the stretches of muddy sand, lay boats turned onto one side, their bottoms heavy with barnacles and sea-life, like beached whales. Carpenters, done for the day, were stepping down from scaffolds set against the ships, where heavy planks were being scraped, repaired, and tarred anew.

"There is the *Denise*." Aubin pointed to a pinnace of middling size, now surrounded by small, heavily loaded boats. On board, men could be seen hauling nets filled with goods onto the deck. "I will get you out there soon, but first let's go higher and find that cook shop Captain Labonte favors. "

Jeanne's belly ached and her feet were hurting. The bundle was growing heavier by the minute. Before them the lights of torches appeared amid bustle and chatter. Cooking smells floated around them—fish, of course --and wood smoke, which stung her eyes. The Sailor's Inn, really not more than a ramshackle one- storey shack, was just ahead.

Jeanne and Pierre, in the old days between voyages, would occasionally come there just to get out of the crowded Dube house and to pretend for an hour or so that they were still courting. Wine, bread, goat cheese, maybe even a bowl of whatever fish stew was on the fire that night, and they'd feel ever so happy just to be together. Here they met others, as they shared the long tables. In those days, Jeanne was shy, and she mostly just listened to sailor's tales, quarrels, and such like, while her husband laughed with his friends or shipmates. Pierre loved to play the married man. He also loved to show her off, "My beauty from Brouage," which one of his friends had amended to "The dark-haired beauty of Brouage," a salute that always left her blushing.

Few of these acquaintances were married themselves, and one by one they had drifted away up the coast or down, or vanished on long, far more profitable voyages east. It felt strange to be at the cook shop again, after so much time and so much loss.

"There's Captain Labonte." Aubin gestured at a large man wearing a feathered hat who sat at the head of a table. Around him sat a group of older men, broad bodies canted forward, deep in discussion. Lower down, Jeanne also saw a few young sailors. Two brightly dressed women of the town joked with them hoping to do some business.

One of the sailors, a short, wiry fellow with a tidy black beard, waved at her brother. "Hey, Aubin! Here you are at last!" He stood with alacrity and then hopped over the bench like a boy, his white teeth flashing against his bronzed skin as he greeted them. Her brother lifted a hand in return.

"Bonjour, Rene! Here we are, my friend. "

The man was not much taller than Jeanne. In the wavering torchlight, she saw that he'd survived the pox, but the beard covered his scars well.

"Rene Mesny is our pilot. This is my sister, Madame Jeanne."

Rene nodded politely. "Pleased to meet you. Your brother has spoken of nothing but returning you to the house of your father. When the tide turns, Madame, we will row you out to *The Denise*. Allow me to take that bundle, and we will find you a place at the table."

His leathery hands reached up. Jeanne was happy to relinquish the unwieldy parcel. Her shoulder ached from the day's work. She sighed and rubbed her collarbone, while Rene swung the parcel across his shoulder as if it was filled with eider down.

The sailors at the foot of the table, she realized, had turned their gaze toward her.

"Leroux, Pouisson! Down to the shore, the pair of you. Find Cadot; learn what he needs done. Make room for this lady. "

Arising at once, despite their curious expressions, the men stood and stepped away making room for her and Aubin. As Jeanne approached the table, modestly lowering her gaze, discarded fish bones and mussel shells crunched under her clogs.

The table was, as was usual in such places, covered with bits of bread and slops of broth and wine. While Rene set her bundle down on a bench, Aubin politely used a well-worn handkerchief to sweep crumbs and bones from the table. Not much later, a steaming bowl of fish stew appeared as well as a new loaf. Jeanne gratefully stuck a spoon into this and turned all her attention to that long-delayed supper.

How strange that this ramshackle inn, the first place they visited on the night her new husband had brought her to La Rochelle eight years past, was now to become the site of her departure. Sighing, she returned her attention to the stew.

At the head of the table, the Captain took his leave of the traders and started the walk down to the shore. It was time to check on the progress of the loading. He called for Aubin to accompany him.

"Good-bye sweet sister. I will see you on the ship."

The rest of the company retreated from the Sailor's Inn which was, minute by minute, growing ever more rowdy inside. Only one gentleman remained, meditatively puffing on a clay pipe. Jeanne used her spoon to sort through the last of the bones and shells at the bottom of the bowl. The fishy buttery fragrance hovered in the air, and she thought that she could have eaten a second bowl with ease.

She turned her gaze toward the port where lights still shone along the harbor and reflected on the ever-vibrant surface of the ocean. The last trader knocked out his pipe and stood. To her surprise, he walked toward her. After lifting his hat politely, he drew out the chair beside hers.

"Good evening, Madame. "

Jeanne, not knowing what to think, simply replied in kind.

"Bonsoir à vous, monsieur. "

"Allow me to introduce myself. I am Captain Abel Martin, supplier to The Company de Canadien. I will soon be doing business with the salt merchants of Brouage. I understand your father, Monsieur Joly, is among them, and that you are journeying there yourself. "

"Indeed I am, monsieur. Going home at last. "

"I also understand that you are a widow. "

"Yes, Monsieur, for some years now. My husband was on a ship bound for New France but never arrived home again. All hands were presumed lost. "

"Alas! You are so young. "

Jeanne did not quite know how to react. One part of her felt the elder gentleman presumptuous to have struck up a conversation as well as opening with such a painful subject. Another part simply felt happy to have company. She had been a little worried that she had been left alone in such a notorious place as Sailors Inn.

"I have sailed to New France several times myself," he continued, "but the journey is perilous especially early in the year when icebergs big as mountains fill the northern oceans. Many ships have been lost on those seas, both ours and those of the Basques and Portuguese who have been fishing in those waters for many years and know them well. "

"Will you travel there again this year, monsieur?"

"I will because I have business in Montreal. I have a son in that wilderness, trading on my account for furs, and a business partner. The colony has not managed to produce salt in any quantity, so salt is always in high demand there. "

"My father and his associates sell fine black salt as I am sure you know. "

"Yes, and there is a demand for that even in New France. The Holy Fathers insist upon their pleasures as do the noblemen in the military. "

This struck Jeanne as a rather dismissive way to refer to the clergy, and then she was struck by the thought that although monsieur Martin was dressed in the conservative manner of a merchant, he was quite remarkably somber in color and style. She wondered if he might be a secret Huguenot as her own grandparents had been.

During her childhood, she'd understood that her grandparents had secretly practiced this faith though the Joly family no longer wished to remember that. Her father went with his wife and children to Mass regularly.

"To be like everyone else is simple and safe," he'd said. "For even the good Duke Henri of Navarre, God rest his soul, knew that to be France's King he himself would have to accept the Catholic religion. "

La Rochelle had once been full of Huguenots, many of them craftsmen and merchants. Jeanne passed their chapel regularly during her years there. She knew some people still worshipped there, but to be a dissenter was increasingly dangerous. In 1627, the city had tried to rebel against Cardinal Richelieu and the young King, Louis XIII. The outcome had been a disastrous siege, 14,000 citizens of La Rochelle had died and the survivors fled to other countries. Jeanne had been taught to read with a Huguenot Bible, but that was, of course, nothing she ever told anyone. Jeanne had taken to heart her Perè's warning, given to all his children,

Her memories were interrupted when her companion asked, "Do you know anything about New France?"

"Almost nothing, except that it is full of savages and the furs are very desirable, Monsieur. "

"It is a most astonishing place. I am impressed beyond measure on every journey I've taken there. It is full of the largest trees I've ever seen, a commodity that is much in demand here--and in all of Europe. But it is also a wild place, for those mighty forests harbor a very dangerous and warlike people. Their ways are as different from ours as those of *le peuple de l'Inde*, and they give no quarter when they fight. We have built some forts and towns along the great river that empties into the sea but have not been as ambitious as those of the English and the Dutch, who have colonies further south where it is warmer. It is indeed a New World."

The Captain talked on and on about this distant New World, painting a vivid picture of the wilderness and telling stories about his fur-trading enterprise in Montreal, and the voyageurs and trappers who supplied him. Jeanne was half-asleep because it was growing late, but her companion was a wonderful storyteller. Beyond them, the ocean grew louder, more of a presence as the tide came in.

A steady stream of carts piled with barrels and casks made their way past to be unloaded and then lowered into longboats that made their way out through the surf to The Denise.

"We came in late this afternoon, and there was no place to tie up at the docks," Captain Martin said. "Captain Labonte was delayed at Saint Nazaire. My sister, Agathe, is on board with me, but she decided against disembarking. We are going to visit family friends in Brouage because Agathe has decided to emigrate and marry that partner of mine, Benoit de Couage, in Quebec. When I next sail from La Rochelle it will be August, and she will sail with me. My dear sister, most probably, will never see France again, so now she wants to visit her friend, Mademoiselle Biscornet, say her farewells."

A momentary sadness flowed across his lined features, and Jeanne understood that the Captain truly cared for this sister.

"You shall meet Agathe on the morrow. "

"I will be honored, Monsieur Captain. I hope you will not be offended, sir, but I must put my head down. I am very tired. I hope that you will not leave me here alone for this place gets less respectable as the evening wears on. "

"Certainly, Madam, I will not be offended. Have no fear. I intend to stay with you. "

His voice went on, while Jeanne, reassured, put her head down on her arms.

Later, she awoke, pins and needles everywhere. Beside her was Aubin. Someone picked up her bundle and Aubin took the trunk. Good as his word, the Captain had remained, and he was the one who helped her to stand and then offered her his arm. Still half asleep, bones aching, she walked across the stony beach and was lifted into the longboat by Aubin, who'd then set the trunk in at her feet.

Jeanne barely remembered the rest of the night or the following day although images flowed past her weary eyes. There was salt spray as the boat was launched, buffeting through the low surf and splashed from the rowers' oars. Then she was hoisted into the boat in a net. When she'd protested that she "wasn't a donkey" and that she could still climb a rope ladder, everyone, including the Captain, had insisted that she go up in the net.

Aubin had chuckled and said, "I can see you have not changed, dear Jeanette, but I am to bring you safe home to Perè and not drown you in La Rochelle harbor. So, for tonight, a donkey you shall be!"

While she was lifted, she'd been glad to be seated, skirts held tight about her knees, in the cargo net. The vessel Denise was taller than she'd appeared from the shore. Captain Martin himself was on deck to help Jeanne onto her feet.

The older man had surprised her. Though gray about the temples, he apparently remained agile and strong. From the rocking longboat, he'd climbed the rope ladder up the side of the ship swiftly like a much younger man.

The next surprise was that Captain Martin showed her down a ladder and then escorted her to his sister's cabin. It seemed it had been determined there was floor space available there between his sister and her maid. Captain Martin explained that the space she had been slated to occupy, a kind of cupboard beneath the stairs, had been accidentally piled high with trunks.

There was a small commotion when their lantern light shone through the cramped room, but it appeared that the occupants had known they would have a new companion. Exhausted, and after wrapping herself in her cloak and kicking off her wooden clogs, Jeanne had dropped to the floor and slept.

The next morning, her roommates awoke and carefully stepped around her. They'd put on their skirts, slipping them on over the undergarments in which they'd slept. Jeanne, aching, still tired, opened her eyes and then shut them again. Embarrassed and suddenly aware of how ragged her clothing was, she wasn't certain exactly what she should do. One of the women she'd seen earlier was very tall, wore a severe expression. The other, the one she took to be the maid, was stout and gray. With very few words, they'd helped one another into their jackets and then departed.

What had happened in the last 24 hours after the years as a poor sailor's wife and widow were now behind her. Jeanne still felt tired and a little queasy.

The ship beneath her rose and fell against the lively swell. She could hear the sailors at their tasks, the sound of someone hammering down below, while above there was shouting, feet hurrying up and down the deck. Without meaning to, Jeanne fell back to sleep.

The door to the tiny cabin opened and the stout woman, the one she'd seen earlier, appeared.

"Ah! Your eyes are open, Madam. I have brought a little water so you can wash before you go up. Mademoiselle Martin is on deck now and she wonders if you will come up to her."

"Yes. I would be very happy too. Thank you for your kindness--Madam. . . ?"

"I am Madam Manie and I travel with Mademoiselle Martin."

The woman held out a small jug of water. Jeanne clambered to her feet and accepted it. She still felt dizzy. There was an odd buzzing in her ears. Perhaps, she thought, it is simple exhaustion.

"That little cabinet by the wall holds the basin and the slops." The woman bent and indicated the doors. "You will pardon me, my dear, but I must go up now in case my Mademoiselle requires me." Slowly and after several hesitations made necessary by the waves, she made her way to the door and then through it.

Jeanne was grateful for the privacy and the water. As she went towards the basin, the vessel lurched. From the deck came shouts and then a thump and laughter as someone lost their footing. She hoped it wasn't Madam Manie who had seemed most unsteady on her feet.

Jeanne poured the tepid water out, and then rested her hands in the bowl.

Examining her hands, she was repelled by how brown and freckled the skin was and how broken and dirty her nails. She knew that she and her skirt probably smelled like fish--at least to those who didn't spend their days cleaning and handling them. She was beyond grateful that before she'd left the Dube home, she'd thought to change to a fresh apron. Now, she splashed her face and washed her hands as well as she could in the little basin and dried them on the apron.

The ship gave another bounce and water spilled. Quickly, she opened the cabinet and then poured the basin into the slop bucket. As soon as that was done, she closed and latched the door, so that it would remain upright inside. As she stood, she noticed a narrow metal mirror fastened to the wall. She moved forward and peered into it, studying herself as well as she could in the twilight of the tiny cabin.

How lined my face! How rumpled my clothes!

She removed her cap, smoothed her hair and then put it back on again before going out and up the ladder, careful to hold on tightly. The ship must, she thought, be tacking its way out to sea.

When she arrived on deck, it did not take long to see Mademoiselle Agathe, thin and very tall for a woman with a wispy halo of fair curls blowing around her cap. She stood with a hand on the rail, gazing at the ocean but turned as the older woman at her side touched her arm and said something.

Overhead the sails were noisy, bellying full. The sailors were busy, scrambling here and there overhead with astonishing ease. The ship must have laid on more sail.

Jeanne had to pause to steady herself and get a feel for how the ship breasted the waves before she made her way to the rail. She still felt lightheaded from the night on the floor and the rush of events.

When she came close, she managed to bob a curtsey and said, "I thank you so much for kindly allowing me to sleep in your room last night, Mademoiselle. That was very kind."

"I wouldn't think of allowing the daughter of one of the gentleman salt sellers of Brouage to travel below. "

Jeanne smiled. It had been a long time since whose daughter she was had mattered to anyone.

"Mademoiselle, nevertheless, I must thank you again for your kindness. As you can see, these days, I am only a poor sailor's widow. " She knew her apron was wrinkled but more or less clean; however, the same could not be said of the rest of her clothing.

"Ah, but your worthy father is bringing you home again. I learned something of your hardships from our good Captain Labonte and my brother as we walked the deck earlier." Agathe offered her a long thin hand. It was white and clean, but the middle finger

41

had a bump and was ink stained. Jeanne thought that Agathe must, like so many women of the merchant class, keep the books for someone in her family, perhaps for her brother the Captain.

"Come! You must be hungry, my dear. I will take you to the saloon to break your fast with wine and fruit. "

Jeanne turned to Madam Manie, who nodded.

"Come along, I insist. Manie, please take her other arm and we can all go together. "

Agathe caught Jeanne's free hand and began to walk steadily across the actively swaying deck. Clearly, she had taken many ocean voyages with her brother. Madam Manie was having a harder time, so Jeanne assisted, helping to keep her upright as best as she could. Spray flew around as they maneuvered their way forward to Captain Labonte's salon.

As her eyes adjusted to the low light within, Jeanne saw bread, wine, water, and glasses, all contained in boxes set into purpose-made grooves in the wooden table. In another, there was a round of goat cheese surrounded by rolls. It was somewhat quieter once they were inside, and there seemed to be less motion as if they had found a smooth coastal current to ride.

"You aren't feeling sick are you?" Agathe asked. When Jeanne shook her head, she turned her attention to her companion. "Sit,

Manie. Poor dear. " She patted the older woman's shoulders. "The ocean will be calmer now. I believe our Captain has found his current. "

Jeanne did not wait to be asked but cut cheese and took a roll. Despite the swaying, at the sight of food, she was suddenly hungry.

"That's right," said Agathe, smiling slightly. "Go ahead. We have eaten. "

Jeanne picked up a glass for wine and indicated that she would pour it for her companions. Madame Manie declined, but Agathe nodded, and Jeanne served her first.

"Water?"

"Yes, please. "

She added water to both glasses. She handed one to Agathe, who smiled. The ship rose and fell regularly now, but Jeanne had no trouble staying upright. She had sailed ever since she'd been little. She feared drowning, naturally, but she had always relished the flying sensation of being under sail with her brother Laurant, their little boat scudding before the wind. It was a pleasure of their childhood when they had sometimes sailed as far out as the Isle de Re.

"Mademoiselle, pardon me, but I must go out again to the deck. I don't feel at all well. "

Jeanne arose again, ready to help the older woman, but Madam Manie, pale of face, gestured her away.

"I can manage by myself, thank you," she said. "I feel a little--unsettled. "

"Please, be careful, dear one," said her employer, "and do not hesitate to return to the cabin if you must. You know I will be fine by myself. If it gets any rougher, please, go below at once and do not worry about me. You know I am a good sailor. "

By themselves now, Jeanne dipped a crust in the wine and then slowly chewed it, grateful for the good bread. Agathe quietly sipped and studied her.

"You do not get seasick?"

"No," Jeanne replied, carefully though, because her mouth was full of biscuit. "At least, not until the sea grows very rough. I often went with my older brothers, and they were excellent sailors. We would sail down the canal and then out to picnic on one of the islands after Mass. "

"Did you ever sail with your husband?"

"When I left my father's house and went with him to La Rochelle. " Jeanne smiled at the bright memory of that little voyage. *How happy they had been!*

"Of course, after that, my husband was often away in the coasting trade, and I had little time for play as I went to work with his mother. Soon enough, I had my little son, too, as well as work in the fish market. Naturally, I helped my mother-in-law in the house and with her younger children. There were nets to mend in the evenings for the

Dube's had a little fishing boat in the early days of my marriage. "

"Ah! Did their boat come to grief?"

"In a way. " Jeanne sighed. "Perè Dube fell into debt and his boat was forfeit. My husband's family had many misfortunes. I did, too, for I lost first my dear Pierre on his first voyage to the Grand Banks. Then, just last autumn, I lost my darling boy. He followed his friends too close to the sea and a great rogue wave came and carried him away. "

Jeanne could not help the tears that still came all too easily. As she wiped them away with a corner of her apron, her elegant companion touched her shoulder with gentle sympathy.

"So much sorrow for one so young! Well, well! I shall pray that loss and grief will follow you no more. I am sure your Perè will be happy to have such a hard-working daughter at home. "

Jeanne sent up a prayer of her own that this would prove true.

"And you Mademoiselle? Your brother, the kind Captain, told me that you are bound for New France as soon as this voyage is done, that there is a gentleman waiting to marry you in the colony there. You are very brave to venture so far!"

When Agathe looked surprised, Jeanne worried that she had presumed too much upon a scant acquaintance, but in the next moment, a slight smile appeared on the woman's long, angular face.

"That gentleman is a business partner of my father's and I shall keep his books. He writes that he has a store in Quebec. Younger men of the company maintain a trading post at the island of Ville Marie where the best fur may be obtained. Monsieur de Couage is older, but not by much. He was in and out of our house for many years before he emigrated, so he is no stranger to me. And," she added, with the hint of a smile, "my Perè knows he can trust me to keep an eye on our interests. "

Jeanne nodded. She had been taught how to keep books by her mother, who had once done the task for her father until her health had grown too poor. Older brothers Laurant and Mathieu had taken on much of the day-to-day work by the time she'd run away. Mathieu kept the books and Laurant oversaw the laborers at the salt ponds and at the port. Merchants still come to her Perè to do business though. She wondered what the situation was now, eight years later.

"Your brother mentioned that you would be visiting a friend in Brouage. "

"Yes. My dear friend, Gillette, who is now Madame Biscornet. We were in school together at Poitou. "

Jeanne remembered the Biscornet family, but they were of higher rank, the kind of people who sat in the front at Mass. She thought that Captain Martin must be a very successful merchant indeed if these were the kind of people with whom he and his sister associated.

"Let us go out to the deck again and walk a little. It will be more congenial than this little room now that the waves have calmed. "

Following the lead of her companion, so tall that she had to duck under the door as they went out, Jeanne wondered why such a well-to-do person would bother to take any interest in her humble self.

The sea was truly calmer now, the rolling regular. They walked where they could, moving around the sailors busy at their work. The business of tacking completed, the level of activity was slower although rope was being coiled. A young lad, thin and wiry, had been set to scrub the deck. From the sour smell that arose as they passed the place, Jeanne knew someone had recently vomited.

"Poor Manie," her companion said. "She is not a good sailor, though, heaven knows, she and I have sailed many times together. I shall be leaving her in my brother's household when I depart at the end of August. She would only suffer in New France. Adventures do not suit her. "

They paused by the rail to admire the gray-green ocean. A fresh breeze blew salt spray in her face, but Jeanne did not mind, nor did her companion. There were a few clouds along the horizon, but none looked threatening. Gulls flew above hopefully following the vessel.

"I have been fortunate and comfortable in my life, but for several years now, I have also been restless, strangely anxious and unsatisfied like a wild bird new-placed in a cage. Agathe turned, her intelligent, pale eyes on Jeanne as she spoke.

"When Monsieur de Couage sent his proposal to my brother, I was surprised, certainly, but not at all alarmed by the notion. At first, my brother Marcel cautioned me, speaking at length of the hardships and dangers of New France, of the cruel savages and the terrible long winters, but that evening I prayed to Our Lady to discover what course I should take. Do you know, Jeanne, Our Lady answered me! As I knelt before the altar in my room, the votive flame leapt high, and I heard a clear voice telling me to accept his offer. " Agathe lifted her chin proudly as she spoke; her plain face glowed with excitement.

Weary as she was, Jeanne was thrilled by the story. She prayed often, yes, and most sincerely, too, to The Holy Mother, but she had never received the blessing of an answer!

"Oh, Mademoiselle. That was surely a miracle. May your voyage and your life hereafter be a fortunate one!" At the same time the hair-raising tales she'd heard about the savages that lived in the new colony crept like shadows around her enthusiasm for Agathe's tales of a holy visitation.

Jeanne hardly knew how to react to all the emotion flowing across her companion's features. It seemed cruel to speak of the infamous story of Father Jogues who had been horribly maimed and tortured by his savage captors. He had escaped, returned to France, and even been given a dispensation to officiate at Mass despite the fact that he'd lost a thumb and index finger. Still Father Jogues had resumed his Canadian mission among those self-same savages.

This was only the first of the intimate conversations Jeanne had with Agathe. For the next few days of their voyage south, they spent most of the time together. Madame Manie did not seem to be jealous. In fact, that lady stayed a great deal in the cabin. Jeanne fell easily into helping Mademoiselle dress and undress and tend to the other small things the lady required. She found that her companion liked to talk about herself and found listening enjoyable.

Mademoiselle Martin had had an interesting life at least compared to the usual conversations Jeanne heard. It was not about babies and husbands, relatives or sewing projects, but about besting her brothers in games of archery, about her horse and her hunting dogs, about traveling with her father and brother to far-off places, to Spanish and Portuguese ports, and to the north as well, as far as Germany.

Her late father had wanted her to marry a widowed business partner who lived in Bruges, next a Rochelais merchant, or at various times, a merchant of Le Havre and most recently one of St. Nazare, but finding his clever daughter a mate had always foundered for one reason or another. Agathe even confided she'd had a private disappointment in love, but Jeanne quickly learned that Mademoiselle Martin was not the kind of woman who pined.

She shrugged and said, "I am so tall, you see, and neither sufficiently pretty nor wealthy enough to attract the sort of husband my father wished for me. "

"You know bookkeeping, and surely that is an asset. " Jeanne had seen her companion at the salon desk, accounts book open, pen in hand, talking trade with her brother.

"Oh, I have been good at that for as long as I can remember! My dear Maman taught me. She was a fine teacher. She wrote collection letters, too, the kind that were speedily effective. Perè would laugh and ask how she'd got those men to pay after he and his clerks had tried and failed. I miss Maman very much. She is not dead, though, you see," she forestalled Jeanne, who was on the verge of offering condolences, "but wandering in her wits. Such an end for our kind Maman is very sad for all of us. "

Sometimes at night they'd stand on deck together, and Mademoiselle would name stars and tell Jeanne the stories of gods from long ago that were connected to them. Some she'd learned from her sailor husband, but Jeanne thought this lady was the most interesting person she'd ever met.

Then the day came when *The Denise* reached the bay that held the canals through the marshes leading to her home, Brouage. The town was embedded in those wide, meandering salt marshes, so the ship dropped anchor in the bay. They would be rowed there by longboat.

From that distance, the town seemed to float amid the morning mist, which lingered even after sunrise. The walled city that had once seemed so large now appeared low and small after life in the larger, bustling seaport of La Rochelle. Marshes stretched away on either side, but even from here, floating far out in the bay, she could hear thousands of birds all of them chorusing as they greeted another day. Soon, Jeanne would see her family again! The idea filled her with a twisting mixture of apprehension and childlike longing.

The storks had already flown south, leaving forlorn nests behind in the trees. It was now August -- nearly eight weeks after her arrival home -- and Jeanne had walked away from Brouage far into the marshes. This was her last day at home, perhaps, forever. Hard to believe! Much had happened in the two months she'd rejoined her family.

On the day of her return, she'd been rowed to the quay beneath one of the brick arches that opened directly into the city. Her father and Laurent had been there to meet her.

How much older her Perè appeared!

Monsieur Joly was well-dressed although Laurent, brown-faced, was in his work clothes, apparently having just come from the salt ponds. Her father particularly seemed pleased to see her although both relatives were obviously dismayed by her appearance.

Falling to her knees before him, Jeanne began a speech that she'd prepared about her gratitude to her father for his forgiveness for her wayward behavior. Before she'd finished, however, he caught her hand, drew her up and embraced her. With tears in her eyes, she continued as much of her speech as she could, but her Perè stopped her.

"Hush now! I am very glad to see you again, my dear child!" To Laurent, he added, "I shall have to provide her with new clothes as soon as possible, *ma petite fille!*" The emotion with which he spoke caused more tears to flow.

Jeanne felt comforted by her father's reception, but she understood that Laurent was holding things back.

Perè handed her his handkerchief. After she'd dried her eyes, Laurent stepped up and saluted her on both cheeks. His expression

was grave and sad, but he said, "It is good to
see you again, *petite soeur*."

Perè explained that Marie-Barbe had
gone out with her maid and that Jeanne
would see her later. Jeanne was relieved.

*I am in no hurry to meet that false
creature again!*

Their home was not far from the
landing, so they walked, her father leaning
on an ivory-headed cane. He ordered the
servant who'd accompanied them to load
Jeanne's few belongings onto a handcart,
which soon jostled over the cobbles in their
wake. As they walked, she'd learned that
Laurent had established himself away from
the family home, living with his wife and
three fine children, the last of which had just
been born.

Marie-Barbe did not appear at supper
that night. While the cook brought a tureen
of stew to the table, a maid with a lined face
appeared to make her excuses.

"She regrets not coming to welcome her
husband's daughter, but after walking out in
the heat of the day, her head is aching and
she finds she is ever so tired."

Perè looked weary, but he said nothing,
simply nodded.

"Tell my wife that I understand, of
course, and please do give her my thanks for
making certain that we have this fine supper
ready on the table."

The maid curtseyed and departed just as
another of Jeanne's brothers, Matthieu,

arrived. Matthieu opened his arms to her, so there was another happy reunion at the supper table. Jeanne was amazed at the way Matthieu had grown. He was just as pale and quiet as he had always been as a boy, but now he wore the somber garb of a clerk, so he too had become a participant in the business of the port. He was, she had learned on the way home, now keeping the books for the family, but he also had an appointment as a clerk at the military warehouse. She was impressed by this, something of an achievement to be placed in a position of so much trust, for Matthieu was young, not some old greybeard. The Joly family must be doing very well, indeed!

The meal was quiet with just four of them. Jeanne learned of the births of more nephews and nieces. Not only did Laurent have three children now, but Jeanne's older sister Henriette now had two. She had married a gentleman who owned a good amount of property near Les Échelles just before Jeanne had run away. Jeanne felt a surge of happiness for all her siblings.

One miscreant in the family is sufficient.

The food was exactly as her Perè had intimated: excellent. After years of scant fare, Jeanne ate far too much. She also drank several glasses of good red wine. Both her father and brothers teased her about her appetite. It was a pleasant reunion even if Marie-Barbe's shadow lay over the room.

As they finished, an elderly woman appeared with a candle to show Jeanne where she would be housed. Jeanne remembered this servant whose name was Madam Guay. She seemed to be one of the few servants from the old days still in the house.

Jeanne happily greeted this old friend, rising from the table, kissing the woman on both cheeks while saying she was very glad to see her again. The woman's bare gums glistened at the effusive gesture.

"Follow me, dear child. I will take you to where the new mistress says you will stay. I am sorry, but your old room, the one you and Mademoiselle Henriette and Mademoiselle Etiennette shared in the old days, is now occupied by Madam's nieces and maids. "

After taking leave of father and brothers, curtsying to her father, and kissing her brothers' cheeks, Jeanne left the room with Madam Guay. When they were quite alone, walking along the passage that led to the area where servants were customarily housed, quite near the kitchen, her companion said, "I am to tend you now. I hope you don't mind that we will also share the room. "

When the door was opened, Jeanne saw in the flickering light of the candle a narrow room with two beds and a washstand, several hooks, and a single window. She remembered that this room had been in her mother's day used for storage although she had sometimes used it as a refuge when

Marie-Barbe had first arrived to queen it over them all. Stone walls, stone floors, now brightened somewhat by a well-worn carpet and two small beds.

"I am sorry for this, but you must remember how it is these days. " Her companion placed the gently wavering candle upon the washstand.

"Never mind, dear Guay," Jeanne replied softly. "These are far finer quarters than those I have had for the last eight years believe you me. "

"Forgive me for being so familiar, but you are even prettier than you were when you ran away with that sweet-talking sailor. I have no doubt that you will find a proper husband soon enough. "

Jeanne nodded, but marriage was not much on her mind. First, she needed time to rest and to look around her, discover what the situation in the family was after all this time. Madam Guay appeared to be pleased by her gratitude.

The sight of a real bed after the days spent on the ship's floor as well as her full stomach had begun to make her long for sleep. After washing hands and faces in the shared basin, they extinguished their light and went to their separate beds. The linen and bedding was worn but clean.

Jeanne wondered if she'd be kept awake by the cacophony of impressions and questions churning inside her head or the washing-up clatter in the kitchen, but full of excellent food and good wine, she quickly drowned in sleep.

Although she awoke just before sunrise to the sound of voices and clatter of pots in the nearby kitchen, her companion had already departed. On a chair, clean clothes were laid out, a complete new set, from undergarments to over-dress. They appeared to be someone's hand-me-downs, but they were clean!

After splashing water on her face and rinsing her mouth, Jeanne put them on and went out to find Guay, now breakfasting in the kitchen. The others--a housemaid and the cook and her helper--gazed at Jeanne warily but greeted her in a polite manner. The youngest housemaid got to her feet from the bench she shared, dish and cup in hand, and waved Jeanne into her now empty place at the table.

There was bread, cheese, and conserves, as plentiful as food for the servants had been in the time of Jeanne's mother. Gratefully Jeanne broke her fast. Later, she thanked the cook for the supper last night, saying how happy she was to taste the food of home again. No one said a single word concerning the new mistress of the house.

Her father looked in and then asked her to come into the family dining area and sit with him. On the way, she heard that Marie-Barbe rarely chose to do this anymore. When the new mistress of the house did appear in the dining room, the temperature dropped. Jeanne rose, curtsied, and spoke politely to her stepmother, who replied with few words and a frown. Next, she turned away and spoke of household matters exclusively to her husband.

On the mornings her stepmother appeared, Jeanne ate silently and quickly. She'd excuse herself and then go out of the house, through the town and out through the gates to the narrow paths that led to the marshes. Here were the beautiful childhood rambles where she'd once spent so many hours. The ocean was present in the distance especially when there was an onshore wind.

She loved to see the green and gray of the marshland, the grazing cattle, little gardens made by *paysans* in the rich muck. These flourished on any scrap of grassy ground available. Farther out, on land cut through with a hundred wandering streams, there ran the sure-footed white marsh ponies, some with their young brown foals, some resting beneath thin trees. In some places, though, the scanty trees were crowded with stork's nests, and the ground below uninviting, stinking from their droppings.

In the beginning, Jeanne walked to her brother's home and visited her sister-in-law to offer her congratulations and any help she could give to her household. Her sister-in-law was polite, but distracted, which Jeanne at first set down to the recent birth of the new baby.

Aside from a little mending or going with someone to the market, no one seemed to expect Jeanne to do much of anything although she did offer to help if she sensed that someone needed it. Not to be busy felt peculiar after those past years of steady, sun-up-to-sun-down labor.

Once, on a quick march through the town in the early morning, she'd seen an ex-suitor of hers, another man of the salt, like her father. He appeared just as grizzled and paunchy as she remembered him, this gentleman who had wanted her to replace his first wife. This fellow had made it plain that what he really required was a strong young woman who would immediately step into caring for a host of his elder relations and half-grown children. On the day he passed, Jeanne kept her head down and hurried along the opposite side of the street praying he would not notice her.

On one of the few occasions when Marie-Barbe spoke to her, she'd brought up the fact that this same gentleman was available once more as, just this spring, he'd buried the widow he'd married after Jeanne had run away.

"I believe that Monsieur Deschalet is an unlucky match, " Perè observed with the ghost of a smile. Jeanne had thanked her stars for his timely presence. Marie-Barbe opened her mouth to say something sharp, thought better of it, and, soon after, found an excuse to leave the room. Blessedly, she did not bring the dreadful man up again.

Marie-Barbe had other gentlemen in mind, however, for during every supper at which she appeared, another candidate was offered. Some were her relations, which made them even more suspect, as most were near-do-wells of one kind or another.

Her father said nothing, but later her usually circumspect brother Mathieu took Jeanne aside to whisper mockingly in her ear, saying these fellows were, to a man, looking only for a dowry to waste.

Both brothers and her Perè were also interested in marrying her off although neither brought up their candidates at the supper table. Most of the men they suggested were almost as unappealing as Marie-Barbe's suggestions, widowers with children, long-time elderly bachelors. At least, Jeanne thought, this selection had money to leave a widow. The only one who was near her age was one of Mathieu's friends, a chinless fellow who held a small government position.

"Ah, dear Guay! Are there no men worth having in all Brouage?" Once, in a moment of weakness, she'd complained to the old woman.

Madam Guay reached to push a stray dark curl back beneath Jeanne's cap. "There are none who wish to consider a woman who once so brazenly disobeyed her father, even one who has been forgiven and who will come to her wedding with a dowry. Even one as pretty as you!"

As the weeks passed, she became aware of ugly rumors, one of which she'd overheard at the market. Some servants began snickering after she passed. One, not bothering to lower his voice, claimed that he had heard "on good authority" that Jeanne had taken up whoring after her husband had vanished.

Jeanne was wise enough to know that confronting them with the fury she felt would only lead to a public scene and yet more nasty gossip, so she'd kept on walking. In despair, she'd fled that day to the hull-shaped Church of Saint Pierre near the town center. Inside, she'd taken refuge before the Madonna altar, shedding tears in the cool, incense-filled darkness.

Jeanne did her best to fill her days but found only occasional tasks in the kitchen garden or minding the fowl. There were two hens who'd quickly lost interest in their eggs. It took some tact to move the still viable ones beneath the skirts of faithful broody mothers who were willing to foster them.

She enjoyed caring for her sister-in-law's children too as she was occasionally called to do and took the little ones for walks in the marshes where their chatter and many questions kept her busy. She found she missed the children of the Dube household. She'd often cared for them when their mothers were too distracted or too exhausted. Laurent's wife, however, managed her affairs well even though she was officially still in childbed and had not been to church yet. However, as time went on, there were fewer calls upon her for help.

No one else seemed to care what she did, so she began to walk out afternoons beyond the walls, to watch the small ships sailing along the canal, all of them loaded with goods either coming to Brouage or going out to the bay. Every day there would be new small ships anchored there.

Sailors would call out to her, sometimes rudely, but more often with genuine appreciation especially when a gust of wind blew her bonnet back and sent her dark curls flying.

Jeanne smiled to herself while replacing her bonnet realizing that was exactly the way she'd met Pierre, and how, barely fifteen and foolish, it had been thrilling to be openly admired by handsome men. Sometimes as she walked she thought about Mademoiselle Agathe, about her learning and her enthusiasm, her many stories and the adventures she had already enjoyed at her brother's side. She considered the unimaginable voyage into the unknown her sea-faring companion was about to take.

During her years with the Dube family, all conversation concerned the daily struggles--how to pay the rent or how to clothe themselves, or the endless family grievances. Adventures and bold actions were for men--for warriors or sailors! Certainly not for mere women like herself.

Jeanne was on her way out one morning to the apothecary with a basket on her arm when Mathieu, unusually away from his office, caught up with her. He was breathless as if he, ordinarily so calm and collected, had, for once, been hurrying.

"Ah Jeanne! Glad I caught you here! Perè says that you are to expect a visitor this afternoon, just before supper. You are to put on the new dress. "

"A visitor?" At once, Jeanne began to fear that another suitor was on his way--one chosen this time by her father and, therefore, one to whom she must pay polite attention.

"Yes! Perè and I were early by the Guildhall, but he sent me home from that meeting to tell you that one of the sea captains present, a Captain Martin, wishes you should speak with his sister, a lady who has been visiting the Biscornet family. Mademoiselle will arrive in the late afternoon. She and her brother will be our guests for supper tonight. It seems they are to sea again as soon as the Captain's business with our father is concluded. She is the lady who made your acquaintance on *The Denise.* "

"Heavens, Mathieu, of course I remember Mademoiselle Martin, who was so kind to me! I also remember that although I looked like a poor fishwife and smelled like

63

one too, she allowed me to sleep in her cabin and keep her company. I can't imagine. . . " Her thoughts trailed away to that strange interlude.

"You are also to tell the cook she is to prepare for company at supper tonight and that it is for business. " He gave Jeanne a kiss on the cheek and smiled. "I've got to get back to my office at once, but I'm glad I caught you before you went roving. "

Jeanne smiled as she watched his trim, black-clad form retreating along the street that led back to the Guildhall. The news he'd brought was surprising, but she quickly resumed her errand to the apothecary and then returned to the house to tell her stepmother at once. It wouldn't do for her to instruct the cook herself. Marie-Barbe would certainly consider that a sign that Jeanne was taking on the duties of the Lady of the House and be swift to take offense.

Jeanne had always believed that the determined, fascinating Agathe would never cross her path again. Now after this astonishing news, she was filled with anticipation. It felt almost akin to watching the quays in New Rochelle back in the days when she watched for her husband's ship to arrive.

Marie-Barbe, as soon as she heard the news, suddenly had an entire list of errands for Jeanne to perform that would fill up the rest of the morning.

"You will accompany the cook to the market for fish this morning, Jeanne. I am certain you will be able to advise her on what's best. "

It was the usual slighting kind of remark that her stepmother employed on those rare occasions she deigned to speak to her. Jeanne ignored it as she always did. Besides, it was true. She was a far better judge of fish than anyone who had not spent years buying and selling them would be. For the rest, she was so pleased at the notion that Agathe wished to see her again that she simply didn't care what her spiteful stepmother had to say.

"Madam Jeanne! How well rested you look."

Jeanne curtsied, but the long pale hands of Agathe raised her up. Agathe was dressed in a somber but expensive dark blue dress, crisp despite all the traveling she and her brother had been doing.

"Oh, Mademoiselle! I am so happy to see you again!"

They exchanged kisses, and Jeanne became aware that servants had gathered surreptitiously to watch. Agathe noticed too. She smiled, a secret, confiding smile.

"Where can we go and speak privately? I have such a deal to say. "

"We will go to my father's study. " Jeanne heard doors opening upstairs and the pattering of feet. It was, no doubt, someone off to announce the news of the visitor's arrival to Marie-Barbe.

Her father's study was cool and dim despite the heat of August. The windows were still covered.

Knowing the room so well, it was easy for Jeanne to reach the first window quickly and pull back the curtains. A ray of sunlight entered illuminating the carved table legs, capacious chairs, shelved accounts books and a large desk. A young maid had followed them in, but before Jeanne could dismiss her, she at once made herself useful by pushing chairs into place around a smaller table which was set to one side by the neighboring window.

"May I bring something from the kitchen for you, Madam Dube?" The child spoke to Jeanne with careful correctness.

"Nothing for me." Agathe spoke quickly to Jeanne.

"Thank youThank you then, Michelle. You may go now. "

"Should I speak to Madam Joly and say you have company?"

"No need. I'm sure she already knows. " From across the room, Agathe sent just the briefest of winks.

"Please close the door behind you. We do not wish to be disturbed. "

The girl curtsied and left but not without an openly curious backward glance at their tall, well-dressed visitor. Michelle was the youngest of Marie-Barbe's poor relations, and she was one among many who now filled various positions in the house, but she always spoke to Jeanne politely.

"The best of a bad bunch," was the way Madam Guay had characterized the child.

They had barely got themselves settled, however, when the door swung open again, revealing Marie-Barbe, all insincerity, her hatchet-faced personal maid at her heels.

There was another delay with introductions, and then Marie-Barbe inquired if their visitor required any refreshment. Agathe, however, surprised the woman by taking her hand firmly and walking her back to the door. The maid, not knowing what else to do, retreated before them.

"I am pleased to make your acquaintance, Madam Joly, but I have come on personal business to Madam Dube. As we told the little girl earlier, we would appreciate being left alone to conduct it. "

Marie-Barbe was so surprised that she couldn't muster another word even when Agathe's long hands closed the door in her face.

Jeanne covered her mouth and just managed to stifle a laugh while Agathe returned to her seat. Outside the door, they could hear an undertone of indignant fussing followed by a loud, heel-tapping retreat.

"I have had my fill of such women," Agathe said as she reseated herself and settled her skirts. "Now, Jeanne, without further ado, as we shall certainly be interrupted again, here is the purpose of my visit.   Madam Manie, as you yourself witnessed, is getting old, and she has never sailed well. She has honestly told me that she fears a voyage across the ocean to New France would be the death of her, and so I have arranged to leave my old companion in my brother's household. This leaves me requiring a new companion with whom to travel. I have thought long and hard on the subject while visiting my friend in Poitiers, and I have concluded that the kind of companion I will need must be young and brave--and intelligent. Therefore, I have come to ask you to leave all this behind and voyage with me to New France. "

Jeanne felt herself gulp as the abyss of the unknown opened before her.

"Candidly, this land has been described to me as 'howling wilderness,' a place with warlike savages and also the longest and most ferocious of winters, but it is also far away from old entanglements and misfortunes, and a place where there are many brave and adventurous men in need of a clever French wife with the courage to help them seek their fortune in this place. "

Jeanne felt her jaw drop.

Mademoiselle saw her reaction, but, with excitement brightening her gray eyes, only smiled.

"Do say 'Yes,' Jeanne! The role of a poor widow, a dependent in your father's house, cannot suit you. "

"I--I beg your pardon, Mademoiselle, but this is a deal to consider! I acted upon impulse and the madness of love when I ran away with my dear Pierre. That choice landed me in friendless poverty from which my generous Perè has only just rescued me."

"Ah, Jeanne, but your husband was your true love, and you have said you were very happy together in the time together that you had. That kind of love I've never had in my life--nor do I ever expect --but now, Monsieur de Couage, who has always treated me with great kindness, has asked me to join him, to marry him--in New France. This gives me a chance to travel to a land that only a very few men have ever seen, a land of many wonders--and, of course, many hardships. "

"And dangers too, from the savage people who live there. I have heard the sailors' tales about the great dark forests of New France and the silent assassins who creep among the trees. "

Agathe gazed down at Jeanne; her gray eyes gleamed with pure excitement.

"I often think sometimes *Le Bon Dieu* placed my soul in the wrong body. My brother agrees. He has told me many times I have the heart of a man. As I told you before, I have resolved not to end up like my friend Gillette whose days are spent with her pets, household matters, and embroidery, or like my bookish *Tante Louise*, mewed up forever in a dark convent . "

"I--I understand very well what you are saying, dear Mademoiselle, and I honor your bravery with all my heart, but I don't know . . . I--I have heard stories of the savages in New France, how they mutilate, torture and kill the missionaries who comes to them in the name of God. . . "

More would have been said, but as Agathe had predicted, there was yet another knock, followed at once by a brusque opening of the door. This time it was Monsieur Joly, not his inquisitive wife who was, however, still outside and trying to look over his shoulder.

"I have heard that you ladies have been making free with my study," he said with a smile, "but be assured, I have let the household know that I have no objection, because weighty discussions do require privacy. "

With those words, he bowed his head politely and quietly stepped back and closed the door.

"It seems that my brother and your father have been talking about things other than the salt business," Agathe observed.

Jeanne was silent for a long moment, then she said, "Perhaps my father has seen a way for me to have a new life. I fear my reputation in Brouage has been sullied by ugly lies. Perhaps it is beyond repair. "

Agathe raised a fair brow but did not inquire further. Instead, she suggested that they go out and walk around the town together.

"This is a great deal for you to consider just as you have said. We will not speak of it again until you wish to, but I must leave in a few days, back to La Rochelle to prepare for the journey. We must sail soon because snow flies early across the water. "

"You are very kind, Mademoiselle. " Jeanne smiled, understanding that the lady's offer had not been withdrawn.

In the next moment, she turned and went to the window. After a short struggle, she'd opened the tall window behind her father's desk and secured it with the help of a prop which was as usual stored tucked behind the curtain.

When she faced Agathe again, she said, "My brother Aubin and I often escaped through this window when we wanted to sail or fish and were tired of lessons. "

Straightaway, Agathe began hiking up her skirts.

"Ah, Jeanne Dube! You are a woman after my own heart. "

Outside the window was a narrow slate path and beyond that a sunlit slice of garden filled with herbs, sage, tarragon, and basil. Getting out was a little more difficult than Jeanne remembered, but Agathe, despite her height and more formal clothing, had no problem following her out.

The only person who saw them take this unorthodox exit was a very young and very surprised kitchen maid whose pale lips made an O as she watched one after the other emerge.

Jeanne helped Agathe straighten her skirts. Then, without further ado, the lady tucked Jeanne's arm into hers. They walked together along the slate path, through the gate, and onto the cobbled street.

The sun was bright, but the wind behind them was brisk, blowing from the land. The streets were full of carts carrying goods to and fro, or going home quite empty. They passed soldiers and servants and occasionally a lady in a chair. The town was far lower than La Rochelle, which had many three- and four-storey houses. Here, two-storeys were the rule. "My father has boats we could use. " After escaping through the window, Jeanne experienced a powerful feeling of elation.

Agathe was smiling widely. Now there was a current of excitement running between them. Jeanne felt ready for anything. "Do you know how to row? To sail?"

"I can do both," said Jeanne.

"So can I," Agathe replied. "Let's go!"

In no time, they were outside the city walls and at the docks.

The boatmen at the Joly dock recognized Jeanne. Marie-Barbe's influence had not reached them; her father and brothers ruled all that had to do with trade. When Jeanne asked, they pointed out a small rowboat near shore they could use.

Without regard for their skirts, they both climbed in while a young, dark-skinned dockman, smiling widely, waded in and pushed them out while they unshipped their oars. To their surprise, he jumped in with them.

"Pardon me, ladies! I am Denis. My Perè, the dock-master, Monsieur Vacay, says I am to join you and keep you both safe. " He moved into the seat facing the one the women shared.

Jeanne was about to protest when someone from the shore roared, "Watch out for that Dutchman!" A ship, a heavily loaded fuste, her sails flapping, came angling toward the docks. Shouts of warning came from the deck.

To drown in the muddy channel was perfectly possible. Both women leaned into their oars just avoiding the lumbering ship. As the fuste passed, sailors called out to them. Some were laughing, others swearing.

Jeanne lowered her head and leaned on her oar, one of Denis's dark muscular hands atop hers. Agathe, in the same situation, threw back her fair head and laughed aloud at the passing ship.

When they had avoided this hazard, they eased off and floated with the tide only using their oars to stay close to the shore and away from the larger vessels. The main channel had a gentle current now going out with the tide. This would carry them into the marshes, past the salt pans, and finally, if they kept going, all the way to the Gulf of *Saintonge* where the larger ships lay anchored.

Denis insisted on taking the oars, and so Agathe and Jeanne had to carefully maneuver to reach the seat before him. No sooner had they settled their skirts then Agathe picked up a gourd floating in the bilge and started bailing. Their feet, of course, were already wet.

The two women stole looks at one another, wondering if their tete-à-tête -- so hard won -- would now be ruined.

Denis kept his eyes on guiding the boat. Jeanne studied the man as he rowed away. The skin that showed through his torn shirt was very brown. His hair peeking from beneath his floppy hat was wiry and cut close to his head.

Men of the sea, she knew, might have children of every color.

"Would you ladies like to see the ponies?"

"Ponies?" Agathe was immediately curious.

Jeanne was amused by how this muddy, sun-burned fellow in his ragged clothes turned out to be so ready to act as their guide although she felt rather irked at having a man--once again--take over the direction of her day. The ponies were a wonderful lure though. Only once since she'd returned had she managed to reach the ponies on foot, wending her way through the heavily dissected, brackish water ways.

They floated down a side channel at this time sufficiently drained by the tide so they could see the muddy bottom. The wind blew and small birds, blue throats, flew up all around the boat as they passed. The area was full of thrushes of many kinds, fluttering between low bushes and arguing with one another.

When they reached as far as the low water allowed, they saw what they were looking for. Not too far away a group of mares and foals grazed on the lush green grass. They were pure white, flicking their tails to keep the flies off, brushy manes lifted by the wind.

Denis jumped out, secured the boat with a rope. Then, without a word, he flopped down full length on the grass and closed long lashes over his eyes.

The women decided to stay in the boat and talk there.

"What a discreet fellow," Agathe whispered. Jeanne nodded.

"He probably needs a rest. I heard my brother Laurant and Perè last evening talking about a ship that had just begun unloading as the sun went down. " After a pause to admire the secluded place, Jeanne said, "Tell me about your visit along the coast. How is your friend? Where did you go?"

"My friend Gillette lives near Palmyre, which is as wild as this place. The countryside is full of water and marshes there too. Nevertheless, her home is very comfortable, I must say. Their *paysan* supply the house with every kind of meat and fish you can imagine, though sometimes I know she longs for a real city. I rode out almost every day, and we went hunting too. Her husband was astonished that I could take birds with a bow--with the help of his fine water dogs--but it seems to me to be the best way to hunt them. Guns simply scare the entire flock away. "

"You are a true huntress, like the Goddess Diana, it seems. " Jeanne smiled at her new friend.

"I think that it is the striking of an elusive target I enjoy far more than the killing. Gillette's cooks saw to it that those birds made good dinners. I have to confess that I also enjoy it when men praise me, for I am no beauty, this I know. It is so rare, however, for men to be impressed by anything that women do. Men insist they are the best at everything. At the same time, what they do are the only things that appear to have any value in this world. "

Jeanne gently shook her head. "There would be no more men if there were no women, don't forget that."

Agathe sighed. "But this argument only states, in the end, that we women have no more value than men's cattle or men's horses. As my Tante said to me long years ago, if having children is the only reason for our being, then she cannot understand why *Le Bon Dieu* gave us minds and the ability to think and learn, just as well--and often far better--than men. "

Jeanne pondered a little before she replied. "I see what you are saying, Mademoiselle. Moreover, if your children die, then you are of no importance. That is what happened to me when I lost my sweet Michel. No matter how hard I worked for the Dube's or the care I gave my sisters-in-law's children, or how much washing I took in, they only wanted me to go away. Pierre's family, you see, are poor people and because of the father's follies and drinking were growing steadily poorer. I shouldn't blame them, I suppose, but it was hard for me to have them turn to treating me like an old hen--only not half so valuable, because they couldn't put me in the supper pot. "

"Is that why you wrote to your Perè?"

"Yes," said Jeanne. Suddenly the whole story of her short life came pouring out, while Agathe, her wise, homely face attentive, listened.

They arrived at the dock as the sun lowered, sending a golden hue across the marshes. Denis pulled up the boat while

Agathe reached deep into her skirt pocket and found a purse so that she could give their rower some coins.

While Denis had slept, they had talked and talked, pouring out secrets to one another. Pierre had risen again in Jeanne's mind, like a ghost. He had been so young, so passionate and handsome--and then, gone--lost forever.

The short years of her happiness, only a memory now, already had pieces missing. Jeanne was dismayed by the realization, but Agathe comforted her by saying that was the way of memories, that she too had experienced losses, where the past became like fragments of a dream.

They began the short walk back into the city still active with people on late errands. As they passed through the gate, they encountered an open air *Stella Maris* shrine, which always had candles burning.

The Blessed Mother of the Blue Robe stood upon a seashell and raised one hand in a graceful benediction. Here was a place where sailors and their women, too, paused to ask for her protection and favor or to spend a longer time silently bowing their heads and praying, especially before going to sea. There was always a small knot of people there.

The two stopped to admire the scene. They crossed themselves, then clasped their hands and asked silently for Her favor. Agathe stepped away to the little flower seller nearby to purchase a small knot of posies.

Jeanne gazed at the statue silently. Her mind, though, was busy, and soon a prayer formed itself.

"What should I do, Dear Lady? Should I leave here and go with this brave woman to take my chances in the unknown? In dangerous New France?"

She closed her eyes and waited.

"A woman who has fallen so far shouldn't be in this good Catholic city among decent people!" The accusation was shouted in her ear. The smell of alcohol enveloped her.

Startled, her eyes flew open. The man had cleared a path with his cane and was now using it to point at her. It was none other than the long-ago rejected suitor, Monsieur Deschalet, now twice rejected. Her first reaction was to run, but the women gathered here were staring. Some recognized her, she could tell.

"You mistake me for someone else, sir. " She tried to sound disdainful, but it was hard to keep her voice from shaking.

"For shame, sir! This is a place for prayer." Agathe stepped through the whispering crowd, the fresh posies she'd been seeking in her hand. "Go back to the tavern where you and your lies belong!"

She bore her tall self proudly, was very well dressed, and not the least afraid. Her voice was clear and strong. She took Jeanne by the arm and began to escort her through the crowd. When Deschalet took an unsteady step forward and waved his cane as if to strike her, Agathe released Jeanne and with both hands she grasped the muddy tip, now waggling at her, and gave a mighty push.

"How dare you! Lout!"

Jeanne gasped as her tormentor, large, but thoroughly soused, lost his balance and sat down hard in the street. His feathered hat fell over his face. Laughter arose on all sides while they walked away.

They arrived at the Joly home just as the sun set. An anxious-looking servant awaited them on the step and promptly opened the door. A maid escorted them directly to the dining room.

Supper was already served. Captain Martin stood at once and came straight to his sister. He looked cross, but Jeanne could see there was also amusement in his eyes as he approached.

"Mademoiselle Martin! Where in heaven's name have you been? Such impoliteness to your host!"

"Indeed." Jeanne's father was clearly annoyed. He did not rise and his eyes flashed.

"You ladies have discommoded the entire household. And you, Jeanne! I thought you promised me when I brought you home that I would not see any more antics!"

Jeanne curtsied meekly to her father, keeping her head bowed.

"I am very sorry, dear father, if our visit to the marsh has upset you. Mademoiselle Martin and I ventured too far. "

"Obviously. " Mathieu from the far end of the table had noted the condition of their hems.

"Monsieur Joly, it is I who should beg your pardon for this inconvenience. . . "

Before Agathe could get well started, she was interrupted loudly by Marie-Barbe. The smirk on her face made it plain that she could no longer hold her tongue.

"My dearest husband. Here it is, just as I warned you." She put her hand on Monsieur Joly's arm. "Here are yet more proofs of her wild ways, despite how you have, ever-so charitably . . ."

"Silence!" Monsieur Joly, red in the face now, wasted no time in cutting her off. He pointedly disengaged his wife's arm and stood.

"What is this about, Jeanne?"

Jeanne had had enough. She'd realized, as she and Agathe walked through those familiar cobbled streets, that the ugliness she'd faced at the Stella Maris shrine would never end. Neither Brouage nor her childhood home, it seemed, would ever welcome her.

Releasing Agathe's arm, she stepped forward, grasped the back of the nearest empty chair to steady herself before she spoke.

"My dearest Perè, dear brother, I intend to leave. I wish to take ship with Captain Martin and his sister and discover what fortune may bring me in New France. "

A stunned silence followed, quickly broken by Captain Martin, who turned to face the room.

"I see that my sister and your widowed daughter have come to an agreement. We hope this decision can be made with your blessing, sir. Madam Dube wishes to become my sister's companion and accompany us from here to La Rochelle. As part of my household, she shall be, from henceforth, provided by us. As I have said, we sail from Brouage as soon as we are loaded, probably the day after tomorrow. From there, as quickly as another vessel, the Company de Canadien pinnace Astrée may be loaded, we shall sail for New France. My sister is to be the bride of Seigneur de Couage, a merchant with shares in the Company, which, under seal from our good King, trades for furs there. "

A profound silence filled the room. Astonishment hung, almost visibly, in the air. A servant, entering from the kitchen with a fresh flask of wine, stopped in his tracks at the door; his questioning eyes scanned the room.

Jeanne's father extended his hand and said, "Jeanne, let us speak further of this in my study. Captain Martin, Mademoiselle, do please join us. "

Leaving the room, now brimming with amazement, they re-entered the study, with those shelves of records, leather books, and maps. Henri Joly took Jeanne's hand in his. Anger had fled. He now appeared concerned, protective.

"Daughter, do you understand that if you take this course, you will certainly never be able to return to France, to your family? Do you understand the dangers of that wilderness?"

"I do not know what I am sailing to, dear father, but it is clear to me now that I can no longer stay here in Brouage. I do not wish to be an object of public scorn, and I do not wish to cause any more shame for my family. "

Chapter 2

Ocean and sky! Ocean and sky!

Jeanne had never before sailed out of sight of land. To see nothing but the ship surrounded by so much deep, deep water and feel herself riding over such massive swells--like hills that endlessly traveled beneath the ship--was a new and frightening experience. Agathe had sailed to the Canary Islands with her brother and all the way down the coast of Spain, too, but even she appeared full of wonder at the endlessness of the Atlantic.

In Jeanne's earlier coastal voyages, the welcome shout "Land Ho" had come quickly, but now a month had passed and they were only half--or, perhaps a third – of the way to their next sight of land. Only time alone would tell. A single heavy two-day storm through which they had passed had made both women seasick and afraid for the first time in all their sailing lives.

They were not alone. The lower decks, where poorer passengers were lodged, stank of vomit for days despite generous applications of salt water.

Jeanne knew it was a high privilege to be housed where she was, in one of the narrow cabins tucked behind the Captain's. The quartermaster on this voyage shared his cabin with an officer on his way to the outpost at Quebec.

Below the main deck were those who were emigrating. A few had wives with them. Some of these folks were tradesmen-- cobblers, coopers, and smiths--who had been engaged to work only for an indenture's term in New France. There were soldiers and some carpenters too. Two of those were indentured, but there was also the ship's carpenter and his apprentice.

As well, peasant farmers were among the passengers, men who were promised land after they served a three-year term of indenture to the gentlemen seigneurs among whom the new land had been divided. Their job would be immense for they would be clearing virgin forest, breaking sod, and facing the savages. After their term of indenture was over, just as such peasants did in France, they would continue to pay rent to the mostly absent seigneurs who held title to the land on which they labored. It was a hard bargain, this Jeanne understood, but she also knew that farmland was almost impossible to obtain in France if you were a younger son. These brave *paysan* were willing to take the chance.

On the next deck were housed the seamen, skilled mariners Captain Martin had engaged for the voyage. Jeanne knew that these poor fellows didn't even have a hammock of their own. One man slept while the other sailor was on duty. Some among the crew, among them the boatswain, chose to sleep on deck under a canvas shelter, except when the weather became too foul.

There were also a few animals, most of these destined for the Captain's table during the voyage. The poor creatures grew subdued and quiet in the endless dark and bad air, and in a few weeks had given up loud protests and simply awaited their fate.

The next level was for cannon, cargo, and, at the stern, lay the galley where the cook and his helper labored. Being so far below decks made their chores even more onerous, especially whatever man had the task of delivering the heated pots up the difficult ladders, all while the ship rose and fell beneath their feet. That room was never uninhabited, as some poor fellow had to always be keeping a close watch on the banked fire.

Jeanne remembered Pierre and the way he'd been so excited before his final voyage because he would sail as third mate. He had been looking forward to all he would learn from this initial step up the shipboard ladder. This three-masted square-rigged ship was larger although in form it was much like the fishing vessel upon which Pierre had sailed away.

She and Agathe ate with Captain Martin, another luxury for which Jeanne was grateful. As she dined beside the Quartermaster, Lieutenant Duplessis, and his aide-de-camp. Jeanne was wary of both gentlemen, especially when they began to flirt with her. She wondered if they imagined her to be a flighty young woman who might be vulnerable to their bright uniforms.

Jeanne's discreet evasions amused Agathe. Finally, her employer made a stern remark to the effect that "the gentlemen will please respect my companion's youth and inexperience."

Captain Martin heard this characterization without a word and with only the slightest gleam in his eye as he watched his sister firmly warn the men off.

There was also a Jesuit and his servant on board. The servant, a dark-eyed, dark-skinned youngster who spoke French with an odd accent, looked terrified most of the time and never spoke to anyone other than the cook to whom he was often sent because the priest, for the most part, ate alone in his cabin. Agathe wondered to Jeanne if this young fellow was from the lands that adjoined Spain in the high Pyrenees, perhaps a Basque, because of his accent.

As for the priest, he might have been a man in the prime of life, but it was hard to tell how old he was because although he stood ramrod straight in his black robe, his face was gaunt, lined, and extremely pale.

His scanty hair appeared either fair, or tinged with silver, depending on the light. On the few occasions he ate at the Captain's table, the meal would always begin with a lengthy prayer instead of Captain Martin's usual, more perfunctory blessing.

When he was present, conversation was subdued, nearly absent. The Jesuit would take a single cup of wine, but rarely ate any of the flesh that sometimes appeared on the table. He seemed to subsist on salt fish, bread, pickles, and cheese.

One evening, in the priest's absence, Lieutenant Duplessis commented on those habits. "Even a good cup of our Captain's stout red wine makes absolutely no change in our good Father, does it?"

After more than a few cups of that same "good wine," Duplessis ceased saying "our good father" and instead muttered about "that black, ill-omened crow. " This amused Agathe greatly, and she discussed it afterward while they prepared for bed in their cramped cabin.

"The sailors say that ships with women aboard are accursed, but I have also heard them say ships with priests aboard are even more unlucky. " She rolled her eyes and laughed. "With both women and a priest traveling on the *Astrée*, I fear this voyage of ours is most certainly doomed. "

"I have heard sailors say that. That is what my husband said, too, although I think in his case, he only half-believed it. He certainly did not seem worried when he and I sailed away from Brouage together. "

Jeanne found herself beginning to dwell on that first voyage she'd made, an interlude of happiness and freedom, but quickly schooled herself to put that old memory aside.

That's a piece of the past best put behind, for although I was happy, I was foolish, too.

Remembering those few sweet days would only bring tears!

But oh! How happy we were, crazy with love, so young, so full of dreams! We imagined we could deal with whatever was to come if only we were together and in love!

"*Amor vincit omnia!*"

Those were the words of the cheerful wandering friar who had blessed their union. He'd assured them that with a few coins to "maintain his ministry" and a few Latin words, they were now man and wife. He'd explained, when they'd looked blank at his Latin, that the last phrase meant "love conquers all. "

After pocketing the coins Pierre had given him, the elderly friar had plodded off, picking a slow path through the rocky shoreline.

Probably in search of a tavern. . .

Jeanne had come to see what had happened clearly with more wisdom and years. Occasionally, she'd even wondered if she and Pierre had been truly married. Such were the questions that arose, but only much later. The Latin had sounded familiar enough although his ceremony had been a far less long-winded affair than she'd heard at other weddings.

At the time, she and Pierre believed what they'd wanted to. Later that day, under cover of twilight, with the sound of the ocean all around them, they'd become one flesh. The story of this wedding day she'd never shared with another soul. Pierre had certainly never said much to his family, and they had not asked either. At first, when he'd brought her to the Dube household, it was enough that they said they had been married and that he'd put a fine gold ring on her finger--and that Jeanne was young and strong and cheerfully willing to do the hard work.

That ring, of course, had been sold and the proceeds spent during that last winter in La Rochelle while she had been sick and unable to stand for such a long time, nearly dead from illness and gnawing grief. She would never forget Madam Dube, standing over her sick bed, a hard, broad palm extended, demanding that Jeanne give up the treasured ring "for the family. "

Agathe and Jeanne shared a bed in the cramped cabin, but as they spent most of their time together anyway, this wasn't a hardship. They had easily formed similar routines before the journey began. Jeanne mostly slept on the outside. As "companion," it was her duty to arise first anyway.

They helped one another dress and bathe in the occasional basin of water that came their way. Their cycles proved to be adjacent, which was easier than if they had both had their monthly flow at the same time. It was a comfort, though, when one or the other's back was aching to have a warm body to lie against, ever more as they began to travel north. On the hot nights during the first part of the voyage, they'd agreed they'd rather walk the decks and get some air before entering the sticky, confined space for the night.

As the journey progressed, Agathe had less to share, fewer stories to tell. Maybe, Jeanne thought, it wasn't that she had come to the end of her tales or to the end of her questions about her new companion, but simply that the ocean around them had sucked all their thoughts away, down into those unknowable depths.

How huge the waves were!

How bottomless that profound darkness over which they traveled, their little ship skimming the surface, floating like a cork above the watery immensity below. It was the gateway to panic if she dwelt on it. How quickly their lives would be over if they fell over the edge or if the ship's hull failed and they sank.

Sometimes Agathe told of pirates and enemy vessels who might, just on a whim, come to attack and sink their ship after stealing the goods below in the hold, to murder and do other terrible things to their victims before the *coup de grace*, the same dreadful things women fear as much on land as they do at sea. In Jeanne's mind, drowning would be better--far more so than the violation and torture women might expect from such vile men, before death took them. As a sailor's wife, Jeanne knew these terrifying stories and, naturally, she had fears.

It seemed that Agathe had been traveling with her brother some years before "in bright Spanish waters" when their ship had been attacked. They had had the good fortune to have excellent gunners aboard; moreover, Captain Martin had been warned of the approach of a strange sail by his crew in plenty of time to do what was necessary to fight.

In the end of their engagement, the murderous vessel had been left behind. A gaping hole at the water line of the enemy had provided assurance to Captain Martin that this menace would not return. To save themselves, these pirates had limped away, but not before Captain Martin's gunners had put a few more balls into the enemy's waterline, destroying the rudder, to be sure the pirates would not make shore.

"Many pirates ply their trade in Spanish waters, by Gibraltar and down in the Mediterranean," Agathe explained. "Some of them come from Tripoli, cruel, slaving infidels. Their ships are strange to our eyes, but if they are not hiding in coves, our men usually see them in time enough to prepare for a fight. Xebecs, their ships are called. They are lateen rigged like our small coastal fishing boats, but these can be very, very large. They are fast, too, and exceptionally well-armed. We were lucky that day not to have fallen afoul of one of those. "

"Holy Mother! What a story! Were you very afraid?"

"Of course! The noise of the cannon, both the firing from our ship and the shots from theirs, was deafening. Musket balls raked the deck, and several of our brave sailors were killed. I hid in my brother's cabin--under his desk, I admit--but my ears rang and my limbs shook for hours afterward. I can't even begin to imagine how the gunners below decks must have felt with all that gun powder on every side and all that hellish noise. The whole time, I was afraid that our hull would be breached or that the sails would be torn apart by enemy shot or that those poor fellows would be trapped down in the hold. I think I barely slept until we were safely back on land. Nightmares about that day still afflict me. "

"I wonder you continued to sail with your brother. " Jeanne shook her head.

Agathe was even more courageous than she had imagined!

A hearty laugh was her companion's response.

"So, indeed, was my poor brother! It took me nearly a year and a great deal of boredom, I confess, before I asked to travel with him again. "

Days passed. *The Astrée* tacked and then tacked again, trying to find the wind. It kept the crew very busy, sometimes taking in and sometimes putting on sail. These *matelots* were not dressed adequately, Jeanne thought, and wondered if some men on such long sea journeys died simply from exposure.

Most of them, though, had been on northward voyages before and had come equipped with coats and hats. They wrapped their feet in rags if they had no shoes even when going aloft. To a man, they wore woolen caps, but as it grew colder, they'd add a tuque or a scarf to their headgear.

Agathe had brought a supply of wool along as well as needles, which she and Jeanne employed making socks and mittens. Jeanne begged some from her mistress to knit a cap or two for sailors whose skull caps were ragged. Captain Martin approved their efforts and promised his sister more wool from the store after they landed.

The aide-de-camp noticed their knitting. He, more irritating than his Captain, was still amusing himself by teasing Jeanne. He said she should not be looking for a husband among poor *matelots* when there were far better husbands to be had in Quebec.

Jeanne fixed him with a severe gaze and replied, "Monsieur LaFranchise, I am the widow of a sailor myself. Naturally I pity these men for their suffering. "

Looking down his long nose at her, he turned away with a new disdain. From then on, his teasing stopped, disappearing like frost in a hot spring sun. Instead of his usual bantering forays, after that interchange he barely spoke to her.

The episode amused Agathe a great deal.

"These noble younger sons who end up in the military are mostly fools in search of a dowry to fritter away. The fact that he paid attention to you before shows his true nature. I am sure there are gossips aboard this ship who could have told him about you if he'd bothered to inquire. Honest women, rich or poor, would do well to stay clear of the nobility. Merchants' prudent sons marry merchants' prudent daughters, which is much the best for both parties. I am sure your mother taught you about keeping the books when you were at home. "

"Dear Mama certainly tried, but she was gone before I learned much, I fear. Father would have surely insisted I continue, but instead he lost his mind and brought that *sirène* into our house. "

"*Sirène?*" Agathe let out a peal of laughter. The bright sound of her merriment cheered Jeanne, for Agathe was growing thin and silent as the long weeks of this voyage went on. Jeanne had begun, in the last weeks, to worry a little about her mistress, who had of late become a restless sleeper and who often walked the deck at night despite the cold and wind.

"*Sirène?* That mendacious lump of flesh?"

Jeanne wasn't entirely certain about what "mendacious" meant, but the implication was clear. Close association with Mademoiselle Agathe was certainly increasing her vocabulary!

"Marie-Barbe was far prettier eight years ago when she married my father. When I came home, I saw that three births and the loss of those babies had changed her appearance. I do pity her for that sorrow, at least."

"I would imagine, however," Agathe replied tartly, "that the deaths of your stepmother's children greatly comforted your brothers."

The journey dragged on and on, seeming as if it would never end. Other passengers came on deck less and less. Some below were ill.

The water had fouled, and all that was left to drink was a weak, vinegary cider, which left those unaccustomed to it slightly tipsy. Lips and skin cracked and the sailors appeared ever-more gaunt. The animals brought along for the table were gone now, even their bones boiled until there was not a spot of grease or goodness left. The only live creatures-six heifers and four young sows-- were merchandise and had farmers awaiting them.

The hens, despondent in the dark, had quit laying, so food, even for the Captain's table, was scant, mostly salted beef or dried fruit. The supply of wine seemed adequate, especially now that Lieutenant Duplessis and his aide rarely joined them at table.

Captain Martin had laughed, saying "They have their own store, apparently, which they imagine we do not know about. "

"Perhaps the Jesuit does too," Agathe suggested. The priest and his anxious attendant had also made themselves scarce.

Jeanne understood that everyone else, from seamen to below deck passengers, was now subsisting on bowls of a crumbled-biscuit, dried-fish, and-lentil gruel concocted by boiling those three ingredients together in the unpalatable water.

One night, a woman went into labor. Her screams, seemingly just below their cabin, awakened Jeanne. Agathe, too, was awake, though she had not arisen. She leaned on one elbow and gazed silently into the blackness of their cabin.

"I will go down to her," said Jeanne. "Women to help are in short supply on this ship. "

Agathe sighed and moved to allow Jeanne to climb over her long body.

"Do you know anything about birthing?"

"Some." Jeanne groped about, found the lantern, and managed, after some fumbling, to get it started. In the shuddering light, she located her dress. "I learned a little while living with the Dubes. Many babies were born in that house. " Jeanne busied herself, getting the lantern secured and then stepping into her over-skirt and covering that with the apron she customarily wore to signal her position as a maid.

"Shall I leave the lantern for you, Mademoiselle?"

"Yes, please. " Agathe was sitting now. Tall as she was even in bed she had to be careful not to hit her head on the low beams of the ceiling.

Upon going outside, Jeanne was struck by a strong, cold breeze that threatened to tear away the cap she'd hurriedly put on. Overhead clouds of stars shone against the blue-black sky. It seemed the sky was rocking instead of the vessel, an illusion caused by those long weeks she'd been at sea. The square sails gleamed, full-bellied and white against the darkness. Wind hissed and banged the ropes. The ghostly forms of sailors moved or stood sentinel.

A few other passengers were outside already carrying lanterns. Having been awakened, some had come up on deck to get away from the screaming. One of them wordlessly offered Jeanne his lantern so she could make her way to the narrow stairs that led down to the lower deck.

Once she'd made it to the bottom, in the distance, she could see a cluster of lights towards which she cautiously made her way. The poor woman's screams rose and fell almost in rhythm with the ship, and the sound grew louder as she approached. When Jeanne arrived, she found two women on their knees alongside a mattress on the floor. One sat behind the woman, supporting her in a semi-upright position. The other crouched between her pale legs, splayed wide. Even in the swaying light, Jeanne could see blood everywhere. Her husband, his face a wooden mask, held aloft a lantern to light the scene.

A sobbing breath; another ragged, hoarse scream. . .

Jeanne was on her knees at once beside the woman trying to midwife the birth.

"It's too early," the woman muttered, shaking her head. "The child has not turned."

Jeanne could see tiny feet amidst the gouts of blood.

Jeanne did what she knew, pressing down on the laboring woman's belly. She tried to extract the baby herself with the first woman's guidance, a feat she'd seen once herself. Perhaps because of her smaller hands, the child emerged at last. Jeanne tried to clear his mouth, and his father could not get him to take a breath, even after swinging him by the legs upside down, or by rubbing his chest, as you would with a sluggish new lamb. The placenta came quickly, but the mother's bleeding was unstoppable, coming in one hot surge after another. She fell into unconsciousness; only the groans of the ship and sighs of the ocean remained.

Another light appeared, but this only proved to be the black-robed Jesuit who'd come to give last rites and to baptize the dead baby.

Dawn came. Jeanne made her way onto the deck. Her apron, arms, and hands were soaked with blood. Her companions--a blacksmith's wife and the cooper's wife -- were still below. The Jesuit had quickly withdrawn after his duties were done. Clearly, he wanted to quickly escape the awful scene. He took the grieving husband with him.

Alone, the women had said their own prayers to the Blessed Mother asking, woman to woman, for her intercession. Then they'd washed the body using salty water from buckets brought down by a sailor. They had bundled the bloody bedding, which they'd try to wash later.

Muslin, even so stained, was too valuable among the poor to be thrown away.

"Shall we wrap her? I can ask the sailors to bring us a bit of sail. "

"Poor little baby! For him, it won't take much," said the carpenter's wife, "but no, Madam, not yet. We will sit with our friend for a while. "

"Yes, her husband may want to sit with her too, before she goes into the sea. " The blacksmith's wife's face was gaunt, exhausted. The deceased, now dressed in a clean shift, lay in repose looking frail and shrunken, barely a husk of the sturdy woman who had come on board.

"We thank you for your help, Madam Jeanne. "

"You are welcome.   I only wish. . . " Jeanne didn't finish. She rose to her feet and nearly bumped her head on a beam. She was not tall, but even she had to be mindful of the low ceilings below deck.

It was a welcome moment when she stepped onto the upper deck at last and could see the sun, now rising through fitful clouds.

Jeanne did not attend the funeral held a few hours later. Agathe said she would go in Jeanne's place. Jeanne had stayed on deck to recover herself and thank the gray-haired sailor who often assisted the passengers below. He had helped them clean up this morning, but now he surprised her by presenting another bucket of icy salt water to her as she stood staring at the expanse of ocean. It, he said, was for her arms and hands and then for soaking her apron.

She had thanked him through tears. The tears had surprised her, for she hadn't shed one, neither while witnessing the ordeal below nor after she'd come onto the deck. She was exhausted, empty.

"You are welcome, little Madam. Women often have the worst of life, I think. "

Jeanne nodded and tried to acknowledge his kindness with a quavering smile but couldn't manage any more words. The sailor, understanding, gently touched her shoulder.

"I think you look ready to drop, my friend," Agathe, coming on deck, intercepted her. "You did all you could to help poor Madam Daleret. Now, you should rest. "

"Are you sure, Mademoiselle?" Jeanne was on her knees beside the bucket. She began to wash her arms in the icy water.

Agathe looked down at her severely.

"Would you be happier if I ordered you to go lie down? I am perfectly capable of managing by myself you know. "

"This apron needs to be washed, Mademoiselle. I fear the blood will set no matter what I do. "

"Never mind. One of the boys will carry the bucket to our door and it can soak there out of the way. The sea is calm--for now, anyway. My brother says he doesn't like the look of those clouds on the horizon, so sleep while you can."

Jeanne obeyed, returning to the cabin. There, she removed her dress, cap, and shoes and lay down. She lay still, while the sun filtered in their single small porthole, her back aching as if she'd been beaten with a stick. After some time in a daze of near sleep, she heard people assembling and the distant voice of the Jesuit, a stream of sound with no discernible meaning.

Then nothing.

She awoke to a roar of wind. Sailors shouted. Sails hissed and flapped, and there was the loud clatter and slap of rigging. The light from the porthole was gray.

Surely it could not be evening?

When she'd righted herself and put on her shoes and skirt and wrapped herself in a shawl, she went out. She moved carefully, hanging onto whatever she could because the ship was rising and falling far more wildly than it had done in a long time.

Overhead the lean forms of sailors scrambled up the main mast and then out along the ratlines, performing the dangerous reefing up the sails. Jeanne steadied herself against the wall that enclosed the cabins and looked up. The sight was dizzying. The ship rose and fell and wallowed, and the men above clung to the yardarm for dear life.

It was exactly how she'd seen Pierre for the last time, sailing out of La Rochelle on a choppy day, in a similar situation as today's sailors. Young, thin, and strong, he'd been intent on his task, his yellow hair flying.

She'd seen him working high up and far out on the ratlines before, but did not feel the fear she'd felt on that long-ago day. This ship was larger than any others upon which her husband had traveled, the yards impressively far above the deck. Standing on the end of the quay, she'd carried Michel on her hip and so had not dared not show her fear or give way to tears.

"There goes your Perè," she'd said pointing. Michel, whose fair mop of hair was a copy of his father's, shaded his eyes with his hand.

"Do you see him?"

The little boy nodded solemnly, his gray eyes intent. He loved the ships. When Pierre was home, he'd carry his son down to the harbor and teach him the names of the vessels and the names of the sails. Michel, barely four, had been an early talker, and he had dearly loved pleasing his perè.

That memory after the night she'd just had filled her eyes, but the wind might have done that too, for a high gust struck just as she made the deck. It felt like a body blow. She gazed up at the roiling clouds overhead and felt a terrible dread.

What if we are going to the same fate that took Pierre--to be lost at sea, where no one would ever know our fate?

Her lips moved soundlessly as she watched the sailors at work so high above, now about their task with the same quick strength her husband had possessed. She could not see Agathe, but believed she was somewhere on the deck. A sudden burst of spray struck her. Waves, great green hills rising and falling on every side, bore white caps.

She feared to turn and look to the rear, but knew she must. The sky there was not black.   Instead, it was an even more threatening greenish gray. This storm, she knew, was probably far bigger than the squall they'd encountered in the early, warmer days of their voyage.

The sailors knew it.   The other passengers sensed it. Those who mostly spent their days on deck were even now retreating below.

"Go inside, Madam!"

Jeanne started when a sailor nearby shouted at her.

"We're in for a bad blow."

"I must find my mistress," Jeanne said.

"In the Captain's cabin! Go to her, quick!"

Obeying him, she did her best to keep her feet on the deck. Like a nightmare, the heaving and rolling--a corkscrewing motion--grew more extreme. The sailor's strong arm came around her, and they staggered toward the cabins together.

As they passed the wheel, near the door to the officers' cabin, she spied Captain Martin. The helmsman was with him, and they were struggling to hold the ship steady. Beneath her feet, timbers moaned and shuddered. Overhead, the few sails still not reefed were bellied taut to breaking as the *Astree* angled to aim the prow downwind.

Ahead a wave the size of a mountain reared high ahead. Jeanne stole a last incredulous look as the sailor who with all his might pushed her against the door to the Captain's cabin.

She grasped the handle and tumbled in. It took all her strength to keep her feet and manage to slam the door shut. Suddenly, everything tilted upwards as the ship climbed the oncoming wave. Next, the prow pointed down again so abruptly she went to her knees. She could see Agathe, kneeling, holding onto a firmly attached bench seat close to the porthole. For an instant, green water appeared through the glass, and then just as suddenly disappeared as the ship sped down into the following trough.

She had to crawl to reach her mistress while searching for something to which she could cling. When she reached Agathe, frozen like a statue, she saw her friend's eyes were closed. Only her lips moved. She did not open her eyes even when Jeanne touched her and cried, "I am here, Mademoiselle. "

What followed was a long ordeal, filled with nausea and flashes of absolute, cold-sweat terror. The ship protested, sometimes threatening--at least from the sound of ear-shattering groans--to break apart. Timbers wailed and creaked; wind howled and shrieked as if a thousand demons had set upon them.

Jeanne had never prayed so hard--or for so long--in her entire life. Finally when both women could do little more than hang on, their heads drooped to touch the cushions. Outside, the storm that had threatened to destroy their vessel, had begun to subside. Somehow, they and their little ship had survived.

The next few days would be spent while the damage was assessed. Some sails were ripped and these had to be lowered and patched. Carpenters were hard at work down below, while the pumps were manned by sailors and passengers alike.

Not many days later, sailors cried out "land!" When people came up on deck to see, all that appeared was a dull gray streak along the horizon.

The ocean here was full of all manner of sea creatures, porpoises that accompanied the ship and sometimes, the great backs of enormous fish, which the sailors said were the famous cod. Sometimes, swift shadows startled smaller fish causing them to jump like silvery flocks of sheep that reentered the water with far-flung splashes. Captain Martin explained that those pursuing shadows were seals on the hunt, swimming fast just beneath the surface.

Though the ocean remained milky for days after the great gale had passed, however, as the sky finally cleared, many new and welcome wonders appeared daily. Sailors and passengers alike were cheered as they realized they'd come most of the way across the Atlantic, that they'd reached the legendary fishing grounds. With no further bad weather, this long, dangerous voyage was daily nearing a safe conclusion.

The sailors managed to catch a net of fish from one of those wild leaping shoals and land it on deck. Jeanne happily joined the sailors in collecting them. Someone loaned her a knife, and she went to work along with other passengers who'd come on deck too.

The fish were large, lively, and needed knocking on the head. Jeanne found herself sorry for them, so very bright-eyed and frightened. They flopped madly, desperate to reach their proper element again. At the La Rochelle market, most of the catch had been moribund, no longer protesting their end. One of the older sailors cutting fish nearby had grinned his bare gums at her and muttered something to the effect that he guessed Jeanne had not been a lady's maid all her life.

"I am a child of the *Saintonge*, Monsieur, and often fished with my family. "

He'd only winked and then put a finger to his lips. The light in his eye seemed to say that whatever less than genteel past she hid was safe with him.

Another welcome sign of journey's end were shore birds who mobbed their deck while they cut fish, only too eager to dive for the scales and guts as they were thrown overboard.

They ate well for several days afterward, from humblest deckhands to the passengers below. How they relished the taste of fresh fish, all grilled by the cook over a pair of three-legged fire-filled cauldrons placed on deck.

Chapter 3

On the rocky bluff high above the Bay of Tadoussac, stood a man bundled in furs. Standing tall, he used a glass to scan the horizon. Brutal winds whipped him and threatened to tear away the scarlet tuque he'd jammed onto his head, despite the fact he'd overlaid it with a ragged red scarf.

The last merchantman of the year from France was expected any day now. Thibaut Babin wondered if they'd made it through the big gale that had swept through a few days past.

Those unpredictable southern gales were dangerous to the ships aiming to make Quebec City during the end of autumn. Soon the Atlantic would be too stormy and that would be the end of new men and much-needed supplies for the colonists of New France and Acadia until the following year.

Of course, a trip begun in the spring also had many hazards, among them the icebergs which the frozen Northland set loose during that brief season of thaw. The bergs, looking like frozen white islands—glittering, beautiful--were ever so dangerous for any vessel to approach.

If the expected merchantman had managed to successfully run before that last storm and stay afloat, it should arrive soon. He and the soldier in charge of the fort, a veteran of five hard Canadian tours of duty, Captain LeBlant, had come to the same conclusion. As a result, for the last three days he'd walked the long steep path that led to the top of the bluff to spend his daylight hours looking out for a ship sailing toward the *Rivière du Canada*.

It was a miserable vigil this time of year. One of the conscripts from below would eventually take over Thibaut's duty, but he knew these Frenchmen were in no hurry to spell him. He also knew he was better dressed for the weather than they, so a part of him didn't mind much. Besides, it suited him to be out of the fort, crowded with the latecomers who needed to trade for supplies before the really deep snow shut everything down. Thibaut Babin was a Canadien, bred to the hardships and customs of the country.

So far there was nothing along the horizon; he leaned behind a rock for a time and peered over the top with his glass. After a little more futile seeking, he blew on his icy brown fingers, put away the treasured glass, and got his hide mittens on again. The incoming ship would need a pilot, which was why he was lingering at the fort so late in the year and why he had not already retreated to winter up the Saguenay.

Squatting, he automatically removed one glove and reached for his tobacco pouch, which contained a small supply of trade post tarry Brazilian *tabac*. His fingers, just inside, hesitated, then withdrew. Instead, he put the glove back on again. He didn't really need it, and he knew that to smoke now was just filling time, behaving exactly like the soldiers at the fort.

Annoying, but the inner voice that restrained him was his mother's, a woman from whom he'd been separated long ago. She had different ideas from his French father.

"You should never abuse the Spirit that lives inside the Leaf. If you are traveling far, if you are starving, if you are freezing-- tobacco will keep you going, so you can catch something to eat or reach a friendly camp. Otherwise, you're just being greedy, like all the other From-Over-The-Waters. . . "

He hadn't seen his mother for years now. The band with whom she lived moved constantly, following the seasons, following movements of fish and game. Thibaut had spent his first nine years as a member of a band. He'd grown up playing beside the other boys and learning Mi'kmaq ways at his mother's knee. Later, as he'd grown taller and stronger, he'd learned from Mi'kmaq husband and from other men of the band.

Then came the fatal day that his father, Simon Babin, traveling with a group of Métis traders located him. That evening, he'd formally asked the tribe for his son.

"I'll teach him to build ships our way, the kind my people use to go far out to sea. I need an apprentice, so let me have him. See the gifts I have brought to exchange for him. "

His French father displayed generous offerings: a large woolen blanket and two metal ax heads. Most persuasive was a large copper pot.

"Do not fear! He can return to you in a few years if he so wishes. "

The band, gathered by a fire away from the traders, had talked it over. Opinions differed as to what should be done.

"From-Over-The-Waters keep coming. They know new things. We can learn from them," one man said. "He could return and teach us. "

Other opinions followed.

"What do we need to learn from these fools? I remember when they first came to our land, helpless as children. They would have died if we had not taught them the ways to live here. "

"Let the boy go and we shall keep his father's gifts. His father wishes him no harm. "

"The From-Over-The-Waters have brought sicknesses, evils our healers do not know how to cure--even their own healers cannot cure them when they fall ill! I believe we need to keep this strong boy for our own good. "

"Those fine ax heads will help us build shelters quickly when a storm comes on. . . "

"But he is a healthy boy who learns quickly. Already he brings home fish and game for his mother. "

"He is one of us, not a captive! It is not our way to sell a child of our blood. "

"That may be, but the big copper the trader has brought is a strong one that will last for many, many years. It shines like the sun. "

Several other women, ones who were jealous of his mother, agreed.

"That big kettle is something we need. "

"Yes, such a big kettle can only be had by trading many beaver pelts. "

After a long back-and-forth discussion, the copper pot weighed most heavily, as so many, not only women, but men, too, needed that strength and durability for their work. At last, it was decided Thibaut should go with his father.

His stepfather was gone hunting three moons past, far longer than was usual. Some were already speculating that some mischance had befallen him.

His mother had shed a few silent tears but did not speak. The generosity of Babin's gifts made this a choice that affected the entire group, not simply her. Thibaut remembered his mother, heavily pregnant and already anxious about the fate of her husband and her place among this tightly knit band. He knew that two of the women had taken against them from the moment they'd arrived. His mother sat through the entire discussion silently, his sturdy four-year-old half-brother leaning upon her shoulder.

Thibaut held back tears of his own but knew he must show no emotion, no matter how frightened he was. At the end, his mother whispered to him to be brave and never to forget her or the wisdom of the band. She assured him that her new man would bring Thibaut back.

"Look for his coming, my son. "

Thibaut had embraced her and his little brother, resolving not to appear weak before the white stranger with the big black beard who had bargained for him. It was all he could do, though, not to shudder when the man placed a large, proprietary hand on his shoulder.

"Don't fear, my son. If you are as smart as they say, you will not only help me but help yourself, too. "

For a year, Thibaut had waited for rescue from this repellant white man by his mother's new man. The promised rescue, however, never came. He would never see his mother again.

Thibaut readjusted himself behind the rock hoping to escape the worst of the freezing gusts, now so full of snow. Though what Babin had said that day had proved true in a way Thibaut had remained, in his secret self, Mi'kmaw. He would always be grateful for the things he'd learned from his mother and the Mi'kmaq elders. If the whites vanished tomorrow, it was Mi'kmaq know-how that would keep him alive.

His reverie ended when his aching feet called him back to the here and now.

I've been squatting too long in this cold.

Awkwardly, he rose and stamped his boots. Thankful as always for his fur leggings and heavy boots, he removed his mittens and again retrieved the seeing glass from the satchel.

He warmed the eyepiece in his hands before facing into the wind and peering through it. Otherwise, the copper rim would freeze to his lid especially now that the cold wind had made him tear up.

Braced against the gusts, Thibaut surveyed the gulf's dark waters.

It was here, at Tadoussac, where the ocean met the outpouring of the river. From where he stood, the expanse was visible. In spring, whale hunters visited the bay to hunt the great beasts.

The Innu, Mi'kmaq, the once-numerous river Iroquois, Huron, Abenaki, and other tribes had shared fishing in this place since time began. Now, of course, the From-Over-the-Waters were here as well in their many tribes. They came not so much for the plentiful meat the whales provided but for their oil. A short distance west, another river joined the gulf, the deep, swift Saguenay, pouring down from what those new men called "Rupert's Land. "

The blinding sun was slipping beneath a deck of low clouds. From beneath that gray curtain, its setting sent a final, blinding flash of light into his eyes. Facing away, to the east this time, he followed the illumination across the gray water. That was when he saw it, something that hadn't been there earlier. There--far, far distant--was a sail.

Was this the expected merchantman?

He stood silently, raised the brass ring of the spyglass against his eye and waited as if frozen to the spot. Incrementally the sail grew larger. Time passed; twilight began.

At last, he saw that the flag, billowing, high on the main mast, was white. It was clear through the glass against the gray sky. With no visible red or orange, it must be the *fleur-de-lis*.

Time to go down to the fort and bring the news! A fire should be lit on the bald rocks above the fort to guide the ship. It was late, but that ship could make Tadoussac tonight.

He closed the glass and tucked it into his bag. What light there was would soon be gone. Just as he'd feared, the man who was to have relieved him had never arrived. Now he must go back quickly without a lantern.

Cold, cold, cold! Jeanne had never been so cold, despite the woolen skirt and fur coat the Martins had generously provided. The great gulf into which they had sailed was finally beginning to reveal shores on both sides, though the southern side had for a long time remained a mere line on the horizon. The wild wind was relentless, periodically full of snow.

As was usual, Agathe and Jeanne were on deck, hoping for a sight of their first destination. They had been told not to expect much, only a small, palisaded fort perched on an extremely steep cliff. Captain Martin would go ashore to speak to whatever military man was in charge, but except for a few sailors, no one else would disembark.

The Captain said he expected to load some fresh water and get news of what conditions were like further west, for winter was advancing quickly. A pilot would also come aboard, a man who regularly navigated the river.

The wind cut, and Jeanne was more than ready to go inside and escape it.

"Come Mademoiselle; let us go in now. It is bitter tonight. You do not want to arrive in Quebec with catarrh. There will be a fire in the Captain's cabin and our supper will soon arrive."

"Since those miraculous fish, there's barely a morsel left aboard worth sitting down for. If you are cold, go ahead. I want to take another look at the north shore before I go inside. "

Agathe pulled her spyglass out again. Jeanne had been intrigued when she'd first known that her mistress had such a device. They were quite expensive, but it was truly amazing how much could be seen through it, once you got the hang of it.

Cold though she was, Jeanne lingered nearby. Agathe--a woman she'd begun to imagine was actually a friend--seemed to be withdrawing. This worried Jeanne as she'd risked this journey under Agathe's spell.

She often wondered now what her life would be like in this strange, wild place especially now that Agathe had become distant and preoccupied. Jeanne had begun to wonder if Agathe was having -- too late -- second thoughts about her decision to make this journey, particularly her decision to marry Monsieur de Couage, a man she hadn't seen in a decade.

The Captain, too, seemed to be testing her resolve, carefully, during the brief breaks he had from his duties to spend with them. The length and ferocity of the storm they'd come through had stretched the entire crew to the limit. They'd lost a pair of good crewmen during the worst of the weather, and he had been affected by it, which he showed in sudden bursts of temper, a side of him that Jeanne had not hitherto seen. He was severe and short with his officers too.

He ate these days mostly by himself, either stationed at the wheel or alone in his cabin.

The ship had required some repairs after the storm. The sails of the mizzenmast had been patched when they'd begun the journey, and some of these patches, as well as where they'd been attached, had been lost or ripped away. Though brave sailors had climbed to those dizzying heights and quickly reefed them in the teeth of the oncoming storm, the violent winds had set one of the jib sails free where it ripped almost apart.

A particularly bitter gust of wind sent a cloud of snowflakes around them, sparkling in the last of the sullen gray light. Agathe suddenly took a step forward and cried out.

"There! I see a fire!"

She turned, her face alight, framed in that bonnet with a fox fur trim, waving one hand excitedly. Above them, the lookout whistled and shouted for he had seen it too.

This was followed by a general cheer from those on deck.

"Come! Come! Jeanne!" Agathe held out the glass. "Do please come and look at once! I see the signal fire. It's just a gleam on that western cliff in the distance. "

Gazing through the glass, standing beside her mistress, Jeanne saw the bright flicker. The landing place still appeared very far away.

"We won't make harbor until after nightfall. What a shame!"

In the morning, they both awoke early. Agathe seemed excited for a change, anticipating seeing the shore and beginning to learn about this new, wild place. Her interest sparked Jeanne's, although Jeanne couldn't understand quite what made her feel that way. Agathe had been so withdrawn before, but since the cry of "land ho!" she'd become full of curiosity once again.

This morning the sky was obscured by clouds, long flat slabs of a stone-like gray. Agathe asked Jeanne to hold her gloves and again took out her glass. On the shore, even unaided, Jeanne could see men in blue coats--French uniform--performing a drill, marching, halting, and then shouldering their muskets before beginning the motions of fire and reload.

On shore, high above, stood a palisade, dark timber uprights enclosing the fort, a structure two storeys high. The French flag was raised, but on this oddly windless, frosty morning, it barely moved. Other men, wearing heavy coats and a variety of headgear, were on a tall wharf, loading caskets into the luggers, no doubt destined to supply the *Astrée*. In the east, across the wide expanse of water, a low sun occasionally managed to send a sharp gleam.

Eventually, the luggers were loaded. Jeanne was impatient, cold, and hungry. She wondered how long Agathe would remain there, eye fixed to the glass.

"What do you see?"

"Just the men loading. It appears there are two luggers out there, both near full now. "

"I am going in, Mademoiselle. I am hungry, and I think I just saw the cook carrying a pot on the way to your brother's cabin. "

"Go on then. " Agathe lowered her glass and turned. "I can't seem to get my fill of having land and a few people to look at. Those pine forests! So dark and mysterious!"

"Merci, Mademoiselle. However, please don't stay out too long. "

In that strange low light, the land looked grim. Snow lay everywhere. Jeanne at once had a feeling that this snow was as deep and endless as those pine trees. Her mind immediately jumped to the most immediate question. *How long before my feet will touch land again?* She was more than ready to have this journey end!

Not much later, in the Captain's cabin, the cook and his helper were arranging their breakfast. A three-legged pot held a watery stew of lentils, and from the smell, a chunk of gray salt pork. It was end-of-the-voyage food, and better than what went to the ordinary passengers or the sailors. Her stomach growled. They were all on short commons.

She thanked the cook. She'd been in his position, while keeping house for her in-laws, sometimes serving the less-than savory food the family could afford. She knew the cook had done his best. He ladled a bowl for her and quickly covered the pot. At this point, they had given up on any ceremony, even in the Captain's cabin. A glass of vinegary cider and a chunk of stale bread would complete her meal. No one would be offended if she helped herself.

"We'll be taking on firewood as well as water," said the cook, "and not a day too soon!"

Jeanne had just scraped the last dregs from her bowl when the outer door opened. The Captain entered, however, instead of the expected Mademoiselle. Behind him came a stranger, a brown-faced, dark-eyed man dressed in the fashion of the country. His calves were swathed in furs, laced up with strips of hide. His long coat, too, was of hide, the fur turned inward.

On his head he wore layers, first a scarf covered with a woolen tuque decorated with a single dangling feather. He turned and carefully closed the door behind him before turning to face her again. He inclined his head, a polite gesture, although the tuque remained where it was. Jeanne got to her feet to stand for the Captain all while her eyes remained on this strange figure. He brought the scent of wood smoke and leather along with him.

"Madam Dube, this our pilot, Thibaut Babin, who is Canadian born. His father

used to perform this duty for merchantmen.
"

"Madam," the man said. He inclined his head to her again. "As I have said to your Captain, I know the river well. " His voice was a pleasant baritone. This time when he'd nodded to her, a short queue of black hair fell forward. His French was accented in a strange way, so with that, and his odd appearance, she imagined he must be one of the Christian savages she'd heard about-- that, or Metis.

The Captain sat in his chair and motioned for Thibaut join him at the table. Jeanne, feeling extraneous to their conversation, picked up her glass of cider and took a small sip. She wrinkled her nose. This was dreadful stuff, but thirst was an ever-present problem.

"Ah, Madam Jeanne, the ship has fresh water at last," said Captain Martin. "It's one of the good things we have taken onboard this morning as well as more food for all, plus a fine venison joint, roasted. Plentiful game to be found in these forests!"

Next through the outer door was Agathe. She leaned back against the door to hold it for the cook's boy, who arrived rolling a small cask, which he set up adjacent to the table. It was immediately opened.

Jeanne stood and picked up an empty jug, which she offered to the boy. The poor fellow had cracked lips as well as cracked red knuckles. Jeanne decided to set to work at once on more fingerless gloves before she left the ship.

Fresh water gurgled into the bottle. Thibaut stood and went to pull out a chair for the Mademoiselle.

This, Jeanne thought, *is the kind of experience my mistress came all this way to have!*

She was, however, a little surprised by M. Babin's manners. All her musings ceased at her first sip of fresh water.

Jeanne poured for Captain Martin and Agathe, but Thibaut refused. Jeanne set the jug on the table and then began to offer the greasy pot lentils to the Captain and to Agathe.

"Not for me. I was ashore where I enjoyed far better fare than that this morning."

The men pulled their chairs closer and began a conversation. Agathe pulled a small sack from her pocket and then emptied it on the table.

"Fetch us the nutcracker, Jeanne, and we shall try these. I am told they grow wild on the southern shore."

The nutcracker was in a cabinet used as storage for serving ladles and the like. Jeanne retrieved this, offered her mistress the nutcracker, and then watched as she cracked open a hazelnut. They had been heated in the shell, but she didn't expect much. When she opened hers, and popped it into her mouth, she was surprised by how good it tasted.

I am hungry for anything that isn't lentils and hard biscuits, even these dry nuts. . .

Both ladies felt the same, for they didn't speak, just cracked shells and ate until all the nuts were gone.

They sailed early on the day following. The weather remained cold, but cleared again, and so Jeanne and Agathe were on deck along with other passengers, although no one stayed there long. Agathe spent more time in the Captain's cabin, her long legs curled up on the long bench, gazing out a window or using an oil lamp to read.

Jeanne found the cold didn't trouble her all that much under her new wool cloak. As long as she could escape the wind and find a sunny patch, she could stay outside and watch the comings and goings of sailors, and pass a few words with other passengers, even though this was not her main interest. She found herself often walking in a direction that would take her up steps onto the forecastle, so she could walk past the pilot. After a few days, she knew she was much taken with this man.

Despite his clothes and his dark skin, he is handsome.

She began to wonder at her own foolishness. Sometimes the man would take notice of her or solemnly nod his head in greeting before turning back to survey the river from his customary post on the forecastle. He even slept there inside a tent he'd rigged up. She had seen other sailors do this during warmer weather, but to a man, they'd abandoned the practice as October had worn on.

Sometimes she would find the Captain there or one of the sailors, those who worked the sails, passing a little time with him, but he was a man of few words and very much aware that he had a duty to perform, so his attention remained upon the river, to the little islands that seemed to pop up regularly or to floating logs. Sometimes the ship would pass a spot where there were native people camped or fishing with nets. Sometimes, with large birch bark canoes pulled up on the shore, they huddled around a fire.

She became used to standing on the forecastle, studying the forests that in many places came down almost to the shore. In one place, a thicket of trees with pale green-grey trunks were still clinging to leaves of shimmering gold. They seemed to tremble in the lightest breeze, these trees of some kind she had never seen before.

Jeanne turned, hoping to muster up the courage to ask the pilot, and found, much to her surprise, that he had been watching her with his dark eyes. The shock of meeting them almost made her forget what she meant to say.

"Madam," he said in his curious accented French, "I see you admiring those. . . ." He spoke a strange word she did not recognize at all. "Your pardon," he said, observing her puzzlement, "Um--ah, yes! I believe your word is 'Mélèze'."

"Thank you, sir. They quiver and tremble as if they can feel this cold, do they not?"

He nodded, and this was accompanied by the briefest of smiles. They found themselves gazing at one another, but remained silent, at a loss for words.

His eyes were very dark.

Was he brown from exposure, or was that the color of his skin?

"For shame, Madam Jeanne," a voice sounded nearby, startling them both. It was Captain Martin, just coming up the steps from the main deck. He smiled. "Don't distract our pilot. "

Jeanne thanked her stars that even a blush would not show on her frozen cheeks.

"I was curious, Captain, about those beautiful trees on the shore. "

"Many strangers to our land ask about those. As I did myself, when I first arrived on these shores. " The Captain took Jeanne's arm and guided her toward the ladder. "There will be many curious sights as we sail in, but there can be dangers, too. Sometimes, even attacks on vessels such as ours by pirates or the Iroquois. Let me remind you, arrows from a good bow man can fly far. "

They had reached the ladder and the Captain gestured for her to go down.

"Go find my sister. She seems to be brooding in my cabin again. She should be out, walking the deck and becoming accustomed to the climate. See if you can encourage her especially on a day when there is so little wind. "

Dismissed, Jeanne thought.

She climbed down the ladder, annoyed. She'd finally found the courage to speak to this intriguing man and their conversation had been cut short! There was so much she wanted to know, but she did as she was told and went toward the cabin. Heaven knew, it wasn't much warmer there than on deck.

She found Agathe swaddled in blankets, her legs drawn up onto the window seat. Her moods were up and down every day.

"Were you on deck again?" Agathe sounded as if she was annoyed by Jeanne's presence. "I am so sick of this journey! I do hope we reach Quebec soon. My brother says we are getting closer, but it will still be several days, especially if there isn't much wind to help us against the current. What a treat it will be to return to land and sit beside a good fire!"

"Yes, indeed, Mademoiselle. "

"Did my brother send you in to find me?"

"He did. I had just seen such beautiful trees. The ones with the golden leaves that we have admired before. Monsieur Babin said they are called 'mélèze.' I was surprised that there is a name in our tongue for them, for I have never seen them anywhere before."

"Nor I," said Agathe. "That man's father must have been a Frenchman. I wonder what region he came from and what brought his father to New France. "

Jeanne was pleased to see her take an interest. Often, of late, when she fell into these dark moods, nothing seemed to interest her.

"So, Jeanne! You managed to speak to our mysterious pilot! Good for you. I have seen you studying him, too. " Agathe managed a slight smile. "If he weren't dressed so outlandishly, he might be rather handsome. "

Jeanne was not deterred by Captain Martin's sending her away from the forecastle. The very next day, she climbed the stairs again and approached the pilot. Monsieur Babin stood tall against the breeze, his fur coat ruffling. From the rear, he seemed to be a kind of two-legged wild animal standing on the upper deck, an idea that made her smile. She was still smiling when he turned and saw her.

A slight smile, the first she'd seen from him, momentarily brightened his features although he quickly became composed again.

"You have good ears, Monsieur Babin. "

He lifted his chin for a moment and gazed down at her before he replied, "Perhaps you do not walk as quietly as you think. "

"Perhaps not. "

"You do not think your presence will distract me? The Captain seemed to think so. "

"I think yesterday he was more concerned with my mistress, his sister, who is weary from this long voyage. He wanted me to go to her. "

"Is it your task to cheer her up?"

"One of them, but she is asleep now. "

He seemed to consider that for a moment and then said, "Come stand beside me. As the Captain has said, I must keep my eyes on the river. The river changes with the seasons, and I must keep close watch. "

She came to stand beside him, not saying a word. Inside she felt a kind of warm glow for at last he had acknowledged her.

"See there," he pointed at a small island close to shore. "A moose. "

Jeanne saw a slow movement in the rushes near the shore. The broad crown of antlers momentarily revealed themselves and then disappeared again.

"The creature can swim?"

"Very well. Sometimes you will even see them further out. Something on shore has alarmed him, so he has come to that little island. "

He began to scan the shore where the woods came down quite close to the water.

"Yes," he said after a moment. "Hunters. Or perhaps they are only fishing."

Jeanne gazed at the line of trees but saw nothing. Sailors' cries arose from below, and the ship began to change, tacking away toward the opposite shore, continuing their slow zig-sagging journey upstream.

"Fish? What would those be at this time of year?"

Again, there was slow consideration on the man's part. She wondered how long he had been a French speaker. There was a certain hesitation when things beyond the ordinary, or ordinarily nautical, were discussed.

"They are flat fish that live at the bottom. They come up the river at this season to lay eggs."

"*Poisson flet*? The flounder? I didn't know that they were here."

Babin nodded solemnly. The silence that followed was even longer.

"The ocean from my land stretches all the way to there, so, I suppose that it makes sense that those fish would be here, too." She thought she probably sounded idiotic.

Heaven knows I cleaned plenty of poisson flet in La Rochelle!

Snow came in hard, the wind incessant from the northwest forcing the Astrée to seek shelter in a bay. No further progress could be made.

Monsieur Babin, Captain Martin, the boatswain and the helmsman spent a long time out in the weather, choosing the anchorage, although it was swiftly becoming difficult to see much at all. Not only the storm but the early sunsets of November left them almost blind.

That night the Captain's table was crowded and the place was a little warmer from all the gathered bodies and the new wood supply. The Captain and his officers did not stay long but ate, warmed themselves with a single shot of hot brandy, and then went back on deck.

After they'd left, much to everyone's surprise, the pilot appeared, swathed in his furs, most of which he shed near the door. His face was raw from the cold and his brown eyes were teary bright. His lashes and brows were frozen. Jeanne handed him a cloth with which to wipe his face and he nodded his thanks before using it.

Agathe had just finished saying that she was warm for the first time in a month as almost everyone was huddled around the small standing stove. While the wind moaned outside-- and sometimes shrieked through the gap where the stovepipe went out--inside, it was stuffy and warm.

Jeanne cleared a place on the table and asked if he'd like to sit down.

"Yes, sit, share a meal with us, Monsieur," said La Franchise. "Thaw out a little. "

"Yes, how do you endure nights up there on the forecastle, Monsieur?"

Babin shrugged. The Boatswain, Haumont, who was the last officer present, said, "Ah, gentlemen! Monsieur Babin is *Canadien*. He was born on this side of the ocean. Isn't that so?

When no answer came, Haumont added more. "He comes by his knowledge of this place firsthand. "

"I have traveled *La Grande Riviere'*- *'Kitcikanii sipi'* my people call it--since I was a boy. "

"And in far smaller boats than this, I'll warrant," said Haumont.

His answer was a nod. Jeanne noted the ghost of a smile. She had seen, on one of the quieter days as they'd entered the gulf, natives traveling in a large canoe filled with baskets, people, and even a small dog that had barked at the ship as they sailed past. She'd watched as Babin had called down to them in their tongue. One of the children had waved his hand the whole time as they floated by.

It was early November when they at last reached Quebec. It was--as usual--snowing, white grains falling thickly from a leaden sky. Dressed in her best, Agathe stood on the deck. Her clothes were covered, of course, but Jeanne had helped her mistress get dressed and also worked on her hair, braiding and coiling it. They both regretted the fact that neither of them had really bathed since the voyage had begun, and it was clear that Agathe's fine fair hair would look prettier if it were washed, but all that would have to wait until they were ashore again and had not only available water but a good fire at hand.

Her friend barely spoke, and it was clear to Jeanne that she was apprehensive about meeting, after so many years, Monsieur de Couage, the gentleman she'd agreed to marry last summer. Jeanne knew how she might feel about having made such a bargain. She could only pray all would go well for Agathe and that this marriage of convenience would work for both parties.

She banished thoughts about her own situation. *One problem at a time.* She, at least, would have food and clothes and be provided for as long as she stayed with Agathe.

Sometimes, though, she wondered if she would ever find a loving husband again. It seemed even more unlikely when she thought about the prospects here--poor farmers and who knew what other near-do-well ruffians who were sufficiently desperate to try to tame these wild shores!

As for the handsome métis pilot, she couldn't imagine what kind of life he was used to. He'd expressed disdain for those enemy *sauvage* who lived in longhouses, so she'd been left wondering where he spent his time during winter.

Not much later, they were rowed to shore, ending at a tall dock. Above them towered a cliff crowned with a large, palisaded fort built of gray stone.

"The citadel took some years to build as you can imagine. It looks finished this year," said Captain Martin who'd accompanied them.

There was a crowd of people milling around the dock, others onshore, simply watching the arrival of what was doubtless the last ship they'd see this year. Some men were military, some were roughneck *Canadien,* with great untidy beards and bundled in fur. Boats left the shore even as they landed heading out toward Astrée to pick up the other passengers and begin the unloading of all those kegs and barrels that had filled the hold. It would be a long process.

Jeanne and Agathe hung onto one another as they stood on the pier as the earth swayed beneath them.

"It will take a while for us to get our land legs again," Agathe sighed. "This is the longest I have ever been at sea, and I hope that it isn't an equally long time before I can stand again without help."

She spoke with a wan smile, but Jeanne knew her friend was extremely dispirited.

A man in a dark suit of clothes and a fur hat was making his way toward them purposefully striding across the snowy pier. Jeanne whispered, "Look, Mademoiselle! Is that Monsieur de Couage?"

Agathe had been trying to maintain her composure, but her sharp intake of breath let Jeanne know that she'd guessed correctly.

Monsieur de Couage was as tall as Agathe, at least, the hat made it appear that way. An icy gust blew over them along with a scattering of glistening snowflakes, but Jeanne could see the man's bright blue eyes. As he approached, Captain Martin paused to bow and briefly tip his hat, revealing scant fair hair with the scalp shining pinkly through. He stepped forward and took the hand that reached for his.

"Ah, Captain Martin! And dear Mademoiselle Agathe! How glad we are that you have arrived at last! We were becoming concerned that the gale might have carried you onto Acadia. "

"We managed to survive it, though," and this was said with a glance at his sister, "not without danger and travail, I confess. With the assistance of *Le Bon Dieu* here we are with all our cargo and most of our passengers still alive. "

"An excellent voyage, then! God be praised!" With that, he turned his blue eyes upon Agathe, whose cheeks flushed with his gaze. "I am so happy to see you, my dear

Lady, at last. With your permission. . . " He had come close and now took her hand and pressed it to his breast.

Jeanne watched them gaze into one another's eyes and realized that theirs was not as much a marriage of convenience as Agathe had led her to think. She heaved a sigh of relief for her friend--and, for herself.

De Couage had brought several rough-looking servants who would pull them along in a cart, and the two women were extremely pleased not to have to walk up toward the fort they could see above, along a steep ascent. The area where they stood was filled with small domed structures made of bark, branches, and hides, all covered with fir boughs. These must be the houses of *les sauvage,* as those original *habitants* of this place were called, but on seeing their lean faces and their weathered brown skin more closely, Jeanne thought they didn't look much rougher than sailors whom she'd observed during those years spent as a fishwife of La Rochelle. These natives, dressed in leather and pelts, might have a bit more of the theater in their garb, with their necklaces and braids, but they no more alarmed her than those La Rochelle sailors did.

The women were both relieved that they would not have to walk for neither felt capable of keeping their balance. The solid ground they'd been dreaming of still swayed and actually felt like waves continuously rising and falling under their feet. Carefully, with Monsieur de Couage holding Agathe's arm, and Agathe holding onto Jeanne, they made their way to the cart.

Around them was a sloping plain, all the trees cut to stumps, and between those stumps the stubble of some kind of plant, one with a thick stem. Here and there were a few lean cattle and three or four goats, every one busy scraping the snow with their hooves in search of something to eat. From the huts of branches and bark arose the smoke of fires. In the rutted frozen mud were men rolling casks that must have just come off the *Astree*.

Suddenly a blazing sun appeared from behind the gray slabs of cloud, so bright, and yet on her skin, still so cold! Everything white sparkled, dazzling bright.

They were led to a mounting block-- another stump--in order to climb into the cart that the men held upright, the back gate opened for them. Agathe, normally so sure-footed, nearly fell, and barely managed to remain upright. Jeanne felt as if this was a dream -- the white land, the frozen mud, the black looming pines, the falling snow, the stark raw newness of the place. Above them she could discern the fort, the wood dark and weathered. Monsieur LaFranchise had explained this had begun in Samuel de Champlain's time, now almost twenty years ago. Champlain--a fellow citizen of Brouage.
. .

"I will leave you ladies here," said de Couage. "At my residence, you will be met by my good housekeeper, and she will tend to you. Just ask for what you need, and she will try her best to provide. I am certain you are both weary. Take this time to rest and recover yourselves. We shall all meet again at supper."

Then the cart, with them huddled inside, was hauled away. They traveled slowly over the frozen ruts, bouncing beside the small trunks they'd had in their cabins. The bulk of Agathe's possessions would arrive later for these were stored in the ship's hold. Captain Martin and Monsieur de Couage had stayed behind to look over the merchandise destined for the store along with others who were apparently store clerks and a few of the *Astree's* officers. The military gentlemen in their heavy blue coats had already begun the long slow trudge uphill to the fort. Jeanne, shielding her eyes against the snow glare, could just make out their cloaks billowing around them.

They too were ascending but not up as steep a slope. Along their way were cabins, trailing smoke. The only signs of life outside were men busy chopping wood, an occupation that must be never-ending in this winter realm.

"I am so cold!" Agathe leaned close.

"And I am too," said Jeanne. She could feel her friend shivering even through the heavy garments they both wore.

"I pray that there will be a good fire when we arrive. "

The journey to the residence seemed never-ending, but at last, they drew up to a long rambling building. The front was gray stone, and behind it was all timber.

The red-faced fellows who had pulled them there blew steam and snot like a pair of horses. While two steadied the cart, the tallest came behind and held up his arms for them as if they were children. Holding each woman by the waist, Agathe was brought down first, and then it was Jeanne's turn. She nearly fell when the man set her down upon a frozen rut.

"Watch your step there, Mademoiselle," he said, steadying her. "Just go through the door and shout if no one is there. "

Carefully, and still unsteady, they entered pushing through the heavy door, the wind and a scud of snow following them. Nearly snow-blind from the glare, Jeanne slammed the door shut and unsteadily turned. They were in a long narrow room with a counter extending along one side. The embers of a banked fire glowed blue and red upon the hearth at one end and shed what heat and light there was.

"Ah, ladies! Come in, come in!" At the back, a door opened and a round, lined face appeared illuminated by the glow of a hand-held lantern.

"I am Madam Hus, the housekeeper. I bid you welcome after your long journey!"

"We are very glad to meet you, Madam," said Agathe. "I am Mademoiselle Martin and this is my companion, Madam Jeanne Dube. "

"Come, come! I will take you to your quarters at once. " The woman's face reminded Jeanne of a wizened apple, round, wrinkled, and brown, and now creased with a smile. "Never fear, dear ladies! There is a good hot fire waiting for you. "

Not only a good fire--so hot that they immediately knew they must shed their furs and coats--but hot water in several kettles on the hearth and heavy sheeting to use for drying off as well as a large basin and a dipper! They hardly spoke to one another as they undressed and used this delightful treat for their numbed extremities. It would be a long time before they finished washing for they wet their hair and took turns helping one another to comb it out all while searching for the inevitable lice.

"Well," Agathe sighed at last, seating herself, her long pale form wrapped in a sheet, "it will be ages before we can scrub off all the dirt, but that was a good start. "

"Indeed. " Jeanne sighed. "How very thoughtful of Monsieur de Couage to have provided such comforts for us. "

The fire had begun to quiet a little and chilly shadows to advance from the corners of the room when there was a hard knock at the door. Without waiting for a summons, in came Madam Hus with an Indian girl bearing a tray with steaming bowls of stew.

"Nothing fancy," said Madam Hus, "and don't go wondering what's in there. I believe it's rabbit and squirrel and perhaps a bit of venison. Winter fare can get scarce even more so after Christmas. "

"The snow will be melting in a few months?" Jeanne asked. She'd never seen such piles of white.

The woman laughed. "Sorry to say, dear Madam, not until May shall we begin to see the last of that frozen stuff, so prepare yourself for the longest winter I dare say either of you have ever seen. "

They were both terribly hungry, but when they reached for the tempting bowls, Madam Hus said, "Best dress first, quick before you catch cold. Lily, rest the tray there on the hearth close to the fire, and go out now. I will help these ladies. "

"Our trunks have not yet come from the ship. " Agathe began to protest as the dark girl set down the trays.

"Monsieur has provided gowns and shifts and fresh stockings for you both. "

She went to one side of the hearth, and there, hanging, were the clothes. Jeanne recognized the gowns as a kind of fashionable "morning dress."

Goodness! This sort of attire was something her mother and her married sisters enjoyed. She'd never had a morning gown herself!

Madam Hus helped Agathe into her robes and left Jeanne to collect her own. Together, by the fire, they redressed, Jeanne modestly staying at a distance from the hearth out of the way.

"Tsk, tsk! My dear Mademoiselle Martin, we shall have to feed you up!"

Agathe flushed, a little annoyed by the personal remark from a servant she had just met. Jeanne, who privately agreed with the older woman's assessment of her friend, replied quickly.

"Mademoiselle will surely regain her appetite now that she is on solid ground again. I have been assured that ours was not an easy crossing. "

"You will pardon me, I hope, Mademoiselle. I meant no offense. Monsieur often says that my mouth requires a bit." She bent to tie the robe, but Agathe stepped away and belted the garment herself.

"I will go out now, but just use the bell pull if you need anything. "

"Some wine perhaps?" Agathe's voice turned sharp.

"Lily is returning with it," said Madam Hus. She quickly dropped a curtsy, collected their bath sheets and departed.

Agathe settled herself in one of the chairs, shivering.

"I already feel a chill. "

"Never fear! I shall put another log on the fire. "

Jeanne attended to this, then brought one of the wooden bowls to her mistress, careful to not unsettle either the chunk of yellow bread resting on top or the spoon.

"Here is a fine napkin," Jeanne said. She first spread it in Agathe's lap, fetched the tray and then got her own. She had no sooner settled herself when Lily slipped through the door. Why she had not knocked was obvious for she carried two bottles and glasses, one set in each hand. After setting them down, she entered the shadows and returned pulling a small table, the wooden feet scraping along the rough floor. After placing the bottles and helping them move their chairs, she awkwardly curtsied and then hurried away. Jeanne took the bowls and placed them on the table.

"Oh, dear, look at her run. " Agathe sighed as she seated herself once more. "News must be already spreading about the haughty Frenchwoman who has come to marry their master. "

Jeanne did not reply although she knew that earlier Madam Hus had assumed a familiarity she did not yet have. She also knew, from her own experience, how servants quickly become part of the family they serve.

There was a loud hiss and then a pop. Sparks scattered along the broad stone hearth.

"What is this--bread?" Agathe muttered. In her long fingers she held the yellow chunk, now sticky on one side with gravy, up to the firelight. Jeanne could see that it was some sort of coarse meal and very crumbly. "Ah, I know! It's part wheat and part cornmeal!" Agathe answered her own question. "I have read of this. It's made of Indian maize, the only grain the natives have."

They both tasted it.

"Crumbly, dry."

"It gets sweeter as you chew it," said Jeanne. "It does soak up the gravy though."

They were both terribly hungry, however, so soon enough their spoons were scraping the bottom of the wooden bowls.

When they had finished, they wiped their hands on the cloth provided and then, without another word, Jeanne went to the bed and pulled back the curtains. The bed was large and covered with furs.

"*Décor sauvage*," Agathe observed. Jeanne had spied a warming pan, the copper glinting in the firelight. She went to the hearth, gathered this up, and crouching before the fire, she used the scuttle to collect glowing coals. The hearth stones were very hot, but she didn't care. Suddenly, it felt imperative to warm the bed for her mistress so they could both subside into it. As soon as that was done, they climbed in, then closed the curtains. Despite the icy places on the linen that her swipes with the hot pan had missed, it didn't take long for them both to fall asleep.

They were awakened by the sound of wood being placed on the fire.

"Ladies, Madam Hus says it's time for you to rise and dress for supper. "

Agathe peeped through the curtain. The speaker was Lily.

First, she stoked the fire, and next, gathered up their empty bowls.

Jeanne had slept on the far side, and she found that though the rocking sensation had left her, she was still in no hurry to get out of bed.

"Ladies--I will return with Madam Hus and clean clothes. "

"Have our trunks arrived?" Agathe sat up, and Jeanne heard the hissing sound of her morning gown as she re-belted it.

"Yes, Mademoiselle. Everything is being pressed and freshened. "

They dressed before the fire in what was provided, in Jeanne's case a linen shift, a heavy quilted linen and wool dress, and a wool jacket faced with hemp and a broad kerchief of flax and wool for her shoulders. Even a new cap had been provided, and this, too, was of lined wool. Though everything was plain, it was carefully sewn and made to be warm and practical. Stockings of wool had been laid out on one of the chairs. Jeanne was astonished and touched by this careful forethought on their behalf. None of the clothes she'd brought, even what her father had given her, were anywhere as warm.

Meanwhile, Agathe was being dressed by Madam Hus, the two of them silhouetted against the renewed fire. Her companion appeared heartened by her husband-to-be's thoughtfulness. It was not as if she didn't have suitable clothing of her own, but it was clear that de Couage had put some thought into taking care of her--and that extended to her female attendant.

"Supper will be ready very soon, ladies. I need to go out and make sure everything comes to the table, so please excuse me now. Lily will escort you and she will fetch anything else you might need. " Madam Hus gestured and the girl stepped out of the shadows by the door into the firelight. Jeanne hadn't really noticed her before. As her clothes were dark and her face was brown, she'd been rendered near invisible.

This entire place, Jeanne thought, is like a cave. After traveling through a world of freezing cold and blinding white, they'd been immersed in a darkness only illuminated by the light of the hearth. The notion sent a shiver down her back. She imagined there must be windows, but these, she reasoned, must be covered with shutters and hangings to keep out the cold. The small oil lamp Madam Hus had carried as she'd led them to this room had hardly cast so much as a shadow on the floor.

Agathe sat down by the fire. "Come and sit by me, Jeanne," she said. "And you, too, Lily. Come closer and sit with us by the fire, here on the stool. "

Lily appeared shy, but after a little more encouragement, she did as Agathe asked, effortlessly lowering herself onto the low footstool. She scanned them quickly, and then, just as quickly, looked down all while gathering her skirts close around her feet. Lily had wary black sloe eyes. A crescent of black hair revealed itself against the close cap.

"Were you born here in Quebec, my dear?"

"Yes, Mademoiselle. "

Silence followed. Agathe smiled and tried again.

"Were you with the Ursaline Sisters?"

"Yes, Mademoiselle. I--I am an orphan. "

"Well, we are very glad you will be here to help us find our way to supper. "

"It is not hard, Mademoiselle. "

Agathe, a little annoyed, sighed, so Jeanne tried speaking to the girl.

"It is so dark, though, and we saw very little on our way. We shall be grateful to you. "

Lily nodded, then ducked her head. Clearly, she did not know how to respond to their attention. Any more attempts at conversation ended when, from somewhere in the house, a bell rang. Immediately, Lily shot to her feet.

"Il est temps de partir, Mademoiselles," she said. Lily gestured toward the door, and then raced ahead of them to open it. Jeanne could almost hear the girl's sigh of relief as she did so. She picked up the nearest oil lamp and followed Agathe out.

Instead of the earlier darkness, they found--besides the omnipresent cold--light, this cast by smoky lamps set at intervals. This was sufficient for them to see that what they had walked through earlier was not a corridor, but actually a storeroom stacked high with casks, baskets, and boxes.

Lily, ahead of them now, turned to discover why they were not following her and saw Agathe staring upward while Jeanne held the lamp higher to illuminate the scene.

"Le grand entrepôt," Lily said by way of explanation. "Come, please, Mademoiselles. Supper is on the table. "

The long room they'd originally entered was now fully illuminated, the long table there was now laid with porcelain dishes and silver on the upper end, the part closest to the hearth, now dancing with fire. The lower end, near the door, was set with wooden bowls and spoons. Clearly, this meal was intended for staff as well as for those ranked above them.

In fact, by the fire stood several well-dressed gentlemen who turned to see the ladies enter. Among them Jeanne recognized Captain Martin, his first officer, Lieutenant La Franchise and his aide, Lieutenant Desjardins, as well as Agathe's intended, Monsieur de Couage, standing beside a black-robed Jesuit, perhaps the religious who would officiate at their marriage. There were a few military men in their blue uniforms with bright sashes. The gentlemen bowed and so she and her companion curtsied. Then, introductions were made.

The military men were officers from the fort, another Commandant and his Lieutenant. De Couage took Agathe's hand and beside Captain Martin they stepped away and began a conversation, the Jesuit in close attendance. Jeanne looked around for Lily, but she had disappeared. Not quite knowing what to do, she remained where she was, hands modestly clasped at her waist.

Then the door opened and men who were more roughly dressed, in buckskin and fur, entered through the other door escorted in by an elderly, limping servant. They began to congregate and talk together at the lower end of the table. Lieutenant Desjardins, although Jeanne had pointedly avoided eye contact with him, made his way to her side. His dark eyes shining, he grinned at her.

"Widow Dube, here you are at last! You look rested."

Jeanne looked him up and down and said, "I doubt you have been waiting for me, sir."

"Ah, but I have! Did you know that there are at least twenty men to every woman in this colony?"

"No, I did not. "

"Do not look so shocked! Your days of being alone will soon be done. So many soldiers--and farmers – are looking for a strong young woman such as yourself. No inconvenient questions about your past will be raised here. "

Jeanne felt a flash of anger. She kept her voice low and answered firmly.

"I sold fish in La Rochelle because this was the trade of my dead husband's family, but my father is a prosperous salt merchant of Brouage. I have no secrets."

Desjardins smirked, and Jeanne had just begun to consider how much of an uproar slapping the sneer from his face would cause when La Franchise intervened.

"Ah, Madam Dube, you look much refreshed since your arrival!" He sent Desjardins a sharp glance, and the nuisance stepped back much to Jeanne's relief.

"Let me introduce you to my kinsman, Commandant St. Mars. He attends the Maréchal here in Quebec. He has served here for the last three years and has acquired a seigneury. He already has some farmers and tradesmen under indenture settled on his land. "

A round-faced gentleman with a big jaw and a long face stepped forward to join La Franchise. All the officers wore wigs so it was impossible to see much more than their face and hands. Even in this narrow room with a blazing fire, Jeanne was aware of the cold gnawing at her toes.

"Commandant. " Jeanne dropped a curtsy. With a name like St. Mars, she was quite certain he was not being offered to her as a prospective husband. Perhaps one of the aforementioned tradesmen or farmers on his land was in need of a wife.

"Widow Dube," he said after a solemn nod in return. "It is always good to see handsome unmarried women arrive on our shores as I suppose you have already gathered. "

"Yes, sir. So I have been informed although marriage was not my reason for accompanying Mademoiselle Martin to Canada. "

He had taken her arm and was moving her away from the crush at the head of the table. In the light of a near-by taper she could see that although the Commandant was no longer a stripling, like many of the aides, he was not old either. Caught in the gleam of firelight, his eyes shone blue and there were crow's feet at the edges, but he didn't look as hard-faced as the other military men here.

"Well, meaning no disrespect, for what other reason would a young woman come to New France if I may ask. "

Jeanne considered. This was a question that often troubled her in the wee hours of the night. Her dear Maman had often scolded her for being "impulsive." After all, running away at fifteen with a penniless sailor had not been a wise decision nor, really, was her sudden determination to accompany Agathe, a lady she'd only just met, into this wilderness. Sailing up that huge river for all those days had revealed a world she had never imagined existed--those endless forests unrelieved by only the smallest patches of cultivation with a few wretched cabins nearby.

Have I come all this way and over that terrifying ocean only to find more hardship? Should I saddle myself with any willing male creature and live out my days in one of those tiny cabins, a prisoner of the snows, just to be a married woman?

"Mademoiselle Martin believed her destiny was here, sir, when she received Monsieur de Couage's proposal of marriage. I--I believe--that it was her strong certainty to emigrate that served to inspire me to accompany her. "

"Well, you are both brave women. A rare breed, certainly, to dare a dangerous journey into the unknown. "

"I thank you for your compliment. I do not feel particularly brave tonight, sir, but here I am. "

"Well-spoken, Madam. Not one of us knew what this wilderness would be like when we set sail from France. You will be able to see more of the country when winter leaves us, but that won't be for quite a while I fear. "

He paused and seemed ready to say more, but there was a commotion by the entryway. Everyone turned back to see who had entered and the conversation around them died.

"Here is the Marchal at last! We shall soon have our supper. " St. Marr smiled and suddenly his round face relaxed. "I hope we will be able to speak again soon, Madam. Frankly, I would like to see my land properly settled. I have under my indenture a stonemason, an honest and skillful fellow I would like to retain permanently. A wife would be just the thing to keep him here; therefore, I would like you to meet this man. I will speak to Captain Martin this evening about arranging it. "

"As you wish, sir, and at my mistress's convenience. "

Jeanne hid her grimace in a curtsy. The proposal had been inevitable, but she'd not seen it coming quite so immediately after her arrival.

Never mind! After all, they cannot force me to marry.

The Marchal had been making his way through the assembly, and her companion had gone forward to meet him, trailed by de Couage and the officers. Jeanne stepped back against the wall, and then skirted the large knot that had formed around the Marchal. Salutations were passed and a path opened before him, leading to the head of the table, all set with fine china and silver.

Jeanne stayed where she was and surveyed the scene, illuminated by the flowing light of torches and the dancing hearth. The lower ranks had gathered near the foot of the table, a few French soldiers of middling rank, and men in leather and fur right down to their boots. As her gaze traveled over these men of the country, with their brown faces and braids, she suddenly saw someone familiar. Thibaut Babin, standing stolidly among the throng. Though she was glad to see him, she wondered why he had not gone back to Tadoussac as he'd originally said.

The upper table, closest to the fire, was now being seated, but at this end, no one had yet moved. Many of them were gazing at her intently as interested in her clothes and person as she was in them. All at once, she realized that she had become isolated, a woman in the midst of a crowd of men, many of them savages! The sensation was alarming.

"Madam Dube, allow me. " A man made his way through the throng, a man wearing

156

French clothing, a man whom she recognized. This was one of the officers from Captain Martin's ship, Haumont. There was a wave of relief as he took her arm.

"We mortals will sit below the salt," he said, stepping up to the table and pulling out a chair into which she gratefully slipped. He sat below her, and she noticed that the place he had chosen for her was adjacent to the china that had been laid.

"Thank you Monsieur. That was uncomfortable."

"It is something you must learn, Madam, for such is the state of this land--women are in short supply. As for the savages, why, they are curious to see our women."

"The Indians must--must--have women of their own."

Jeanne could still feel eyes on her. From their faces, she knew she would not like to hear their thoughts. She felt like a mare at a horse market.

"Yes, but their women do not come to such gatherings."

The noise around them was mostly of chairs being moved, and there was only a murmur of conversation, most unrecognizable. The Metis and Indians took seats, but many of them appeared decidedly ill at ease. Her attention returned to her plate when something close to an altercation began on the other side of the table. This was Thibaut asserting his right to be seated across from Jeanne between a pair of French soldiers.

"Gentlemen, please!" Haumont stood up. "Monsieur Babin and I have things to discuss. You will be able to speak with Madam Dube after supper."

Jeanne forced a smile and nodded to them, which silenced them. Immediately the company was called to order as the Jesuit would offer a prayer before the meal was served.

This was done, and then servants carried trays of meat, bread, and some baked brown knots that Jeanne had never seen before. Faster than she would have thought possible with such a crowd, they were served, their servers being mostly half-grown Indian children, the girls dressed in heavy skirts and aprons, the boys in woolen trousers, each one wearing a big wooden cross around their slender necks.

Across the table, she gazed into the dark eyes of Thibaut. She thought she saw a gleam there which seemed as odd as his apparent determination to be seated close to her, an inclination he'd never displayed on shipboard.

The table was near quiet for a time as everyone applied themselves to their meat or to their bowls, each filled with a creamy, steaming corn and bean soup. The strange brown lumps, on closer inspection, were some kind of root that had been baked on the hearth. She watched Haumont choose several and cut them open.

"What are those?"

"Topinambour, a root that grows wild here. In this form it seems rather like the Indian potato but does not taste at all similar. The root of this plant forms below clumps of tall thick stalks with many small yellow flowers. Even in times here when all other crops fail, these produce. They are bland, but filling. " He set one on her plate. "I've learned to be glad to have them. "

Jeanne picked one up, although it was still rather hot, and then bit into the flesh. It was bland and somewhat stringy, but she went on chewing with determination. After all, this was the kind of food she would eat here. It didn't taste like much of anything-- certainly not offensive, though it was rather gluey. She had, she reasoned, eaten worse at the end of the sea voyage.

"Madam, that root will fill your belly when food is scarce. " It was Thibaut speaking to her from across the table. "Indians and Frenchmen alike are grateful to find them when the game fails. "

Surprised and pleased that he'd spoken, she smiled, which apparently pleased him, because she was rewarded with one of his rare smiles in return. Jeanne lowered her head and took another spoonful of soup. This soup, her tongue told her, had been made with game bone broth. Cattle remained in short supply in this wild place.

Game of many kinds followed, venison, elk, moose, and tough wild geese. Some meat was salted, some fresh. She'd learned that here the cold was so reliably intense that meat could be kept in a frozen state until needed. Eels and white fish were also presented, food to which she was more accustomed.

Jeanne ate, listening while Thibaut and Haumont spoke across the table. In this way, she learned that Thibaut had been engaged by Benoit de Couage over the winter to guard the stores and to do whatever else was needed. One task would be to accompany Captain Martin to Montreal by dog sled where the Captain would have a chance to look over a small, new trading post there and visit local merchants.

Agathe and Benoit de Couage were married the next afternoon at the Governor's house. Jeanne was in attendance as well as many of the colonial gentry and the expected large military contingent. As she listened to the service, she watched her mistress, who seemed more resigned than happy. Agathe was almost silent, lost in thought, even her gestures subdued. Jeanne knew that the face behind the veil was a mask.

She understood that the marriage contract must have been signed yesterday evening after the banquet. Her friend had emerged from the room in which that piece of business had been conducted in company with a notary, her brother, and her intended. At once, Agathe had dismissed Lily, who'd dutifully appeared just as she and Jeanne left the supper hall.

"Is there water in our room? Very good! We'll go to bed on our own, so attend us again tomorrow morning, Lily. " She'd quickly followed this with, "Come along, Madam Dube. I am terribly tired." She'd walked off as soon as the words were out of her mouth.

Jeanne, catching her withdrawn mood, did not attempt any small talk until after they were within their room. When she spoke of the supper and the wealth of fine game, Agathe had simply shaken her head and sighed.

"I am exhausted. I wish to retire immediately. Help me out of this dress. "

Jeanne too was tired, but she wondered why her usual voluble Lady, who normally would have shared her impressions of the meal and the people in attendance--if not the private business-- suddenly had nothing to say. Perhaps it was as Jeanne had imagined at the end of their voyage. Agathe was having second thoughts about this great leap into the unknown.

"Our marriage will take place tomorrow in the afternoon. The Governor has graciously offered to host us at his residence. I will need the veil in my trunk to be ironed early and carefully laid out. Will you see to this for me?"

"I will, Mademoiselle. " Jeanne thought that ironing was not something at which she excelled. It was not a skill called for at the Dube house, but certainly the convent-raised Indian girls who served them would be able to do it.

She undressed her companion then folded and hung her clothing. Agathe settled before the fire with a hairbrush in her lap while Jeanne unbraided her fine hair. The only sound in the room was the fire settling. Water gently simmered in a kettle upon the hearth.

Jeanne went to get the basin. After setting it down, she brought a towel. Agathe used this to wipe away her powder. Afterward, she began to brush her hair.

"I will brush it, Mademoiselle, if you wish. "

"I can do it. Just warm the bed, please, and then we'll retire. "

Jeanne did as she was told, getting the warming pan from the stand and picking up a shovel. She carefully maneuvered the necessary number of coals from the hearth inside. After that, she closed the lid and carried the copper pan to the bed.

While she heated the sheets beneath the blanket, paying careful attention to the bottom of the bed, Agathe finished brushing her hair, put on her nightcap, and checked her face once more in the tin mirror to be certain she'd wiped the powder and rouge away. After that, she tied the laces of her cap neatly beneath her chin. They retired without another word.

Now they stood in the official residence at the very crest of the city with most of Quebec society present. The Governor's house was a fair copy of an aristocrat's country farmhouse, made of limestone, the front door guarded by soldiers. There were wide board floors and servants in livery to welcome them in.

Hangings softened the walls of the private rooms. In one of these, a dining room with a hearth and a lustrous mahogany table, they now stood. Every wig in the colony must have been donned for the occasion. The military men and various local officials looked grave. Even Captain Martin, who'd given his sister away, wore one.

Agathe looked quite elegant in a blue silk dress and a wig of silver, an item Jeanne had helped her into, both of them rather anxious about it as Agathe was not much accustomed to wearing such "frippery." The entire business was now covered with a veil as befitted a maiden lady coming to her husband.

Jeanne stood nearby. She knew she'd be relegated to the bottom of the table again beside the lower-ranking military men. They, like the gentlemen last night, would want to meet her, to size her up as a candidate for marriage.

She had only been here two days, and she was already tired of it. She'd made up her mind that if marry she must, she would not be forced into accepting just anyone because he wore the King's uniform or was some ne'er-do-well cast-off from a titled family.

She was also beginning to nurse a heartache.

How greatly Agathe had withdrawn once they'd reached New France!

Till then, she'd enjoyed what she'd believed was a genuine friendship, unequal though it was, with that clever, assured woman. After all, it had been Agathe's vision that had spurred her on when she'd been smarting from public humiliation on the streets of her birthplace. Nothing could have made her situation clearer: that in Brouage there were those willing to believe her to be a woman with a sullied past.

Now she began to feel that although in Quebec there was enough to eat and clean clothes to wear, she was right back where she'd started, as a dependent in someone's house. She'd simply traded her father and selfish stepmother for the merchant Benoit de Couage and Agathe. . .

Her father, forgiving though he'd been, remained roped to that spiteful woman who would never stop making her life miserable. To escape such a fate, she'd fled a world away from Brouage into the vast unknown of New France. With only the dowry her father had provided, she must steer a course to whatever safety might be found in this dismaying place.

Always such a bitter cold! Newcomers were constantly regaled with the dangers of the season. Nevertheless, it was hard to always be in the dark, smoky interiors of the trading post. The place did have a few glass windows, but you could catch your death sitting near them as so much cold streamed in around the sills. Sometimes, a thread of snow would slither inside to cover the window ledge or the glass would be obscured with frost that made elaborate, unworldly patterns across the surface, a frost that could be scratched with her fingernail.

The wind outside was relentless. It howled like a pack of wolves around the walls. Snow piled on snow, deeper than she could ever have imagined.

Agathe now slept with her husband, so Jeanne was now lodged in a small room with Lily, Madam Hus, and Marthe, another orphan the nuns had raised. Agathe spent most days trailing her husband and his accountant. De Couage was in earnest about familiarizing his wife with the fur trade.

When Agathe talked to Jeanne now, it was often of things she'd just learned from her husband or from the elderly clerk who had been managing the accounts. These days, what interested her were the duties owed to the *Communaute' Habitants*, which held a license from the King, or the rate of exchange for beaver pelts, moose hide, and *pelleterie*, furs which could be worn. There were many other hides and pelts that were traded, and each had a value according to quality.

"This is a kind of business of which I know little. De Couage says the Indians have changed their tastes since the days of Champlain. Trinkets, such as ribbons, beads, and pins, aren't desirable as they were before. "

Jeanne listened while Agathe spoke of rasade, glass beads sold by the pound, gunflints, lead shot, woollen blankets, vermilion paint, and copper kettles, the latter in high demand, and of how many pounds of beaver pelt each was worth. It was not the colorful, fanciful conversations of before. Instead, Agathe's head was full of little else but business. She did not seem disappointed or unhappy now that she was married or that the suitor of her youth had been replaced by a stolid, mature man of flesh and blood.

There were, certainly, newlywed concerns about which Jeanne was able to give advice. She hoped Agathe would confide in her if she became pregnant. Her mistress was no longer young and child bearing held more than average dangers for older women. However, her shipboard friend, who'd once shared so much about herself, was wrapped up in her new husband's business striving to fulfill her new duties as chatelaine of a frontier trading post.

Her husband seemed content, though more like a friend than a lover, but that was, Jeanne thought, often the way of things. Among proper bourgeois, marriage was a contract between two parties plain and simple.

Most people do not throw everything away for love as I did.

Jeanne had to keep reminding herself that things would necessarily be different this time.

I am older, wiser. This time, I shall marry for security. I shall find a man who is making his mark. If I am fortunate, perhaps he will also be one with whom I can imagine sharing my bed.

"Would you care to venture out today?" De Couage addressed Agathe as she and Jeanne sat sewing. "The sun is shining for a change. "

Jeanne's eyes were sore and itchy from tasks done in dim, smoky rooms, ever with cold feet and hands. At the idea of something new, she looked up quickly far sooner than her mistress.

"May I go out with you, Monsieur, Madam?"

De Couage, who did not address Jeanne frequently, smiled. His gray eyes shone pleasantly.

"So eager, Madam Dube? It is very cold and there are mountains of snow. "

"I miss the sun, Monsieur. I would be glad to see it, no matter how cold it is or how deep the snow. "

De Couage touched Agathe's shoulder gently.

"What do say you, Wife? Your companion longs to see the sun. "

"Will you be with us?" Agathe gazed at her husband who was often absent, traveling by dogsled here and there despite the terrible weather. Jeanne suspected that her mistress also felt confined.

"Not for long, my wife. I have to attend business along the river, but I thought Babin could accompany you. He can teach you both how to use snowshoes if you wish. Here that is the only way of walking in winter. "

So began their first snowshoe lesson, really their first outing in weeks. Jeanne could scarcely believe how high the snowdrifts were. Their path had been dug through a veritable mountain of snow with a slice of daylight overhead. At the end, there was a wide ramp of snow, stamped down by many snowshoe-wearing feet. Babin had coached them both in the narrow entry area that led into the building, an anteroom now lavishly floored with icy mud.

The snowshoes were not hard to get into, but walking in them took a great deal of effort. The women were stiff and unaccustomed to much effort after months aboard ship followed by weeks of huddling around fires. Jeanne found herself panting before she even reached the top of the ramp. Agathe, too, labored as she followed.

As soon as they emerged, there was another trial. It was sunny, fairly windless as de Couage had said, but the effect of weeks of living in that twilight, smoky world of the post rendered them, at first, snow blind.

The first flare of noontime sun bouncing off the frozen white actually hurt! Blinking, teary, Jeanne took the first few steps on faith that there would be solidity beneath her clumsy, bound feet even while blinding spirals pinwheeled before her eyes.

"Ladies, can you see?" Babin asked.

"My eyes are so full of tears!" Agathe cried. "They sting!"

"You both have been inside for a long time. " One at a time, he helped them each turn back toward the dark wall of the building.

"Stand still and wait. "

So they did, tears trickling down their cheeks. Slowly, squinting, Jeanne began to open her eyes sufficiently to see where she stood. Down the snow tunnel was the door they had entered weeks ago. Now they looked down on that same door because the slope they'd just ascended had led steadily upward.

Jeanne turned slowly, awkwardly. The frozen river and the dark line of the opposite shore swam into view. On all sides, the land appeared to be frozen solid. Here and there, further down the bank, snow-wrapped cabins, just roofs visible, sent up smoke.

Breathing hurt their lungs too, and they both began to cough. The only motion visible nearby was a man, buried in furs, shuffling along on his *racquets*, pulling a sled piled with stubby logs. From somewhere nearby there came the ring of axes as some folks labored endlessly to stay ahead of the cold.

Neither she nor Agathe lasted long on this first trip outside although they managed to walk slowly back and forth before the de Couage establishment using the strange gait the snowshoes required. The outbuildings and cabins they saw were half buried, doors sunk between drifts of shadowed blue. Jeanne gazed at the cabins and wondered how many people were huddled inside each one. She also wondered if this would be the kind of wretched life she'd end up living.

"Fine cabins," Babin pointed as they shuffled about. "Chinked up tight, some with stone chimneys, too. If you've enough firewood and food, winter is not bad. "

Jeanne almost laughed out loud at this immediate counter to her self-pity.

"Have you lived in such a cabin, then?" Agathe asked.

"My father just made a stone house for himself about ten years ago after his first cabin burned. "

"Were you there to help him?"

"No, that year I was wintering with the Huron who live upriver to the west, far, far beyond Montreal. Whole families live together in long houses covered in bark, as do our enemies, the Iroquois. "

"What kind of chimney would your father have?" Jeanne asked. "Those appear to be timber. " She pointed at the cabins below.

"Well, clay and timber work if the fire doesn't get into the chimney. When I first came to live with my father, his home was roofed with branches, hides, and bark. It was not much different from how I'd lived with my mother's Mi'kmaw people except he'd made a table and had benches to sit upon. Women here do not go out very often during winter, whether they be rich or poor.

"It's like the cricket and the ant," Agathe said. "Everyone who lives in New France must be an ant if they want to survive this kind of winter. "

Babin looked at them, a question in his eyes, so Jeanne explained. "It is a story we tell of how the ant works hard all summer storing food and the cricket does nothing but sing. So the poor cricket dies when the weather gets cold and the ant stays safe in his house beneath the ground with plenty to eat. "

Babin had given her all his attention. When Jeanne had finished, he nodded.

"I see. That is a teaching story. "

"Yes," Agathe said with a smile. Jeanne again wondered how good this man's French was. Sometimes he seemed--except for his clothes--just like an intelligent *paysan*. Sometimes, though, she had the uncomfortable feeling that he was studying them exactly as they were studying him.

"You wintered among the Huron? What were you doing so far away from the great river, Monsieur Babin?"

"The fur trade, Madame de Couage. I was among the paddlers returning with a party from a journey to the trading post at *Michilimackinac*, far, far to the west. "

Jeanne could see he was surprised by their interest.

"All those furs are carried in those big bark canoes. Isn't that right?" Agathe asked.

"Yes. Mi'kmaq make the best canoes. They are light but very strong. "

"My husband says there are many portages between *Ville Marie* and that far off trading post. "

"I counted thirty, Madam, between *Ville Marie* and *Michilimackinac,* which lies between two great freshwater seas. I remember each one well because I was younger and not as strong as I am now. The packs I carried through the portages seemed far too heavy. "

They walked a little more, panting slightly. It seemed mad to have to work so hard simply to walk!

"How difficult it is! It's far harder than I thought it would be. " Agathe seemed to be having a harder time than Jeanne, something that clearly annoyed her.

"You could not walk at all without the snowshoes," Babin said with the hint of a smile. "You would sink into the snow. "

"I understand that, but, oh! This is not easy, Babin!"

"It takes time to learn. "

"That I can tell. " Agathe's cheeks, at least what could be seen of them beneath her fur hood, were bright pink. Each breath came out as clouds of frost.

After they were inside again, out of all their gear and close to a fire warming their hands--fingers frozen to the bone after just such a brief time--Agathe said, "I can feel my legs aching!"

"Well, as Babin said, it takes practice. It's going to be a very long time until spring, and although snowshoe walking is difficult, I was really happy to see the sky again and breathe clear air. "

"Indeed," Agathe said. "Although my nose is still frozen. " She fumbled for her handkerchief and then blew into it. "Imagine! My husband says this is a good time of year to hunt because the game can't go any faster than he can. "

"Did you see Babin? He wasn't even breathing hard, while we were both blowing like old horses. "

"Yes, I know. That long voyage without exercise has made me feeble as an old woman. The Indians often travel at this time of year, great distances, or so I've heard. Sometimes they conduct raids on our people who live south of the river. Not too long ago, they even killed some farmers who were out cutting wood at *Ville Marie*. "

"Hard to imagine," Jeanne replied, although it really wasn't now that she'd seen how easily Babin moved over the snow, almost as if this was his normal gait.

The next morning they both had aching legs and backs, but the weather had remained fine, so they asked to go out once again. They agreed that they would love to stand on the banks of the nearly frozen river and look across.

Monsieur de Couage, who accompanied them this time, reminded them that the southern banks were almost a kilometer away.

"The river does not entirely freeze, you know, for there are still tides here. If you were to taste the water here, you would probably taste salt. "

"Yes, it certainly took us a long time to sail here from Tadoussac," said Agathe. "We were so hopeful when we reached here that we would soon be in Quebec, and then disappointed that it took so many more days to get here. "

"There is a great deal of tacking against the west wind to get upriver especially in November. "

Sometimes Captain Martin would visit his sister, but he was living at the fort for the winter. He too chafed for spring, or just a break in the weather, so that he could begin to get his ship repaired, launched, loaded, and ready for the long return journey to La Rochelle with the valuable cargo of furs and square-cut timber he'd acquired.

Sometimes, there were suppers at the house attended by officers and notables of the colony. Jeanne realized that among these were always some attendees who had come to size up a potential wife.

"A comely young widow with a modest dowry. " This, she'd learned from Agathe, was how she was described.

She had found that here no one danced around a proposal. Of course, a regular, proper marriage--unlike her first--was a business contract. However, in New France, she might be seated next to a gentleman one evening and receive a proposal upon the following afternoon. A young woman born in France, apparently, had a certain *cachet*.

After the first occurrence, she was no longer surprised when a proposal would be made after a brief, pleasant, but superficial conversation. No one of significant rank was among her suitors though there were two from the lesser nobility, seasoned military men, the kind who had come here young, often fleeing trouble at home, who had endured, survived, and carved out something for themselves.

Jeanne was thankful that Agathe had been nearby the first time because the abruptness of the proposal had taken her by surprise.

"Madam Dube has never had such a direct proposal, sir. Her father, of course, chose her first husband, who now, sadly, has passed to his reward."

Jeanne covered her mouth with a handkerchief to disguise her smile at Agathe's quick--and fantastic--intervention.

"Ah! Was this loss recent, Madam?"

"Some years passed, sir, but I had not thought. . ."

Agathe cut her off, briskly taking the situation in hand. "Madam Dube has made this arduous journey with the decided purpose to begin a new life in New France."

"Indeed, sir, so I have." Jeanne gathered herself and managed a smile for the burly, gray-bearded officer at her side.

"If your duties allow it, sir," Agathe continued, "please visit tomorrow and you may both continue the conversation in a quieter situation."

There would be others in his wake. In a scant two days Jeanne had two offers to consider. Each man had property here, one in town, the other on a farmstead he oversaw for an absentee seigneur. Every time an offer arrived, however, she felt rather shocked. The reality here was different from anything she might have experienced at her father's house in Brouage.

Benoit de Couage was often an amused onlooker. Not at the offers, it seemed, but by Jeanne's incredulity.

"You are a handsome woman, Madam Dube, or has this fact escaped you?" He leaned back in his chair and smiled at her. He was just as burly and robust as the middle-aged fellows whose offers she was now considering.

Much to her annoyance, Jeanne felt herself flush.

"And," Agathe added crisply, "her father has been helpful with dower, too. "

That Jeanne could not dispute. She had been surprised by the amount her father had put into Captain Martin's keeping. In fact, when she saw the figure, she'd burst into tears. She had not expected that he would bother to do much, especially with her brothers and Marie-Barbe jealously eyeing one another over the family fortune.

"We must do some traveling together with Captain Martin, Madam Dube, to see with our own eyes what each one of these worthy gentlemen has to offer," said Monsieur de Couage. "Dog sledding over the snow and across the ice is the way to go at this time of year. A journey in winter here is bitter, but believe me, it will be easier than in the spring when the ground everywhere turns to swamp and the black flies swarm to suck the marrow out of your very bones!"

Agathe wanted to travel with them, but she was in the early stages of pregnancy and morning sickness had her firmly in its grip. Besides, she was still thin from the voyage and had just endured a feverish spell. The bouts of coughing she'd started in January continued to make her short of breath. As things stood, her husband would not hear of her chancing a winter journey.

"Gabriel Le Blant I am well acquainted with. You could do worse, Madam Dube although he is no longer young. I know Mousnier and Lescaroux less well although they are reputed to be decent fellows and I know they pay their bills. Of the younger two, and especially that dandy, Lieutenant Jouin, I know nothing. "

"Husband, please take good care of my friend," Agathe said. "She should not have to take a pig in a poke after so much risk coming here. I know I don't feel well today, but I do wish to smooth her path toward such an important decision. "

"I shall miss your sharp eyes, dear Madam de Couage. " Jeanne replied with tact. "But you must not risk yourself by traveling in this weather especially now. "

What she wanted to say as well was that Agathe was no longer young, and it was clear that the long sea voyage had been hard for her, far harder than it had been for Jeanne, who was not only a decade younger but far more used to discomfort and short commons.

Moreover, a certain resentment toward her benefactress had begun to take hold. After all, she, Jeanne, was no longer any kind of inexperienced girl. Agathe, she now saw, was entirely certain she knew what was best for everyone. It was clear, too, that she enjoyed Lily and Marthe very much and relished the way both girls looked up to her and the way they followed her about like anxious little dogs.

These native girls, convent raised, had never had such a mistress, one who wanted to teach them about things other than religion, needlework, and obedience. As Agathe had dazzled Jeanne, she now dazzled her maids.

Daily, Jeanne could sense her importance dwindling. It was clear that the time of their close association was near an end. Agathe had a husband and a new occupation as wife to a man who ran a difficult and chaotic business in a place where danger was all around them and in so many ways neither of them had ever imagined.

Profits here, Agathe had explained, were not guaranteed. Profit in New France had as much to do with Europe's desire for furs as it did upon the tenuous supply lines from the West, these subject to wars among the natives as well as those between the French and the active, fast-growing Dutch and British colonies to the south. Her mistress now spent long hours closeted with the accountant or accompanying her husband on business with officialdom in the stockade.

The projected dog sled journey never happened for some alarming news regarding an expected shipment of furs arrived. The Iroquois had struck again destroying a group of traders who'd been bringing in a winter shipment. Not only were good men dead, but the furs had been stolen probably now destined for the Dutch traders down in Fort Nassau.

Monsieur de Couage dropped everything and traveled by dog sled to Montreal to assess the situation. He stayed there longer than anticipated all while news of murderous raids on farms arrived every other day.

Agathe was agitated, fearful for her husband's safety and concerned about the business. It was during this time that she began to travel into Quebec City to pray with the nuns. It was no secret now that during the last few months Iroquois raiders had stolen many large shipments of furs bound for Montreal.

The "good Indians," the Algonquin tribes (Huron, Wendat and others) with whom the French had allied long ago, were now under constant attack. The Dutch at Fort Nassau had allowed many traders, both

Dutch and British and those of other nations, into the markets at Fort Nassau. They sold, besides the forbidden spirits, modern weapons to the Iroquois, a trade in arms that had been forbidden in French territory.

Now, the original French trading partners, principally Huron, Montagnais, and Wendat, were under constant threat from opponents who were better-armed. The Iroquois, from a seasonal menace, now seemed to be on a mission to conquer every other Indian nation, whether by wholesale massacre or by absorbing captives into their tribe. The Huron, the first allies of the French, many of them Christian, were in danger of being destroyed. Many had already fled west.

When Monsieur de Couage returned at last, wind-burned and exhausted, he retired immediately to his chamber. It was clear to all that there had been even worse news from Montreal and the western traders.

"Benoit is tired and needs to rest. " This was all Agathe had to say on the matter. A cloud of anxiety hung over the post; it was clear that a great deal more trouble was on the way.

The worst of all the stories that arrived from the West was news that Jesuit Father Jean de Brébeuf and his assistant, Father Lalemant, had been captured, tortured, and killed along with most of the Huron tribe with whom they had been living, their mission and their town burned to the ground. The end of those brave missionaries was horrible--even to hear about. Everyone knew the lengthy tortures the native people inflicted upon their captives before they died.

Even before her New France voyage, Jeanne had heard the story of Father Isaac Jogues. That missionary had been tortured and mutilated by the Iroquois, a gruesome tale, which had even long ago filled her with horror. At last rescued from his captors by a Dutch trader out of Fort Nassau, a man called Arent van Corlear, Jogues had been smuggled down to New Amsterdam. From there, he'd returned to France.

Upon his return, the Pope himself called Jogues "a living saint," and had given a special dispensation to the mutilated priest so that he could continue to offer the sacrament. Jogues, undeterred, returned to New France. Not much later, he was once again captured, tortured, and this time killed along with the worthy Fr. Jean de Lalande who had accompanied him.

Now this latest news concerning the fate of Fr. Jean de Brebeuf and Fr. Lalemant dampened any relief they'd begun to feel because the sun shone for a little longer with each passing day. There were many tears and many prayers at Mass. More men than usual appeared inside the church to confess and pray. The Lord himself had died after terrible suffering, and now it seemed that these brave Jesuits had followed in his footsteps to their own bloody martyrdom. The people of Quebec felt it deeply.

As she was no longer so much called upon, Jeanne often found herself in the warmth of the large kitchen. It was a place where she felt comfortable, among the kitchen maids, servants, and traders. Here she heard almost-daily stories, most of which did not bode well for the colony's survival. While picking up what tasks she could, helping to prepare meals or using the warmth and light to sit and sew, she kept pace with the comings and goings of the colony.

Jeanne learned that spinning hemp was far harder than spinning wool, which was more flexible and softer, easier to turn into yarn. There were not many sheep yet in the colony and hemp was a crop that grew quickly in the short summers. Like flax, it had to be retted in water and the outer sheath peeled away from the stem and carded, a process that required tough fingers, a vigorous arm, and a strong shoulder.

The resulting "fleece" was wrapped upon a dowel, at last ready for hand spinning. This could be done with a drop spindle, like wool, but Jeanne had never had a great deal of practice as cloth--new or used--could be easily purchased in La Rochelle.

Here in Canada, so many things were different. Everyone, to some extent, lived like a *paysan*, hand to mouth, so here she must learn to spin hemp for she might yet end as a farmer's wife. Still, it was hard to draft the fiber, the fibers were shorter and far more prone to break than wool.

The kitchen was an interesting place to spend her time. Sometimes, however, the stories she heard as she labored at the recalcitrant hemp were so disturbing she would stop and simply listen to the traders and porters who warmed themselves near the great hearth.

"Those devils, the Iroquois, used to raid at certain times in the summer, and we were ready for them--at least those of us with a whit of sense. But for the last few years, their raiding parties may appear anywhere at any time. They fall upon our canoes both up and down the whole length of the river, steal our furs, and slaughter everyone."

"They just murdered my friend who had a farm near Trois Rivieres and carried off his wife and son. "

"Neither Huron nor Wendat can help us anymore now that the Dutch have given the Iroquois the new arquebuses. They are so much easier to load and fire! When one of our Good Indians happens upon a nest of Iroquois raiders these days, he just takes to his heels!"

"And why should he not? To risk being captured and tortured by those heathen fiends? Besides, we all know that our leaders -- *Imbeciles* -- went behind their backs and signed a secret peace deal with the Mohawk. How those governors, men who live so well on the profits we earn--at the risk of <u>our</u> lives--ever thought such a betrayal could long remain a secret, I do not know. If we, *fils de paysans,* know one thing, it is that the promises of rich men aren't worth the paper on which they are written. "

"The wind from their mouths is as foul as the wind that blows from their assholes!" (This mutinous remark was followed by a communal bark of laughter.)

"Beyond our sorry double dealing, it is well known that since plagues have killed whole villages, the Huron and the Wendat are few and can no longer protect themselves from the fury of their enemies. The Iroquois want to destroy us all, Huron, Wendat, Mi'kmaq, Montagnais, and French and give it all to those thrice-damned Dutch or to the perfidious British. "

"I am told Iroquois have attacked the Montagnais to the east and even raided north, high up the Ottawa river. "

"And they have gone west, too, into the land of the Petun and the Neutral. They are intent on destroying the entire Huron nation and all their relations. "

"They want the fur trade for themselves. Those mongrels who now flock to Fort Orange trade the finest new guns for our stolen furs. They have made the most dangerous of all these savages into the best armed."

The grizzled beards and lined faces of the speakers, men who'd survived life in New France for many years, proved to Jeanne that these words weren't coming from ordinary disaffection. These were true tales spoken by men who were well used to the hardships and perils of New France.

Sometimes she saw Thibaut in the kitchen, among the others, silently listening as he ate a bowl of soup or warmed himself by the fire. After eating, he generally retired into the shadows at the back of the room where he often fell asleep. He rarely spoke.

One day, Jeanne took notice when he slipped out the door. Abandoning her task basket, she followed him out.

"Babin!" she called after him. "Wait, please!"

Her "wild man" stopped and turned. He recognized her although his expression was, as usual, unreadable.

"Please tell me the truth. Are we in danger from the Iroquois in Quebec? I have heard so many terrible stories. . . "

"We are always in danger, Madam Jeanne. This world is full of evil, especially now that the Iroquois are on the warpath. I do not think they will dare to attack here. However, they grow stronger and stronger as each year passes. The plagues have weakened us--I mean, the French allies. "

She heard him correct the slip, for he'd aligned himself with his Mi'kmaq side. It pleased her, though, that he had let down his guard even this little.

In the dim chill corridor that led to the outer door, Jeanne came closer. Babin was beginning to shrug on the heavy jacket he'd shed in the kitchen.

"What happened to the native people who used to live here, the ones who were our friends? The trapper back there, Damien Roy, spoke of plagues that killed those people, and you have said something similar. Those Hurons and the river people I've heard about, the ones who used to build their villages here in the time of Champlain. What new sicknesses were those that killed them?"

"I think you ask about the sicknesses that arrived even before your people did, that is what the old people told me long ago when I was a child. The fishermen from over-the-water who spent summers on *Sipekne' katik*, brought them.

There is la petite vérole, the disease of pustules and the fever that burns the body and devours like fire; diphtérie, which chokes off the breath as surely as a rope tight around the neck; oreillons, swellings cover the face and underarms; and many others, all of which come with terrible fevers. My grandmother and many others believed you from-across-the-waters were demons. When my mother went with my father, Babin, she knew her mother would go into the woods and mourn for her as if she had already died. "

"But did those plagues only come to the allies of the French?" Jeanne stumbled, realizing that the subject was painful for him. *So much here was so strange!* She wondered why smallpox and those other diseases would only kill those who had become Catholics or who were friendly to Catholics?

"The sicknesses your people brought came to every tribe, including our enemies. Many, like the Iroquois, believe that if there are deaths in their villages, they have an obligation to replace those lost lives with captured people. That is called a mourning war. So, you see, the new sicknesses, as well as trade with your people for metal, pots and guns, has made fighting among the tribes worse than ever. The Iroquois have, perhaps, lost as many as our friends have, but now the Iroquois capture whole villages and force those they have taken to join them, to take new names and new clans. Either these captives do as they are told or, after suffering days of agony, they die in the fire. "

Jeanne shuddered. She wanted to speak more to him about this, but he was noticed and summoned by one of the servants for some task for M. de Couage. Of all the things she'd worried about while making her decision to emigrate, she had never considered the fact that this new land, as well as all the other dangers, was in the midst of a great civil war. In so many ways, it was no different from France torn apart by wars of religion.

The long dark of winter was wearing on everyone, particularly Agathe, who found the forced confinement almost unbearable. The last time they'd been out to practice on snowshoes, Jeanne had been going along quite capably even to the point of reaching the top of a hillock of white, a nearby drift with an incline. Waving from the top, she'd called Agathe to join her.

"I can see right across the river!" she'd cried feeling triumphant. For once, it was not snowing. The day was blue and clear. There was even a hint of warmth coming from the sun and a soft southern breeze. At the end of February, at last, the weather gave a hint that spring was--however distantly-- stirring. Just the idea lifted Jeanne's spirits.

At first, Agathe was game to try the drift, but her long coltish body would not cooperate. She'd slipped, fallen, and rolled down the bank. She had been having far more trouble than Jeanne in getting the hang of the racquets, perhaps because her limbs were longer. After scrambling to her feet, she tried again, but near the top she'd fallen once more. This time she'd gone face first into the snow.

Jeanne and Lily had rushed to her. They'd helped her up and gently brushed away the snow from her face. Once they'd gained the crest though, without a word,

Agathe had shaken them both off and gone shuffling back the way they'd come. After exchanging a glance, the two followed her.

At the threshold of the post, Agathe had called for Lily to help her remove these "*ces maudites raquettes,* and hurry!"

Once that was done, she'd gone straight to the door.

"Attend me, Lily! Hurry!"

Standing there, her glove on the handle, her heavy coat covered in snow, wisps of her fine hair hanging wetly about her thin face, Agathe added, "You seem to be enjoying yourself, Madam Dube. Continue your walk, why don't you?"

Jeanne had stood, stunned. Lily rushed behind her mistress. The door slammed, leaving her in the cold.

Agathe had never been so unkind before. She stood at the top of the incline staring down at the door. Her face felt hot and red as if she'd been slapped. Her eyes stung.

How alone I am in this icy place!

She wiped her checks hastily in case there were tears. Someone was coming swiftly over the hill, someone who was well accustomed to snowshoes.

She recognized him as soon as he appeared at the top. The low southern sun illuminated him, tanned face, his fur coat and leggings, his red tuque. Jeanne waved but he already heading down the slope with alarming ease on his *raquettes.*

"Madam Jeanne! What are you doing out here? The other ladies have just gone in. "

Jeanne was angry enough not to mince words.

"I was dismissed, told to please myself out of doors for a time. "

"It is very cold, Madam. " Babin, at her side now, gazed at her with some concern.

"I know. " Jeanne felt a lump rise in her throat.

"If you are to remain outside, you must keep moving. That is best. " After a moment, and possibly noting her teary eyes, he said, "We could walk together for a little if you wish. "

"I do wish, Babin, and I would be very happy for your company. "

He offered his arm and she took hold though it was awkward with the *raquettes*.

"I know a place you might like to see, but it is by the water. Do you think you can go that far?"

"Yes, if I have your help. " She was cold, but the desire to be with him was strong. She also knew she was angry with Agathe and definitely did not want to be in her company right now. It was imprudent, but right now she didn't care.

They started down the path, well beaten as it led up to the trading post. Soon they were among the warren of huts and improvised shelters that had grown up by the landing.

The ever-moving river was stilled now, glittering, iced into silence and topped with a scud of snow. Shielding her eyes against the glare of the low sun, Jeanne paused to admire it. Her breath came in puffs of frost; keeping up with her companion had been an effort.

Thibaut, now a few paces beyond, stopped and effortlessly came back to her.

"Tired?"

"A little, but this view is worth it. "

Despite the shoreline clutter and the chimney smoke that sometimes swirled around them, the vast frozen river, the dark line of the southern shore, and the blinding blaze of the sun upon it astonished. It reminded Jeanne, in a strange way, of the vistas of the open ocean at La Rochelle. Here was raw Nature on glorious display!

He stood beside her almost, but not quite, smiling. Jeanne had noted the impassive, give-nothing-away faces of the Chiefs who sometimes came to visit Monsieur de Couage. They might be dressed in all kinds of exotic finery, with feathers and necklaces of bones, and fur robes, but in their silence and erect carriage, they equaled the dignity of any French military official. Thibaut shared their quiet authority.

"*Kitcikanii sipi*. Our great river. " He looked down at her and observed, "You are shivering, Madam. "

"Yes, I get cold as soon as I stop moving. "

"Well, let us walk. With your permission, I will show you what is inside these cabins. I am wintering in one. It is just along here, a short way. "

They continued along the scuffed-out trail. As the drifts encroached, they began to work their way back up the slope. Jeanne hoped it wasn't too much farther. The "short way" was longer and more uphill than she'd imagined. Finally, they reached an area where a tiny cabin stood by itself.

There was a small nudge of anxiety, but Jeanne was too cold now to entertain any unpleasant fantasies when he said, "I will help you remove the snowshoes. We lean them on the wall. " Without another word he bent to her feet. She looked down seeing the red tuque and the black queue of hair that trailed along his broad back. He shed his mittens onto the snow and then she felt his fingers unlacing her feet from the frozen hide laces.

It did not take long. He did not get up though but moved his attention to his own snowshoes. Soon, he was upright again offering her his arm.

"Come in, Madam. " With the other arm, he opened the door partially, pushing it against the snow that had been drifting across the entrance.

Then she was inside standing in a smoky, only slightly warmer, darkness. She heard him moving away toward what was apparently the hearth wall, followed by the sound of him blowing. Next, there was a glow and then a flare of red as he began to add the small shards of wood that were used for starting fires.

She was shivering again, belatedly wondering if this was a great misstep, entering an isolated cabin alone with a man. Light suddenly illuminated him, crouching, blowing, busily adding more kindling.

When the flames stood a little higher, he got to his feet again and turned towards her. Above him was a low ceiling, barely higher than his head. They stood upon a floor of rough planks. A single broad bench extended the length of the wall with folded blankets, furs, and a single stool were the only furnishings her eye encountered. On either side of the hearth there were a few pots of varying size, a stone crock for grain, a little trunk, and a trivet. Hanging upon the wall beside the hearth were a long spoon and fork, and two shovels, the larger probably for ashes and the smaller for cookery.

Everything a bachelor might need...

"Is this yours, Monsieur Babin?"

At that, he shook his head and actually smiled.

"No, I am still too much of a wanderer. I am fortunate this winter because my friend is trading, wintering in *Ontari:io*. When he is traveling, though, he needs someone to look after it for him."

"It is well provided. "

Thibaut nodded. "Filion likes to be comfortable. " He picked up the stool and set it down by the fire. "Please sit for a moment and get warm. . . if you wish. "

Jeanne did. She had never spoken alone with this interesting man and, she reasoned, she might never again. She took the few steps it took to reach the hearth and sat on the stool. Although it was a bit tall--probably to suit the owner--the seat was broad and the legs fit squarely on the floor.

"Thank you, Babin. I will. " Although the stool was tall, she could touch her boot toes on the floor, and the warmth of the little fire felt good. She even pulled her skirts up a little, to the tops of her boots because her toes ached.

"This is very comfortable. You are fortunate to be here away from the barracks. "

"Yes. That life doesn't suit me. We won't stay too long because it's a long walk back to the stockade. "

"Yes, I agree. "

She watched as he gracefully folded cross-legged onto a mat of grass laid to one side of the stool. She couldn't understand how he could do that although she'd certainly seen Huron at the trading post seated in this manner.

"Is *Ontari:io* an island?"

"No, it is the name of one of the big freshwater lakes that lies west. There is an island in the next lake, Lac des Hurons, you call it. This island is called Michilimackinac, which also may be where Filion winters. He has spoken of friends there. "

"Huron?"

"Yes, and a few other tribes who are cousins of the Huron--or as they call themselves, Wendat. They speak a similar tongue and live in peace, mostly. "

"You seem to know all the languages. "

"Oh, no, Madam Jeanne. There are as many other languages I have never heard on this side of the great salt water. There is a way of signing with the hands for trade and that I know. I am told there are many different languages in your distant land. "

Babin smiled at her as he spoke. Looking up at her in flickering firelight, he almost appeared boyish.

He is so handsome. . .

Hastily, Jeanne interrupted her thoughts to ask, "Captain Martin told me that there is another great salt sea far to the west, and that distant sea is the way to far away Chine, wealthiest of all nations. "

"Is that what your people came here seeking? The Kingdom of far away Chine?"

Jeanne had to think before she answered. She really knew very little about the English and the Dutch who had landed on the northern end of the new world years after the Spanish had conquered the famous Kingdoms of Gold that lay to the south.

From what little she had seen, New France was very cold and covered in dark, deep forests. *So much work would have to be done if there were ever to be farms!* Jeanne did know a little about the great man who had come from Brouage, just as she had, the sea captain Samuel Champlain, the man who'd been trusted to become the first leader of the King's new plantation here. She had seen his new grave in Quebec City, on the heights above, now placed beside the recently reconstructed Notre-Dame-de-Recouvrance. The original church, she'd been told, had burned to the ground.

"I think my people followed the Basque fishermen here for codfish, but then learned of your many fine fur animals. These days every gentleman in Europe must have a beaver hat. "

Thibaut nodded. "My father lived beside many Basques when he first came to this country. " He paused for a moment before speaking again.

"But when, I wonder, will your people begin to truly see our beautiful land?"

Silence fell between them. Jeanne didn't understand what he meant.

Thibaut withdrew into his own thoughts, and they sat silently for some time. Jeanne focused on warming her feet, but already the small fire had begun to fade.

"We should go back. They will think you are in trouble. "

"Yes, of course. " Jeanne got up and moved away so her companion could bank the fire. She retreated toward the door, which was, after all, only a few steps away and watched as he used a piece of kindling to carefully bank and then push the embers deep into the hearth.

Soon they were back outside. In the cold, Jeanne worked to fasten her snowshoes onto the boots. The wind had quickened. A high scud obscured the sun. Already their trail to the cabin from below was covered in snow.

"I will break trail ahead. "

"Thank you, Babin, for your hospitality. " Jeanne said the words, but the wind blew so briskly she didn't know if he'd heard.

Next, a hard trek--at least for Jeanne--followed as they ascended the slope to the post. No more was said, and Thibaut managed to make a swift retreat as soon as a servant, standing outside the post door, recognized Jeanne and began waving his hands, shouting questions about *où au nom de tout ce qui est saints* she had been off to?

* * *

Now that Jeanne had begun to master the wide swinging gate required by snowshoes, she walked out for brief intervals on her own. She sometimes wished that she could wear trousers, like the men, because her skirts caused her all kinds of troubles especially when the hem was weighed down with snow.

She didn't dare go too far as it was, no doubt, as unsafe for a woman on her own here as it could be in France--never mind that the terrible weather could quickly freeze you to death. She hoped to see Babin again, but for a time, de Couage kept him busy with travel.

Then the day came when they did meet just as she was about to turn back from what had become an almost-daily outing. She was in the habit of laboring to the top of a nearby white dune from which she could see down to the river, now sheathed in ice. The only exception was a central black stream that still appeared to be moving. Near this, she saw--oh, so far away--the moving shapes of geese and other water birds who flew down to rest on the ledge between ice and water.

Sometimes they'd fly up in a great cloud, shouting alarm when an eagle or great red-tailed hawk swooped down falling from the sky like a meteor. When the hunter struck, like a dragon from some ancient tale, feathers flew. Away the dark-winged hunter would fly with the limp body, neck broken, grasped tightly in its talons. She'd watch as the great bird, an eagle, hurtled away, meal secured.

The first time she'd seen it in New France, she'd gasped, and instinctively covered her mouth with both hands, filled with a sudden horror. Tears that stung painfully sprang into her eyes.

In her mind, she'd been the goose flying high, beautifully alive. In an instant, the freedom she'd been imagining had ended in a single, deadly strike. Heartsick, she'd watched as the flock scattered into the blue, crying with distress. She stood for a long time frozen in place, with the wind swirling around her.

Then someone approached moving along quickly toward her. She did not want to speak to anyone and hoped they would soon pass her by.

"Madam Jeanne? Has something frightened you?"

Thibaut.

Still unable to speak, she'd turned to him, minding the snowshoes. He recognized her distress at once and held out his gloved hands, hands she grasped gratefully.

His dark eyes surveyed her. She hoped that he could comprehend her distress, her tears. She did not want to be ashamed of her emotion, not even before a man who had doubtless killed many living creatures.

"We all must eat," he said, but gently, almost as if speaking to a child. She was grateful for in that moment a most tender part of her was exposed. "Yes," she replied. "Of course. Everyone eats meat, and I have killed ever so many fish, and--and--chopped the heads off chickens, too, but. . . " To say that she had been flying with that goose seemed mad, but, somehow, although at this moment, it was the truth.

"Perhaps," Thibaut said slowly, "the geese are your spirit companions. "

When she looked puzzled, he explained, now a little embarrassed himself. "It is a belief of my mother's people that we all have a spirit guardian who watches over us, one who comes to us in the guise of an animal. "

Jeanne nodded slowly. Perhaps that made as much sense as anything, that connection she'd been feeling with the bird.

"My mother's people have clans--like your family names--who are called after winged creatures. *Kitpa* is "eagle" and *Kokokwes* is "owl," but I have never heard of a goose clan. " His eyes brightened as he studied her.

"Come," he said. "Let us go down to the river and see the ice."

Jeanne was so happy to hear this that she forgot how cold and sorrowful she'd felt. She went along with him gladly, angling along the slope until they reached a spot where a small creek came down from the plateau above and emptied into the river.

The creek was frozen now like an icy ladder leading ever downward. This terminated in a low hollow, today a solid pool of ice. As Jeanne drew closer, she saw that there were different textures and colors to it, some rough, some parts were smooth as glass, others, milky white. Still other patches were like lace because air bubbles had frozen beneath the surface. Peering down into this was like looking into another, magical world.

"Ice fisherman!" Thibaut pointed toward the southern shore, and Jeanne saw men here and there sitting, some on low stools, others on boxes that they'd carried out. At lower elevation, the river appeared completely frozen.

"What do you catch in winter?" Jeanne was at once interested.

"Do you want to go out and see? I have a jig in my bag. " He indicated his ever-present hip bag. "You must go out carefully," he added, "because the ice can make it difficult if the snowshoe isn't purpose-made for walking on ice. Here," he said, extending a glove. "hold my hand. "

The first time they went out, they did not go far, just far enough to see what the nearest fisherman had caught. As they approached, Jeanne saw the fisherman busily drawing his line up and down, not steadily but in an erratic fashion. Frozen on the ice beside him was a string of small fish.

"What are they?" Jeanne asked, after the man had turned and touched his brow in a polite salute.

"Yellow perch and crappie, Madame. Not large, but enough for supper. "

"And better than spending the day tending the fire inside in the smoke," Thibaut added.

"Or chopping wood," the fisherman added with a truant grin. "Thank heaven for strong women. . ."

This was the first of many walks to the river because now Jeanne was keen to try her hand at ice fishing. She was proud of herself for putting so much effort into learning to use the snowshoes because it was a long, cold jaunt to the trading post and, even harder, back up the slope. If she had not built up her strength with these outings, she wouldn't have been able to endure the effort.

She made an agreement with Babin to meet by the water in the afternoon on the same day of the next week although they both understood that his orders--or hers-- could supersede their arrangement. For the next few weeks, the weather cooperated, as did their duties, and they ventured out onto the ice together carrying boxes upon which to sit.

The first time they went out, they didn't catch much. Babin had arranged to make use of a hole one of his friends had made. When they arrived, after a little difficulty in locating the exact spot, they set down the stools they'd brought. Jeanne sat, and Babin helped her remove the raquettes.

"Be careful now," he said as she stood. "The ice will feel different from snow. "

He'd brought a jig in his bag. The lure was a carved piece of horn attached in such a way that it would whirl and twist when drawn through the water. The flashing would attract the attention of a larger fish. If they were lucky, they might get a bite.

The cold was almost exhilarating when she first gazed across the great expanse of ice. She could almost feel Thibaut's presence beside her. Here she was in the New World! The season was bitter, cold, strange, and even more threatening than the old – but somehow she felt stronger here, freer.

Or was that the company?

The ice was always beautiful. The color changed every day, sometimes stone gray, sometimes sparkling, eye-shattering days when her nostrils were nearly stopped with frost. When she smiled her teeth ached. When she put the stool down and sat, her feet began to freeze almost at once. Nevertheless, every moment here, released from the dark trading post, beside this man, brought her to life. Glancing down at the ice in the hollow when they returned, Jeanne stumbled on numb feet.

Her hands burned and throbbed, but there again was that frozen lace, motionless sea-foam, the flow arrested, each bubble stationary. As cold as she was, even knowing how hard the trek back would be, she'd always pause, take a moment to gaze at it, hoping to fix the beautiful images in her mind.

"Come, Madam Jeanne," he'd say. It was a summons, but delivered gently. "It is very cold today and you have stayed long."

"This cascade, all frozen, reminds me of something, but until today I've never been able to think what. Now, at last I see that it is like a wave, like the crests of waves as they roll onshore, all foaming, ever changing, like the ocean at La Rochelle. Only cold as it is, these waves don't move."

One of his rare smiles appeared, just a slight curl of his lips and brightening of his dark eyes. The day she'd made that speech he'd nodded, seemed to understand.

He took her gloved hand in his. "Time to go now, Jeanne. They will wonder where you are."

"What about our catch?" Usually a few of the fish Babin kept, but most they left with a family wintering in one of the huts where he knew the man of the house had fallen ill and could not work. On those days, they had not lingered, only knocked, summoning one of the children to the door to receive the catch.

For Jeanne, as he'd predicted, it was an effort getting back up the slope. Her ankles burned and her toes passed through throbbing to pain to nothingness. When she finally made the door of the post and went inside, he followed to help her unfasten the snowshoes. It was the last moment they'd be together again until the next week. Jeanne treasured everyone of these outings.

When she bent to dig the icy snow off her boots, he always helped with his own tough fingers. It brought their heads together. Breath mingled in the chill, a brief moment of closeness, where she could hear his breath going in and out. It made a connection, although one without any palpable touch, it was one she could feel.

"Is this where the lady has been?" The door that led into the living quarters opened suddenly. A shadow stood there. The speaker was de Couage. The tone was amused, but the expression on the face was disapproving. Even in the twilight of the room Jeanne could see it. At once, Thibaut stood and made the customary gesture of respect, removing his cap.

"My wife requires Madam Dube at once. She has had everyone in an uproar looking everywhere for her. She had better go to the kitchen first and use some warm water on her feet and hands. Let me remind you that a woman loses her value here, Madam Dube, just as in France, if she loses her toes or fingers—not to mention after losing her nose."

"Sir, if you please, she has not been out of doors long enough for frostbite."

"That is not for you to judge, Babin. The lady is new to this land and still not accustomed to our climate. From now on, Madame Dube, you must speak to my wife and receive her permission before going out."

Jeanne was furious. She was not indentured or any kind of servant! Still, she knew she had better not express that opinion just now. It was clear that Babin would receive a sterner lecture after she had gone.

In the kitchen, many of the women looked at her with knowing eyes. No one spoke to her. Jeanne collected what she needed, water and basin, and retired to a corner of the room where she unlaced her boots. She hated the very thought of what came next but went ahead anyway, sinking her dead feet into the basin, gritting her teeth. No doubt more discomfort would arrive when she reached Agathe's rooms.

Agathe was, as expected, red-nosed, angry at showing her feelings, angry at her confinement, angry at everything.

"You have journeyed away from an impossible situation only through my good graces, but today you are nowhere to be found when I need you! It is quite intolerable!"

Jeanne said nothing. She, too, was angry and knew she could not trust herself to speak.

"I am ill! You know how dreadful I feel—every day--and yet you desert me!"

"I only went out to exercise and feel sun on my face, Madame de Couage, just as you would yourself if you were in better health."

"Don't you dare justify your dereliction! Don't you dare!" Agathe began to sob. Despite herself, Jeanne was moved by the sorry spectacle. She had never seen a woman whose strong spirit had been so entirely reduced by pregnancy. She would never have imagined seeing Agathe in such a state.

"I am sorry I went out without asking. You will feel better soon. The doctor says so as does Father Marchand. You mustn't worry so much."

Tears were the only response. Jeanne came closer and laid a hand on her companion's shoulder. Agathe pushed it away.

"Don't! I hate it when people pretend to be sorry, and I hate being sick!"

"I am not pretending. I am sorry to see you so. Come, Madame! I am here now. What would you have of me?"

"Sit here, beside me. I miss your company."

Jeanne did, sitting on the reclining couch while Agathe adjusted her legs to make space. Her toes still ached, and she longed to rub them. She hoped that the atmosphere of this room would soon cure it for the fire was built up high and there were many candles blazing all around Agathe's couch.

The cost of so many lights Jeanne could scarcely imagine. . .

"Where have you been?"

"Ice fishing on the river."

"With Babin?"

"Yes, Madame. He had time to escort me there and back today."

"And why do we never see any of those fish, here in our kitchen?"

Jeanne understood that Agathe was determined to remain angry. She seemed to be waiting to catch her out over something. It was another unpleasant trait she had never expected her benefactress to show—pettiness. She, Jeanne thought, could put the Dube women to shame at that game because Agathe was far cleverer.

"Because if we catch them—and you do not catch many at this time of year—we take them to people in the huts who are hungry."

Agathe sighed and readjusted herself. "Why don't they fish for themselves? Surely a line and a lure are not difficult to obtain."

"There are children, Madame, and the parents are sick—perhaps with the same catarrh that has so troubled you this winter."

"You pretend to charity, Jeanne, but you are spending time with that handsome Metis, instead of tending to your business here."

Jeanne shot to her feet. "And just what is my business here, Madame? What would you have me do? Since the Feast of Our Lord's birth, you have been unwell and closeted in your chambers spending every hour with your convent girls. I think I ought to learn more of this country, one in which I shall take a husband, instead of sitting about in the kitchen listening to gossip. I sew and I learn to spin hemp if there is work of that kind for me. If you think I would be better occupied scrubbing your floors, then I will, but you must give the order."

At the end of this speech, she tossed her head angrily.

Agathe has no idea of what life has been like for me here. She is intolerable—even to someone as beholden as I am!

"Stop being dramatic, Jeanne! I would never expect you to scrub the floors, but every time you walk out with that Metis, a man who is a simple jack-of-all-trades--a soldier, or a sailor, or in the wilderness doing God knows what with those savage *Coureurs de bois*—you – you remind the gentlemen of Quebec, the very gentlemen you should be encouraging—that you might have a past you are attempting to escape by coming here, and that, perhaps, you are not quite a lady. "

Jeanne boiled over with anger. She wanted to throttle Agathe. Instead, in silence, she turned on her heel and headed for the door.

"Jeanne Dube! Don't you dare leave me!"

Jeanne's mother must have come to her aid then for when she turned back to Agathe, she lifted her head proud and high and said, "Maman always said that civility is the true mark of a lady, but just now, civility is in short supply here." She didn't wait to see or hear another word just marched away through the door.

Despite this uproar and new eyes upon her, she managed to see Babin a few more times afterward, always heading to the ice.

"Excusez-moi, Madame. I have lingered too long already. I must go now. " Since the day of her altercation with Agathe, Thibaut had grown formal again. It was far more difficult to meet and go out walking together now for both of them, but he was always willing to go if he could and if she could manage to meet him.

On this day, instead of allowing him to go, she followed him all the way to the outer door. The attraction that had affected her so strongly when they'd first met aboard the *Astree* remained although she'd dutifully tried to put it behind her.

Why oh why couldn't her heart be like her mind--sensible, practical? She simply must make a suitable choice for a husband and do it soon if for no other reason now than to escape being beholden to Agathe. The gentlemen of Quebec, however, were to a man, either too old or adventuring younger sons, born to privilege, the kind who were liable to abandon a lady not of their class as soon as a better opportunity presented itself. She knew that the man she must find was an honest fellow, a bourgeois.

At the door, Thibaut turned. He paused for a long last look, one that was unmistakably full of desire.

"Adieu, aimable Madame Jeanne. Je reviendrai quand mon devoir sera accompli – et je te retrouverai. . . "

As the heavy door opened, a gust of freezing air struck her. Snowflakes entered too, invaders from the bitter white world beyond. Even that could not erase the blaze of hope those words had ignited!

"I will return when my duty is done and find you." He'd spoken to her as if they were intimates, family--or lovers!

Darkness fell as the door closed. Jeanne knew that he'd be putting on his snowshoes ready for a trek to wherever he was going. She could hear foot-stamping and the sound of cheerful, muffled greetings of others by the threshold.

She knew she should leave that frigid little space and return her recalcitrant fingers to the task of spinning hemp in a corner of the warm kitchen, but she was immobilized. At last, she'd learned that Babin was attracted to her too, but she also understood that he might never dare cross the gulf that lay between them.

She sighed heavily, leaning back against the cold stone. Months could pass before she would see him again.

Or, perhaps, never.

That afternoon, Jeanne remained outside. She walked a little more until she felt calmer. When she entered the house at last, she walked to the kitchen to find a task to fill her hands and occupy her mind until supper.

At that time, she'd asked herself if it was wise to marry in haste to escape what was becoming an increasingly uncomfortable situation. After all, it was as easy to marry the wrong man here in New France as it had been at home! All this turmoil, while the man her heart beat fast for was even more of a mystery than her carefree sailor had been.

The unhappy memory of that interchange resurfaced while she leaned against the wall in the now familiar "mudroom." This narrow space was equipped with a long bench and floored with rough planks covered by puddles of ice. A host of snowshoes crowded the walls.

She knew that another basket of hemp awaited her attention back in the kitchen, but she was immobilized by a stubborn wish to do nothing but brood. Lately there had been several more of these episodes with her patroness.

Of course, Agathe was breeding, often suffering the discomforts of early pregnancy--nausea, vomiting, and fatigue. It was hard, though, to never receive any indication that the lady might be sorry for her short-tempered behavior or that she was even aware of it.

Just as Jeanne was considering where a place might be that was not only secluded but warm, the door opened again. Light and a cold gust of snowflakes blew in.

A sturdy, bearded man entered, swiftly closing the door behind him. Before she could escape, he spoke.

"Bon après-midi madame."

"Et à vous monsieur."

"Do you know if Monsieur de Couage is in his office? I have traveled from the Seigneury of St. Mars to discuss business with him on behalf of my master. My name is Luc-Gabriel Fleury, and I have a letter of introduction. "

"I believe that Monsieur de Couage is within, sir. If you will accompany me, I will show you to his rooms at once. "

Although the poorly lit anteroom was dim, she could see Monsieur Fleury studying her.

"Excuse me, madame, but may I know your name?"

"Je suis la veuve Dube. Please, follow me. "

"Merci, madam. "

They began to walk, the gentleman close behind. She always placed the "widow" first when she introduced herself to any new men. It was, at times, a handy defense against the kind of attention often visited upon single women. The gentleman appeared to have taken the hint for he followed her in silence.

"I do not know if he will be at leisure," she finally said as they walked through the twilight of the corridor. "However, I am sure he will find time to speak to you today. "

"It is good simply to be out of the weather. It has turned cold again, and a storm looks to be coming from the west. That little break we had last week was pleasant, however, just enough to make us cautious crossing the river. The dogs, fortunately, hear the ice crack sooner than we do. "

"Did you come from the south shore then?" Jeanne slowed to walk beside him. She had heard tales of sleds falling through "rotten" ice.

"Has the ice become dangerous?"

"Well, it will soon. I hoped when I set out that the thaw had not yet begun. The seigneury where I am employed lies just a little west of Quebec on the south side of the river. The land is now farmed, and I have nearly completed a mill for the Sieur. Now, I am constructing a fitting residence for him. "

That was the moment Jeanne remembered the first winter supper after she and Agathe arrived, and the way Commandant St. Mars had kindly relieved her of the sneers of Desjardins.

This man must be the mason of whom the Commandant had spoken. Does he truly have business here or is this by way of introduction to me, a marriageable widow?

She wouldn't ask. It seemed much easier to simply let events unfold as they inevitably must.

When they arrived in the anteroom to de Couage's study, a clerk met them. It seemed that de Couage would be busy for a little longer with one of the notable landowners of Quebec.

"You are welcome to wait here by the fire, monsieur, especially since you have traveled over the river today. Some brandy, Monsieur Fleury? Perhaps, madam, you could bring some food from the kitchen?"

"Certainly, right away. "

In the better light of the anteroom--by the table where the clerk was at work--Jeanne saw a man not much taller than herself. She helped him out of his heavy coat and saw a sturdy fellow of early middle age with clear blue eyes, a high forehead and an aquiline nose.

Not much later she returned with a platter of what was to be had at this time of year--flatbread, smoked sausage, and a cup of hot, peppery broth. Fleury was still waiting for his interview. In the meantime, he and the clerk had struck up a conversation. Jeanne set the tray and a hemp napkin down on a corner of the rough table that served to hold the clerk's books.

The men had been engaged in study of a map and talking about *les Indiens*, but when the food came in, Fleury carried the stool he'd been sitting upon around the table to the place she'd made for him.

"Thank you, madam," he said, smiling at her. "As I have not eaten since dawn, this is most welcome. " He crossed himself and murmured something before he reached for the steaming cup of broth. While he drank appreciatively, Jeanne curtsied before she departed. She felt certain she would see and learn more of Monsieur Fleury at supper tonight.

It was no surprise when she learned that she and Fleury would be seated together. To her surprise, however, Commandant St. Marr arrived at supper too, and he took time before they sat to formally introduce them.

"I wanted Fleury to come to speak to you before the ice breakup," he said. "My friend here is a far more worthwhile partner for a lively young woman than any of those old soldier compatriots of mine. " With that, he smiled, nodded his head, and then went to sit by de Couage and Agathe at the top of the table.

"I assure you I am capable of speaking for myself, Widow Dube. " Fleury was clearly embarrassed by his patron's remark.

"I did not doubt it, sir. "

Relieved, Monsieur Fleury smiled. "After speaking with Monsieur de Couage today about some other matters, he was kind enough to bring to my attention the particulars of your situation and that your father has provided towards your eventual marriage. "

"Yes, he has, sir, and that was good of him, all things considered. "

"All things considered?"

"As my mistress has been privy to all my trials, I am certain that these matters have been made plain to her husband and, therefore, doubtless, to yourself. "

"I would like to hear the story from your lips. Otherwise, anything Monsieur de Couage has said--and I make this remark with all due respect--I must regard as hearsay. "

Jeanne studied him. She believed him for his eyes were thoughtful and curious, and his expression honest.

"Only if you will be as honest with me concerning your situation as I am about to be with you. "

"You have my word, Widow Dube. " The mason acknowledged with a nod and a good-humored smile.

Jeanne drew a deep breath before she began. She had an intuition that this meeting would be fateful.

"I was born to Monsieur and Madame Joly. My father is a respected salt merchant in Brouage. When I was fourteen my dear mother died after a long and terrible illness. My brothers and sisters were all surprised and saddened when our father took a new wife in less than a year after her demise. This woman arrived along with a swarm of poor relations, whom she clearly preferred to her new husband's family. I had met a sailor at the Port of Brouage--not a suitable match, but handsome and gentle. I ran away with him to escape my stepmother and her unkindness. We were young and married by a mendicant friar. After that, I lived with my husband's family in La Rochelle and bore him a son. The family was very poor, but I was not proud. I was a good daughter-in-law and learned to cut fish and sell them in the market as did the other women of the family. I scrubbed floors, sewed, cooked, mended nets, minded babies, and did all the things that a seafarer's wife does. After four years, my husband, along with his ship, were lost on a voyage to Terre-Neuve. Not two years passed, my precious boy was swept away by a wave while he played on the rocks near the harbor. When Mademoiselle Martin, as she then was, met me at La Rochelle, she spoke with high enthusiasm of her voyage to New France and of the kind gentleman she would marry here. By that time, I had reconciled with my father, but I did not want to add to the family quarrels with my presence. I also soon learned that my reputation in Brouage was lost. Despite knowing all these things, Mademoiselle Martin was generous enough to ask me to be her companion on the voyage, and so, here I am."

"Thank you for your frankness, Widow Dube. That was a bold step to take."

"My stepmother was still in residence at our house in Brouage, and she had spread so many lies about me during my absence. Although my father had at last seen his new wife for what she is and now understands the bad bargain he's made, he agreed with my desire to emigrate. Coming to New France will, I hope, be a way for me to begin my life again and avoid further discord within my family."

She paused and raised the glass of red wine to her lips. The trading post--and, of course, the residences of officials in the city--were the last places where such refreshment remained available. Some of the transients who were overwintering here had made wine from the plentiful pumpkins, or so she'd heard. It did not sound inviting, but apparently it was sufficiently strong to leave those who imbibed a quantity "to feel no pain."

"A foul practice, probably learned from that rabble of English and Dutch seafarers who infest the ports. " At least, that was how M. de Couage, importer of wine, brandy, and cider, had described it. Still, to Jeanne, it seemed that it was unsurprising, especially among the rough fellows she'd observed stumbling down to their miserable huts, holding one another upright, sometimes laughing until they puked. Quebec must be a joyless, miserable place, she thought, for men forced to overwinter in those dark, smoky hovels.

Fleury studied her with his light eyes. He looked and sounded like a man from the North, perhaps from Le Havre.

"Thank you for your candor, Madam. Now," he said, "it is time for me to be as forthcoming as you have been. " He sighed. They were momentarily interrupted by a server, a young man with dark sloe eyes and plump brown cheeks who offered them a platter of cheese, once a large piece and now much diminished. A powerful smell came along with it as this was also the remains of the last autumn ship's bounty. Jeanne shook her head and so did her companion, so the Indian boy moved on.

"I was born to a master mason and his wife of Rouen and learned my trade from him beside my brothers. I am a younger son and so have had some ups and downs in attempting to establish myself. In time, I made a small reputation and felt secure enough to take a wife from a family of carpenters. Marie was an excellent helpmate and a faithful companion. We had two living children when I was introduced through a reliable client of mine to a nobleman who had a large project in hand. At that time, I believed I trusted that gentleman and believed I was on the eve of lasting good fortune."

Another sigh followed. She could see that the tale to come would be painful to recite.

"However, as has happened to so many of our stations as craftsmen, I was deceived by this gentleman and left with debts for materials and also without funds to pay the laborers employed by me. I did find the money to pay my workers what I had promised and also managed to pay a small part of my debt out of small savings, but my dream of a settled life was gone. For several years, I was forced to travel across the north to find work, and creditors pursued me.

My wife found refuge with our children in the house of her elder brother whose helpmate had recently died. I continued to travel, found what work I could, and sent the most I could to her. I have St. Marr to thank for offering me a living here, and as there are yet not many in New France who have such skills, I see a chance to find some measure of security at last. I received word last spring that my dear wife, Marie, had died. My boys are apprenticed, thanks to my brother, but neither will finish their term for some years. "

While he had spoken of his ruin, Fleury gazed past her into the middle distance of the smoky room. It was clear that this story was difficult for him to tell. He spoke without any obvious rancor or excuses; his pride in himself had remained intact. At that instant, Jeanne knew that before her sat a courageous and honest man.

"So, that is my story, Madam. I am now a widower as you are a widow; a man whose children may or may not wish to emigrate. Much will have changed as they have grown in the last six years. "

"I, too, appreciate frankness, Monsieur Fleury. You have behaved with honor, although the nobleman did not. During my life that is not the first such tale I have heard. They call themselves "noble,' but, assuredly, many of them are not. "

***

222

Black fly season had come along with the first green buds and gushers of meltwater from the snowpack. Stinging insects were a plague despite every precaution she'd take against the black, biting swarm that landed on any exposed inch of flesh. Her flesh, which had been longing to feel those first sun rays, had to be covered as quickly as possible. Nevertheless, those little demons penetrated every opening they could find, and itchy, hard welts appeared on whatever naked flesh they could find. The itching was terrible; it was hard not to scratch until the blood ran. Although that provided relief, it was only for a few seconds and soon, all too soon, the maddening itch would return again.

Veiled as much as she could against the tiny bloodsuckers, Jeanne persisted in going out if only for the sensation of sunlight. She learned that windy days were best for the flies were fewer.

Over the next month, her view of the river showed that the ships careened during the winter were being launched. Now some floated once more in the river. The ice pack had flushed out to sea a few weeks back, the noise of grinding and crashing so loud that they were often startled by the thunderous tumult even inside the often-noisy trading post.

Down along the shore, men hauled casks filled with fur down to the shore, to the boats that would row them to the newly floated ships, now busily loading whatever cargo there was--from fur to lumber to pitch--bound either for the northern port of La Havre or to her own La Rochelle in the west.

"What are you looking for while you walk out there getting bitten by those horrible flies and soaking your boots in that quagmire?" Agathe asked. She sounded impatient, but Jeanne refused to let her patroness's' irritation at the daily walks she took bother her. Agathe's swift changes of mood, she'd learned, were now inevitable.

Once a rangy Diana with a bow, Agathe was today nothing but a wife, a pregnant, pale-faced woman who'd spent the winter huddled inside that smoky cave of a house. It was clear that she was having second thoughts about the path she'd chosen. She sometimes took her frustrations out on her little maids or Jeanne or, for that matter, whatever servant happened across her at the wrong time. She also spent a great deal of time on her knees, praying.

Sometimes, Agathe, taking either Lily, Marthe, or Jeanne as companions, traveled to the Ursuline monastery. This had been built only a few years ago thanks to the largesse of a pious aristocrat. It sat above the old lower town of Quebec City.

Here, Agathe might visit Mother Marie De L'Incarnation, from whose tuition both Lily and Marthe had come. Sometimes she was confessed by the Father who provided priestly care to the nuns or attended Mass or whatever devotion was then being celebrated. That winter, Jeanne sometimes thought she spent more time on her knees before the Mary altar than she ever had in her life.

"It's *who*, I think, is the proper question, Madame. "

Jeanne ignored Madame Hus's mischief-making and continued tightening the laces of her soft indoor boots.

"Surely you aren't suggesting that Jeanne is watching out for that wild Babin?" Agathe, disapproving, shook her head and sighed. "I certainly hope you are not entertaining any such notion! My husband says that those Metis are half-wild, that they wander about all summer, chasing fish and game. In winter, they live in huts made of hides and branches exactly like the savages! No! No! Impossible! That is not the match your father wished you to make!"

"That Babin is very handsome. " Madame Hus continued in that same sly tone. "But, sadly, 'tis true Madam de Couage, his kind come and go like the deer. Besides, I have just heard that the governor has authorized a company of our young men, Metis, and Huron to form flying patrols along the river. He hopes they can help to keep us safe from those Iroquois devils. If Babin is part of the governor's patrol, he could be anywhere along the river, from Ville Marie to Trois-Rivieres. "

Jeanne had heard that bit of news already. Still, she wondered if Madame Hus knew more than she did. She certainly wasn't going to ask the old busy body if that was what she was fishing for!

Her heart sank.

If Babin had returned to this part of La Grande Rivière, why had he not come to see her, as he had--so nearly--said?

"Monsieur Babin is not my anything. " That much was certainly true, especially as things stood.

Madame Hus smiled knowingly to herself, then lowered her head and picked up her sewing.

"May I fetch you something from your room, Madame de Couage? Another wrap, perhaps?" Jeanne knew Agathe was often chilly, but suddenly she was in a hurry to escape. She wished to be alone with her thoughts.

"No. You may put another log on the fire. I wish you to stay right here, with me-- for a change. " Agathe pointed to a chair already occupied by Marthe.

"You go sit over there, dear," she said to the girl, who jumped up, surprised and a little injured at being summarily evicted from the place of honor beside the mistress.

"Come, sit beside me, Jeanne, and tell us all of what you have seen outside that has kept you away from us all this time. "

With a heavy heart, Jeanne tried to comply. Of late, her mind was elsewhere most of the time. The enforced idleness of winter had brought night wakefulness and along with that had come unwelcome ruminations on the past.

Did I make the right decision? Am I nothing but an exile now with no hope of ever returning home.

She felt that she was once more an outcast. She'd become an outcast among the Dube's after Pierre had disappeared and her beloved Michel had died, an outcast after her return to Brouage--and now, here. Agathe, who had taken her up so enthusiastically, didn't seem to have much interest in her anymore--except at moments like this when she demanded attention only because of her own boredom and anxiety.

Jeanne knew she was beholden in all kinds of ways to this woman. Now she chafed at the situation.

The more she thought, scarcely listening to the idle chatter around her, Babin seemed an even more inappropriate choice for a husband than Pierre Dube had been. The mason, Fleury, appeared decent and solid, a quantity that could be known.

Across *La grande rivière*

The crossing of the great river to the Seigneury belonging to St. Marr was on a beautiful day. Jeanne enjoyed herself watching the southern bank grow closer, and the little gray houses of Quebec and its palisaded fort slip away behind her. Fleury sat beside her. One of the things she enjoyed about him was that he did not fill the time with endless chat. If he saw something worth noting--another Chaloupe sailing with the wind down the river, or a large bark canoe filled with natives, or even a moose, breaking its way among the little islands that dotted their passage--he would comment. Otherwise, he was silent.

Otherwise, he stayed silent. Jeanne was perfectly happy with this, viewing the wide blue-green water around them in this clean bright fresh new world with birds sailing above and the bright green of the shore as they approached.

They drew closer to the landing place, which was up a wide-mouthed creek. The shallow draft they negotiated reminded Jeanne of the canals of her homeplace. Although it was June, snowbanks on the north-facing slopes of the hills were still melting their traces seen in long pale tongues of silt, pushing their way toward the main body of the river.

The men, Fleury included, used poles and a small square bow sail--for the wind came today from the north--to push against the flow. After a brief time, Fleury pointed out the gray sides of a mill, a tower that he had built on a hill that still lacked the sails. Their landing place was a low pier.

"This is narrow, but it never dries up, according to *les Indiens,* so that was why St.

Marr chose this place to build. It's sandy loam here, but inland there is black soil, so the *habitants* who are settled here have been successfully growing wheat as well as barley, oats, and maize. In Champlain's time, there was a Huron town here. We found the remains of their palisade close by while we were digging the foundations of our new houses. "

A few men labored nearby shoveling into a swampy place where they planned to make a pond. Further up a soft slope, Jeanne saw a new palisade. Within that, she caught a glimpse of a big stone house and a few cabins.

"Inside the palisade are our homes. Some of the laborers have families they've made here if you take my meaning. "

Jeanne nodded. That was one of the first things Canadienne women shared with marriage-minded newcomers. That Frenchmen took native women to wife was a custom a newcomer had to understand, especially if you were dowered and therefore equipped to bargain with a potential husband. Not all marriageable men had the problem of native wives and Metis children, of course. A few had families at home to whose memory they remained faithful, however, men were men! Why be surprised?

Off hand, Jeanne wondered if that was the reason for Monsieur Fleury's wish to bring her here with the understanding that she would return to Quebec to consult

Monsieur de Couage before any marriage contract was signed.

That Fleury was a man of business pleased her. Although he was indentured to St. Marr, he was clearly a man of standing, respected by his laborers as well as his employer. The behavior of the rough fellows he'd greeted while they landed seemed proof, their salutes, smiles, and greetings appeared genuine. To Jeanne, their respect mattered as she hoped to find a husband with a just heart even if there could never be another golden sailor like Pierre in her life.

Within the palisade stood a long barn-like structure made of bent saplings and covered with slabs of bark in the native style. A thin wisp of smoke trailed from a roof hole as the morning fire died away. There were other small structures that appeared to be animal pens. Two small cabins had also been constructed, but in the center of the enclosure was a low stone house with two stories that reminded Jeanne of homes she'd seen along the wind-swept coasts of her home.

"If you agree to be my wife, we will live in that small stone house, just behind the larger one. When St. Marr and his wife come down from Quebec in the autumn, they will occupy the great house that stands directly before us. The interior has yet to be finished, and so the men who are performing that work are currently using the downstairs as their shelter. " Jeanne saw the imposing gray stone mansion, set in the exact middle of the stockade. On every side, both inside and outside of the stockade, the trees had been cut. Stumps stood everywhere.

"I thought I'd heard that St. Marr was coming here quite soon."

"He should be here shortly, by himself, as usual. The fact is that his wife is anxious about living here instead of the safety of Quebec City. When he does come over, then I shall be at his beck and call. He is most particular about the way he wants work done. "

A woman wearing a head wrap emerged from one of the cabins, a child in one arm and a work basket in the other. Fleury noticed Jeanne gazing at her.

"That is the wife of Renaud, the trusty fellow who has labored in this seigneury the longest. Perhaps you would like to speak with her while I go see what's been done while I've been away. She can tell you about this place and about what life is like. "

When Jeanne hesitated, Fleury said, "She's a plain-spoken soul, honest as the day is long. She's French, a *paysan*, but she's lived here with her husband for a long time. She's usually forthcoming, so she will be pleased to speak with you. "

With that he turned away and left. Madame Renaud sat on a stool in a patch of sun and deposited a hefty toddler on the ground.

Nothing else to do but explore, Jeanne thought. She wondered if this weathered creature would have much to say to someone clean and wearing new clothes, but as Fleury had turned to speak with one of the men who'd been hovering since they'd landed, she kept walking and put on a smile.

The woman did not bother to stand, but she raised her head and nodded a greeting. One scant lock of her dark hair hung by her ear, braided with rasade--trade beads like a native.

"*Je vous salue, Madame*," the woman said. At her feet, the child looked up curiously. He had a cap of wavy brown hair and green eyes. He wore a little shirt but was otherwise bare. In one hand, he held a grubby piece of crumbly cornbread.

"And to you, Madame Renaud," said Jeanne.

"Are you Monsieur Fleury's new wife?"

"Not his wife yet, Madam. I have come to see where and how he lives. "

"From Quebec City?"

"Yes. My name is Jeanne Dube, and I sailed here last year before the snow. "

A long pause followed.

"You look strong enough, and that is a good thing to be in this country. "

"I see you have hemp in that basket. Do you grow it here?"

"Yes, and many other things too, but it is still too early to put seed in the ground. "

"It has been warm for a few weeks now. "

The woman nodded. The child, suddenly anxious, crawled to his mother and pulled himself up onto her lap.

"The winds often play tricks on us here even in June. It will blow from the south and be warm and then it will turn north and send us sleet and cold again. It is north again today, so we cannot yet be certain that the frosts are gone. "

"I see. "

"Do you know how to hoe and plant?"

"No, Madam Renaud, but I will learn. " Jeanne saw a skeptical expression slip into the woman's eyes, so she added, "I lived by the ocean, so I know how to sail and how to catch and salt fish, how to spin hemp, how to make nets and to sew. "

"Eels sometimes enter our creek here. We don't use salt much, except for fish we trade away. We have little salt in this country, but we do have the long cold for keeping. "

"Your winter is the worst I've ever seen," Jeanne said. She'd been astonished to learn that so much here was simply gathered just as autumn arrived then allowed to freeze. Afterward, it would be stored in huts and laid into pits among the pines where little sun ever came.

Jeanne took a seat on a nearby stump. The ground was dotted with them.

The child had been grumbling and squirming in Madam Renaud's arms. Without ceremony, she opened the top of her loose dress and offered him a pendulous, surprisingly fair breast. Silence, at least from that corner, followed.

"A fine boy." Jeanne observed his chubby legs and dirty feet. "Do you have other children?"

"Three. There," Madame Renaud nodded, "are my girls."

Jeanne turned to see two girls struggling with a bucket near the gate. Drawing water was one of those endless tasks of a poor woman's life and one with which Jeanne was familiar. These girls had been set to the task early.

"My oldest is working with his father, over there. " She pointed with pride, and Jeanne noticed a slender boy among some men who were chopping limbs from a freshly downed tree.

At supper that night, taken inside the unfinished great house, Jeanne saw that everyone appeared not only curious but pleased to see a new face. The food was what she'd come to expect in spring, rabbit stew, bread of wheat and oatmeal, and the bland *topinambour*, those roots that remained in everyone's larder. There was, however, a genuine treat in the form of a fresh goat cheese as well as a pudding made of milk, cornmeal, and flavored with dried fruit and molasses. A broad-hipped Metis woman,

Noelle, was their cook, so Jeanne made certain she complimented her on the excellence of the supper, particularly the pudding!

"Seigneur St. Marr has provided this farm well. We already have an orchard with apple and pear trees now beginning to yield, two fine oxen for hauling timber and plowing as well as goats, sheep, and ten cows. " Fleury explained.

Jeanne smiled. She'd been here long enough to understand that was a goodly number of livestock. The fruit trees were even more of an achievement. Their presence meant the Iroquois hadn't attacked this place in many years.

"The Seigneur truly means to settle himself here?"

"Indeed he does. It's not easy to begin farming in this wilderness, but he has put a great deal of thought and money into his plans. He has brought his wife here, but she does not look happy when she is here. "

That night Jeanne slept in the big unfinished stone house sharing a bed with the housekeeper, Madam Garand, a woman who'd been raised in Acadia but who had come here with a husband, a soldier, an older man who'd been a farm tenant in the seigneury. When he died a few years ago, St. Marr had taken her in.

"I didn't expect Garand to die so soon, but he did, Bless God! Dropped like a stone just outside our door while he--for once--

was chopping wood. The Seigneur said I could stay at that farm if I took another husband, but I saw no one I trusted, so he sent me here. There is always plenty of work for a woman to do wherever she lives. "

"You were born in Acadia?" Jeanne was tired, but as curious about these Canadienne as they were about her.

"Yes. My father was a Portuguese fisherman who made many voyages, but in the end, he stayed here, took a wife, my mother, in Acadia. Garand came there as a soldier. One day, he saw me hoeing our garden and he asked my father for me. "

Jeanne noted the set of her eyes and her dark hair and skin, neither remarkable among the native people nor for a descendant of the Portuguese. She was a handsome woman despite her weathered skin. Her nose had been broken and had healed askew.

"That is a long way from this place, your Acadia?"

"Indeed it is, Madam. "

The candle flickered, and the woman's rough brown fingers extended to pinch it out. Conversation was at an end.

Darkness descended; candles were a luxury. In the darkness, Jeanne felt her companion settling in beside her. The rest of the story could wait if the woman felt inclined to speak more about that tomorrow.

Silencing her curiosity, Jeanne lay down, resolving to learn as much as she could about her and the other women who lived here. They would tell her what she needed to know about this life more, far more, than any suitor could or would perhaps be inclined to.

The next day began with a birdsong chorus and gray light, which entered through a gun slot in the wall above. Jeanne arose with her companion, and they pulled overskirts over the long shirts they'd slept in. From her bag, she took a brush, but the other woman simply put on a cap, stepped into her clogs and said, "I must go get the milk. "

When Jeanne nodded, she went out. Immediately there was the sound of wooden clogs rapping down the stairs.

Jeanne continued to unbraid her hair. She would brush it out and then braid it once more. then she would follow Madam Garand as soon as she had this done. When she had her own cap in place and her boots on, she made her own way carefully down the dim, narrow stairway.

In the kitchen, she saw the welcome light of a morning fire dancing. Noelle bent over it adjusting a pot on a crane.

"Bonjour, Noelle. How may I help you this morning?"

Noelle turned, but she looked uncertain.

"Porridge?" Jeanne joined her and glanced into the pot containing a combination of Indian meal and wheat groats. "I can cook that. I am sure you have many other things to do especially with the arrival of the Seigneur so close at hand. "

The woman considered her for a moment and then after tapping the wooden spoon on the side of the pot, she offered it to Jeanne.

"Merci, Madam," she said.

Soon they were tending the fire side by side, Noelle used her shovel to move coals around, placed a trivet over them, and set a heavy skillet with fatty meat to render. Next, Madam Garand entered bearing a basket of eggs. Behind her came a youngster with a bucket of fresh milk.

"We will be making cheese later," she said. She placed the eggs on the table and took the bucket from the child.

"Is that milk from the goats?" Jeanne asked. It made her mouth water to see so much foamy goodness.

"Yes, and some from the cows. All of them are nursing young now, so we don't take much. The Seigneur wishes the herd to grow. "

"I've milked goats before," Jeanne said. "I will be glad to help you tomorrow if you wish. "

Days passed quickly as Jeanne's help was quickly accepted. When she assisted in the daily chores, no one complained. In fact, they were able to clear and dig a small new vegetable patch in a sunny spot around the stumps, then haul manure from the pile and fork that onto the ground.

Fleury was not around much because he was absorbed in his masonry, cutting and dressing stones with a son of one of the farmers who was his apprentice, so Jeanne spent most of her days with the women learning the daily rhythm of the place.

From the others, she learned how to concoct a healing salve of local plants for the bites and scratches that came with outdoor work. There were also tasks she'd never done before, such as cleaning saved seed from the year before as they prepared for the rush of planting that would begin in the next weeks. She washed ragged clothes, then strung up lines to dry them. Later, she'd cut old fabric with scissors that had come with her. Everything that could be saved would be used for patches.

Sometimes her back ached from breaking the rough ground or from sewing while seated on a stump; sometimes she was so tired she fell asleep before supper. Sometimes, however, as she stitched up rips, patched, hauled water, hung clothes, or sat beside a milking stand, her head resting against the warm, softly gurgling side of a goat, her thoughts went wandering.

She would think instead about the strange dark winter just past, about snowshoeing, traveling by dogsled across great white dunes, or lying on the frozen river peering into a fishing hole--all adventures she'd had with Thibaut. It was not easy to push him out of her mind, his rugged strength, or the wonderful moments when his dark eyes so gravely considered her. She kept reminding herself she must be practical and make, this time, a reasoned choice in a husband.

"We are so happy, Madam, for your help. " It was Madam Garand who spoke up one afternoon as they--Noelle, Madam Renaud (whose given name was Louise,) Marie Denise, and Mathurine (two laborers' wives)--were all taking a well-deserved rest sitting in the afternoon sun.

"When we heard Fleury was bringing a Frenchwoman here, we did not know what it would mean for us. We feared that you would be *dame impuissante.* "

Jeanne smiled at "helpless lady. " She was exhausted here most of the time, bug-bitten, hands roughened and bruised from lugging kindling and water, but it felt good to be out of doors in the sun. It was good to meet these brave women labor alongside them.

"That I would be proud and distant?"

"No, worse! That you would be *dame qui s'évanouit* and make even more work for us. "

"And I have not fainted once, have I?" Jeanne smiled.

"No, though you do fall asleep easily. "

Everyone laughed then, because for the last two nights, Jeanne had rested her head upon the kitchen table after they'd finished the evening's washing up and fallen asleep straight away.

She remained most curious about Madam Garand, about her odd accent, about her ability to speak with the Algonquin who occasionally came traveling by. The Indians wanted to bargain for iron pots, cloth, and, of course, gunpowder. The last was too dear to part with; however, Fleury had brought things for trade back from de Couage's store, but nevertheless at this time of year all supplies were low. When the first ships arrived--soon, everyone hoped--they'd have more. What those Indians brought was meat and hides and, most importantly, news of Iroquois movements.

Jeanne knew that Belinha (for this was her first name) had been born to a native mother. Bit by bit, as Madame Garand became more comfortable with her roommate, Jeanne learned more of the lady's past. After Jeanne talked about losing her husband and son to the ocean, and of the unkindness of her in-laws, Belinha gradually became ready to share a story of her own.

"My mother was a widow of a Mi'kmaw, a fisherman who had become friends with you foreigners. She was born Algonquin, but in the days of the new diseases, every one of her kinfolk died. One of the last men in her village took her to a Mi'kmaw family he met while they were all gathered at a creek netting eels, and they took her in.

As that kinsman never returned, she was married soon after to a man who moved between forest and ocean as they did. Her first husband had become friendly with many of the fishermen who came across the sea every spring--Portuguese, Basque and French--a few of whom had made Acadia their home.

After the sea took her Mi'kmaw husband, a Portuguese neighbor, Ribiero, married my mother and so he became my stepfather. "

Jeanne learned that Ribiero had sailed across the ocean many times, but after surviving a shipwreck, he'd decided to stay in the new world, in the new town.

"My mother taught me Huron and Mi'kmaq; my father spoke Portuguese and French too. Where we lived there were many French people. When the French soldiers came to keep order there, Garand saw me. With my sisters, I was hoeing in the garden. He asked my father for me the next day. I told my father I would not go with him for he was ugly and looked so old, but my father struck me and told me I would do as he said. "

Her story ended as suddenly as it had begun. She heaved a sigh. Jeanne could see her face by the smoky illumination of the reed light.

"You are lucky, Madame Jeanne, that you have a choice. "

As Jeanne worked beside the other women and the days passed, she heard something about each one, how they had come to be here with these men. Louise Renaud told her more about Belinha Garand's past, for her husband had been working for the Sieur for the longest of all.

"Belinha and I have known one another for years now. I remember when Garand came and began to work his arpents for the Sieur. The Wendat once lived here in great numbers. They had cleared large areas for their towns and gardens, but too many died of the plagues that came upon us. After that, the Iroquois began attacking us every autumn. Those Wendat who survived took their kin and went west, leaving this land behind. That is what I learned from the few unhappy people we found living here when the Lord brought us, his *paysan*, to begin to take charge of his grant--oh, maybe ten years ago. "

Jeanne, wondering, interrupted her to ask, "I thought the Indians took care of their people. "

"Well, the ones who were left were people who did not want to leave. Some were too old to undertake a long journey, others had lost their kin and had no one to help them. There was one hearty grandmother nursing her daughter's baby because the younger woman had died in the winter and the baby was too young to take anything but milk. The grandmother was called Otter Standing. "

Jeanne shook her head, amazed, but Louise explained that once you have nursed a baby, it is possible to get milk to return by putting a suckling child to your breast.

"I am told the baby was screaming and frantic until the milk came again. I had not known this could be done until this woman showed me her grandchild, an active boy, who was in those days playing at the door of her *wi'koum*. She was determined she would not lose her grandchild after all the other losses--her husband, her daughter-in-law and her son, and all the rest of her kin. "

Louise's weathered face creased into a gentle smile as she remembered. "That old woman taught me much about the ways of this place--how to make thread and nets from *orties* and where to place weirs to catch fish and eels, and places to hide if the Iroquois came. She knew about the medicines that grow in the forest and helped us in many ways during our first years here. "

"What happened to this wise woman?"

"She died two winters ago. Her grandson lived with us until this spring, and soon he will go his own way. You have met him, I think. He is called Adelard. "

Jeanne had indeed met him, a shy young man whom she'd taken for a Metis orphan. He lived with two other lads in a bark summer hut at the edge of the forest.

"He wants to go with the *coureurs de bois*, but neither Renaud nor I are happy about it because that is very dangerous, but I fear he will go just the same. "

Louise sighed. Jeanne, wanting to hear more about Belinha, prompted her. This was the most forthcoming woman she'd met in this place. Perhaps it was because Louise and her husband were French, and she missed such talks with other Frenchwomen.

"Belinha, yes, we were speaking of her. Garand brought her to us when he came here to work his arpents for St. Marr. She was another raised in Indian ways. Her husband was the son of a *paysan* who'd turned soldier, and Renaud always said Garand wasn't much of a farmer. He would disappear for half the year trapping, leaving his wife behind to tend their garden, feed his stock, clear the brush, tend babies, and get through the winter as best she could. She lived in our stockade every winter for we insisted and Monsieur Fleury too. At first we had a hard time persuading her because she told us she'd been bred in this country, but we feared she might perish out there alone especially if she had a little one."

"She has never mentioned any children."

"No. They all died of one thing and another."

Jeanne heard the rest of the story: how Garand would return in the spring with a little script from his trapping, a few supplies, and plenty of brandy. He beat her when he

245

was in his cups and that was how her nose was broken. He'd broken her nose three times. Any time they'd seen her, she was either bruised or had a black eye. The last time he'd broken her nose it hadn't healed well.

"Poor woman!" Louise Renaud sighed. "She has had more than her share of trouble, but she is a strong one! She knows the forest like the back of her hand, and she has taught us many useful things. "

Life here was hard. Jeanne understood it ever more clearly as the relentless work of spring commenced. She'd been a fishwife, but she'd never done the work of a farmer's wife. Calluses grew on her feet and hands. Her back ached as did her hands and wrists from digging and hoeing hills for corn, beans, squash, and cabbages as well as the endless toting of water and wood.

The winter seed came out of storage, was sorted to find that most likely to sprout, and, thereafter, in the ever-lengthening daylight hours, was planted. Earliest came cabbages, then wheat and oats, the men ploughing behind the oxen and the women trudging behind, stumbling among the raw clods of earth, scattering seed. Next, a variety of beans and peas as well as some Indian corn were planted in manured garden patches. Last came the pumpkins.

Afterward, they cared for sprouting vegetables. Children were set to many tasks, such as picking slugs from the greens and the cabbages or throwing rocks at the birds that came for their seed in the wheat fields.

One day, a crow was caught. Afterward, he was tied by the leg to a stake in the field. His cries for help warned others who, after surveying the situation, would leave. If they didn't, the boys would use slings and try to drive them off. Intruding rabbits often ended in the stew pot, thanks to the better-aimed shots of older boys. Men mended fences and built fences while the domestic animals were moved daily to fresh grazing areas where they had to be watched over.

While all this went on, the women had their other daily tasks of sweeping out, the hauling of water, washing of clothes and dishes, and preparation of food and meals. Everyone was almost too tired to speak most of the time, which suited Jeanne. There was no time to brood about the past, either distant or recent, just the days marching-marching-marching, doing whatever tasks were most pressing in the race against the coming winter.

They had to use the sunshine and the good weather while they lasted!

It seemed selfish to leave and return to Quebec although she was always very tired. Here, she had found a community of women and quickly began to feel close to them. She became involved in their trials and their celebrations especially because they had so quickly warmed to her. The daunting task ahead of them--carving farmland out of the forest--engaged her in ways she'd never imagined.

After her long inactivity over the winter, Jeanne had had to build her endurance and strength again, but she stuck with it. Weeks passed; she stayed far longer than she'd originally projected.

She wanted to watch over the new crops she'd helped to plant, to tend the animals and the children of the place. Simple pleasures began to quiet the ache in her heart. Perhaps, she dared to hope she'd found a group of people with whom she could belong, a place where she was welcomed and valued, a place that might truly offer her the home and belonging she'd so often craved.

Everyone seemed pleased by her fortitude and her willingness, Fleury most of all. His smile, when she served him his supper, was real and welcome. No one cared how she'd come to be here because she'd proved that she was willing to work hard and smile while she did it.

Chapter 4

Babin had taken a small canoe he'd found in the scrub near a burned homestead. He'd been fighting for months and traveling with other frontiersmen, Metis and soldiers, first chasing and then engaging Iroquois bands whenever they encountered them. Often, however, as at today's site, they'd arrived too late to be of much help except to any survivors they encountered. Sometimes they found children alive, usually ones old enough to stay silent and hidden so that the raiders had not discovered them. The bloodied bodies of infants were a horror that, each time they found one, infuriated every man among them, driving them onward in their pursuit of vengeance.

Once they'd found a very pregnant woman who had hidden with four children. She'd taken the little ones into an old badger hole inside a clay bank, the entrance heavily screened by brambles. Babin and his comrades had arrived while the Iroquois fighters were making a last search of the area. They'd managed to drive them off and kill two into the bargain.

Several male *habitants* and a native woman—probably a wife fighting beside her husband--were also found dead at this site. The defenders there had been fairly well armed and had fought bravely, wounding and killing many of their attackers before their shot ran out.

Other homesteading families, alert to the sight of smoke rising over the forest, had escaped, some fleeing into boats on the river, others rowing out to hide among the many small islands. The homesteaders left their precious livestock behind, always a heart-wrenching and expensive loss.

Although the raiding parties were not large, they were well armed, effective fighters, intent on inflicting as much destruction and terror as they could. The coming of spring seemed to be time for withdrawal, though, as the snow was disappearing. Mud and black-fly season was coming fast. Apparently, the Iroquois had gathered sufficient captives and livestock, so for now, they'd disappear into the woods, heading south toward their own villages farther south. For their purposes, it was best to make a start before the mud season began in earnest.

Babin and his companions were exhausted in every way—minds and bodies. They'd covered many leagues on foot hoping to protect the scattered small farms that had begun to grow and flourish along the river. Now, supplies and shot gone, it was time for them also to retreat, to lick their wounds and care for those they'd saved. This new year had seen some of New France's deadliest fighting in years.

Babin paddled and floated as he went toward home. He was traveling east with the current toward his father's home up the Saguenay. It had not taken long, although he'd had to be attentive because floating ice and logs came down river at a good pace, and the banks were ever-changing because of the speed of the high water in the river.

He'd given the arquebus he'd carried to one of the Metis soldiers hoping that would make him, now traveling alone, slightly less of a target. From a distance, he'd appear to be a poor *sauvage* in a small bark canoe. All he had was a good knife and a short ash spear he'd fashioned using items scavenged from ruined farmsteads in the last few days before the company had parted ways.

The blade of the spear was a large, beautiful, and extremely sharp flint he'd happened upon when they'd dug a grave for one of the brave men he'd fought beside, a legacy from the old times before the *from-over-the-waters* came. Thanks to the training of his early life, he saw it for what it was--a work of art as well as a deadly weapon. He'd kept it in his pack for the last two months. Despite its long burial, it was still sharp as any steel.

Thibaut was tired, but the pinch of hunger and the cold nights kept him pushing on. It was not all that hard to catch fish though, and at night, he'd find a landing spot and, screened by scrub, make a small fire in a hole, coat his fishes with mud, and bury them among the embers. He knew he'd not look much like a Frenchman by the time he reached Tadoussac. He'd need to rest a day or two before he tackled the current of the mighty Saguenay--or walk, if the river was too strong—back north to his father's home. Fortunately, his father had not settled too far up that wild river.

The dangerous task of hunting Iroquois for the last four months was over, at least for now. He was utterly worn out. He could fall asleep anywhere. He could count his ribs through the layers of cloth, flannel, and furs that he wore.

Fighting was like that. In the midst of warfare, your senses were constantly on fire, ever alert. If they weren't, you didn't survive. He knew how to remain in that state and how to do what must be done to survive. After all, he'd been in a battle for survival one way or another most of his life.

First, as a child, whether as a Metis in a band who wondered if his white half would keep him from measuring up and later as a Metis among whites who looked down on him because he was "half savage." Afterward, living as a waterman, he'd been constantly on the lookout for robbers as well as the now ever-present threat of Iroquois raiding parties.

Thibaut wasn't a fighter by nature. Perhaps, the plain truth was that few are born that way. Most people had to be taught to kill. If you did too much killing, however, you might come to enjoy it and the thrill of the dark power such violence conveyed. In his travels, he'd met men like that. He feared them.

Thibaut fought because that was what he had had to do in this world; he intended to survive and to protect those who depended upon him. Killing had not become a thing he enjoyed nor had battle become a kind of poisoned intoxicant.

At the Tadoussac fort, he showed his script from Quebec and they let him in. This gave him the right to obtain food and a place to sleep if he wanted. He ate what was offered--the standard poor fare of spring--a piece of hard tack and watery stew of pounded, dried fish--with gratitude. That night he slept inside a smoky hut with other soldiers, feet pointed toward the central fire. He rarely did that because sleeping among strangers could be dangerous, but on this night, he took the chance. He badly needed to be warm overnight.

A few days later, following a narrow trail along the cliffs, he arrived at the cove where his father had his home. He had walked because the Saguenay was flooding, crammed with chunks of ice, torrents roaring and foaming over the rapids, chewing away the scrub-covered banks. In summer, the inlet at his home was shallow, the bottom covered with gravel and sand, but now, it was deep, filled with whirlpools, and treacherous.

The clearing carved into the scrub had grown wider every year, as the trees--low pines and birch--were used up by the people who'd come to settle there. The slope down to the water was low, making it a good place to launch his father's old *chaloupe,* careened now, awaiting repairs. From the chimneys in the clearing--his father's rubble stone house and the cabins clustered around it--a cloud of morning smoke arose.

Dogs made an unholy uproar as he approached, lunging against their tethers. Wolfish creatures those sled dogs, so it was best they were kept tied. A man came out of the nearest cabin warily, arquebus in hand, but his approach was forestalled when the front door of the stone house opened and a burly figure wearing a faded red blanket like a cloak hobbled out.

"It's only my boy, Thibaut, come home to us at last! Never mind. "

Although bulky, it appeared his old man was lame this spring. He approached, leaning on a cane.

"I wondered when--or if--you'd reappear, my boy. Did you stay in *Kebec* for the winter?"

"Greetings, my father. I did for a time but after that I went hunting Iroquois with the soldiers trying to keep the *habitants* along the river safe. Our enemies are thirstier for blood than ever. They have burned farms and killed many on the south shore and also at *Ville Marie.* They have even raided north, up the Ottawa trade route. "

He'd extended his hand, but his father, instead of insisting on formalities, threw his arms around him.

"I am grateful that *Le Bon Dieu* has sent you home to us, Thibaut! I feared when you did not return that they had set you to some dangerous work. "

When his father showed affection, it always took Thibaut by surprise. Nevertheless, it was a good feeling even if it lasted for only a moment.

His father quickly broke off the embrace with a shoulder slap and a halting step backwards.

"Those devils are more active than in many a long year. My old friend Bear Paw, the Innu, has warned us to be ready for they've been seen on this shore too. "

His father's unruly black hair now showed streaks of iron gray. His right cheek was yellow, the flesh puffed unnaturally high.

No doubt more teeth lost! Winter must have been hard on the old man.

"Ah, stop looking at me like that!" The elder Babin took his arm and began to lead Thibaut to the house. "Just had some teeth knocked out, but they were rotten anyway. It will be a while before I can eat anything but soup. " He paused, turned, and used his free hand to pull back his lip to display a ragged hole in his jaw.

"Bonne has been cosseting me, but it will be a long time before I get the feel of some good fat meat between what's left of my teeth. "

"What happened?"

"Eh! Kicked by that crazy Perrette while I was pulling a thorn out of her back leg. Damned lucky thing for her she's got a fine calf at her tits, or I would have made stew out of her. "

A round woman in a brown blanket coat stepped out the door.

"Come in at once, Babin, out of that cold. You've left your cap behind again!"

"Stop fussing at me, woman! Is the kettle on?"

Thibaut knew well that his perè would never kill a productive animal simply for kicking him. Perrette had always been unpredictable. Thinking of the testy cow brought a smile to Thibaut's lips. Perrette had kicked him, too, when she'd still been a heifer. The blow had nearly broken Thibaut's leg. He'd limped for months after. Perette was a fine milker though, and she raised strong calves.

Soon he was greeting those within the house, his half-sisters, Marie-Lucrece and Therese, with their shiny dark hair and rosy cheeks. Their mother, Bonne, pulled up a stool for him by the fire and then began to brew chicory. After he was seated, a mug of broth was placed in his hand, something "to warm you" before the chicory had finished steeping.

As he looked around the room, past and present merged. He remembered how frightened he'd been when this big, bearded white man had taken him away from his mother and everything he knew and had brought him here. He'd hidden the fear as best he could by not speaking for a long time. After all, he'd known but a few words of French as his mother had seen no reason to teach him.

Clearly, she had never imagined that Babin would come searching for the son she'd taken with her when she'd run away. Of his father, all he'd ever heard from his mother was: "Fool of a white man! Lying on the ground drooling and stinking, full of demon brandy! I swore I would never again live with such a man whether he be from-over-the-water or one of my own people. "

The Mi'kmaw warrior with whom she'd decamped had taken her to his band, then camped near the mouth of *Kitcikanii sipi*. As winter was coming on, they'd moved inland hunting before the heaviest snow came. This particular Mi'Kmaq band had never taken up the Cross and had no truck with the Jesuits. Except for trade, they rarely associated

257

either with the French or even with the Christian members of their own tribe.

His father still took a drink now and then, but even when he did, his behavior did not much resemble his mother's stories. It seemed his father had at last realized that those bouts of liquor madness weakened him, a circumstance his pride and a powerful instinct for self-preservation found intolerable. The shock of losing the labor of that fine, strong woman, as well as the sturdy toddler, had jolted him into better habits.

Babin Perè had realized that he wanted to continue to sail, fish, and trade the river in his beloved *chaloupe*. To do this, he had to keep his wits about him, first, so he could keep his scalp, and second, to make a living. He'd begun to truly want to settle down. These days he kept Bonne Marie and their daughters well fed and no more bullied than those of any other hard-working white man. He'd built himself a permanent home on this cove and since those old days, gathered friends around him.

First to build huts had been hunters and fur traders who came and went, but then old friends from Acadia had arrived, bringing families. Most important among those was a smith, Paul Surette, who arrived in a ketch filled with iron scrap. He could make many necessities, like knives, ax heads, nails, and pots. In fact, scrap metal was part of the trade his father sometimes plied. He and Surette would search out wrecks taking with them whatever metal they found. They hunted, too, and traded furs for metal rods at the fort. They also traveled to *Trois Rivieres* where a few industrious men were making bog iron. There they traded dried fish or even the valuable and hard to obtain script for the precious resource.

Other people settled, too, hoping for safety in numbers. Most of them had been born in New France and were almost as untamed as the creatures of the surrounding forests. There were children brought by parents, and new ones born. Some, like Thibaut, lived to grow up.

A family who kept goats arrived. The original clearing widened at a steady pace after that aided by the all-devouring goats.

As soon as smoke began to rise from a few more fires, the religious had appeared in their black robes. They'd settled a little deeper in the woods high on the cliffs above. Here they'd built a little mission and tried to save a few souls while scratching out a meager living from the soil-poor land. The last time he'd visited his home, Thibaut learned that the religious now called their settlement "Sacred Heart."

His father had often likened the religious orders to ticks "feeding on the flesh of working men. " However, the last time Thibaut had visited the cove, just before he'd taken on the task of piloting the Astrée, he'd been surprised at the sight of a priest taking his ease at the family table.

Father Marchand was a cheerful man who'd lived in Acadia for years and who understood his parishioners. Not that Babin senior had become a regular at Mass as were Bonne and the girls, but it seemed the old man had decided that, at his age, it was best to keep at least one foot in the door of heaven. After all, even all those long years earlier, his father had managed to find a priest to baptize Thibaut after he'd been dragged out of the woods to "become a good Frenchman. " A proper Frenchman was Catholic after all!

A few days of eating, sleeping, and occupying himself with daily chores and Thibaut found himself wondering why he had chosen to come here instead of returning to Quebec with his squad. Certainly, he was happy to see that his father and the small community were doing well and had not been burned out during his absence. Bonne was a good woman, but she'd arrived when Thibaut was sufficiently grown to believe he needed no mother.

It was comforting to see these familiar sights, safe from the unremitting dangers and exhaustion of the past months. In a single week, however, he began to feel restless, and his thoughts returned to Quebec, to the pretty, curious Frenchwoman there, and how she had not treated him condescendingly. Instead, she'd been eager to learn from him. Her determination to master the *raquettes* and to endure the cold had impressed him.

And those ice-fishing afternoons, when she'd been as delighted with her catch as anyone could be, had charmed him. Also, the look on her face when she gazed out across the snowscape, transfixed by the perilous beauty of the great, frozen river, exactly as he often was! She had welcomed his attention – even to his daring use of the familiar during their last interview. The tender expression she'd worn there in the twilight entryway as they'd made their farewells continued to haunt him.

Then he'd realized that neither his mind nor body had yet recovered from the bloodshed of winter. He needed to gather his strength. He needed to allow the nightmares to die away just a little more before returning to Quebec.

Each night Thibaut slept in the loft behind some casks. His sisters slept on the other side. His father and Bonne Marie slept in a bed in the main room of the stone house behind a screen, a nicety that was a new addition to the house.

Everyone arose before dawn, but his father often returned to his bed this spring while his wife and daughters made breakfast, milked goats, and drew water. Thibaut got into the habit of helping his sisters carry the buckets. They appeared surprised by this, but were pleased, too, because the buckets weighed heavily on their slender arms. This morning, after he'd poured some water into the stone jars set on the stoop beside the kitchen door, he went in for breakfast.

There Bonne Marie was busily frying cubes of salt pork on a tripod griddle set over the coals she'd raked forward onto the hearth. A plate of heavy cakes, still hot from the griddle, steamed on the table. Made of wheat, rye flour, a dab of melted fat, and a pinch of salt with a little water, they were the end of the winter flour. Bonne daily let her husband know they'd nearly come to the end of last year's provisions, but after the last few months of scant fare, everything smelled good to Thibaut.

"Thank you for helping your sisters, dear boy. " Bonne took her eyes away from the griddle and smiled at him. A lock of hair had escaped from her cap and her round, brown cheeks were red from proximity to the fire.

"Come and plate this for me, Lucrece. I need to sit for a moment. "

She moved back to allow her eldest to pass through to the griddle. Thibaut pulled out a chair for Bonne Marie. She smiled at him, amused at his politeness. He smiled in return and bent to kiss her moist cheek.

"Have you come home to stay? We all hope so. "

"I will stay for a time. The last few months were. . . difficult. I need to rest a little. "

"Well, Thibaut, you came home with your scalp, which you <u>might</u> want to enjoy having safe on your head for a few months more before you go chasing off down river again. " She lowered her voice and added, "I know your father needs your help to ready his boat. "

Thibaut sighed. He had no intention of staying too long. He would help them bring supplies from the store at Tadoussac as he had script from his service to spend, and he'd help complete work on the *chaloupe*, but after that, he'd be going west again.

The image of Jeanne smiling up at him from the ice that last bright day they'd fished together and the evenings when she'd asked him questions about this land and had listened, ever so attentively, kept entering his mind no matter how much he tried to push them away. In vain, he'd remind himself that she was probably out of his reach, a woman who could read, who knew how to write! Doubtless, she had come here to marry one of the French traders. . .

Then the usual, personal hesitations set in. *Am I ready to take another wife?*

So much love and so many future dreams had died along with his beautiful Sylvie and his little ones! He believed he couldn't endure another happily-ever-after destroyed by the violence that endlessly bloodied the river.

"There is a new Perette in the cove now. " The younger girl, Therese, came to lean against his chair, breaking his reverie.

"What are you talking about, *petite soeur*?"

"Don't bother Thibaut, Therese. He needs to eat his hot cakes while they are still hot, skin and bones that he is!"

"Ah, but she's correct!" That was his father emerging from behind the screen. "A pretty girl, that Perette, all of fourteen now. She's a strong girl, not at all like our mad cow. "

Thibaut gazed at his father. Of course, he had not been sleeping but listening! There was a yellowish cast to his winter pale face that he'd never seen before. The limp, as he came to the table, was at its worst in the morning.

In a reflex from the past, Thibaut stood, greeted his father then helped him into his seat.

"Good to see you still with us this morning," the old man said.

His father turned and took a moment to stroke his eldest daughter's round cheek as she brought him a plate of eggs. In earlier days, he would have been up and about before any of them off to business in the gray pre-dawn light.

"Some pretty young women right here in our cove, and summer is the best time for courting. You should get you a new wife and settle down here with us. "

Thibaut cleared his throat so that he could speak, then found that he couldn't organize his thoughts sufficiently.

Sylvie and their sons, her smile, the bright eyes of his children! Now, forever lost!

Yet, somehow, this dreadful memory, which had once reliably unmanned him, was followed by an image of Jeanne, her dark eyes, her kindness, her endless curiosity. She had been so unlike other Frenchwomen he'd met.

Thibaut collected a dense pancake from the plate before him and pushed his stool back with a screech. Without answering, he stood and walked out the door, taking the path which led to the "shop," a shed surfaced with bark. Before him, under a leaden sky, the rocky shallows of the inlet foamed and gurgled as the Saguenay purged itself of the last of the ice.

How easy, once he helped with this, it would be to take a canoe and ride the current down to Tadoussac! The ships from France would be coming now, and the river traders would be busy. He could quickly get work on a boat that would take him back to Quebec.

Instead, standing, he pushed the pancake into his mouth and chewed it, gritty and warm. Then, he ducked inside the shelter that covered the old chaloupe.

Best to just concentrate on what work was before him!

His father was not as strong as he'd once been, and repairing his chaloupe had been unavoidably delayed. However, by this time it must be June. At supper the night before, he'd heard enough back and forth between his father and Bonne to understand that the fisherman who had engaged to use it was fretful.

Of course he was! Everyone knew the whales would be by Tadoussac any day now. It was past time to get ships ready to hunt them.

Thibaut pushed the image of Jeanne away. There was guilt as he surveyed the state of things in the shop. His father was failing; that was clear. He gritted his teeth. He'd hoped to get the holes patched and the rotten planks removed and replaced as soon as possible, take his script down to Tadoussac, and get whatever supplies he could and then be on his way.

The little vessel rested on a low jig. The shed stood close to the water, but everything was ready for the day's work to begin. He sighed then went to take a closer look. He hoped that Surette or one of his boys, Charles, the one who'd been learning carpentry and helping out his father last year, was available to give him a hand. Fixing this old scow would take longer than he'd hoped and time was wasting!

Chapter 5

"So, you will marry and leave me. " Agathe sighed, lying back among the pillows.

"I thought you wanted me to marry. " Jeanne grumbled, but Agathe simply waved a pale hand as if to brush her protest away.

Her patroness was even paler than usual, but her cheeks were flushed as if she was feverish. Jeanne hoped that came from the heat of the day and not the pregnancy. It seemed impossible that after the long winter they would ever feel hot in this place, but the last few days had been ferocious, a circumstance that, everyone assured them, didn't happen often.

"This awful heat is sure to end in a nasty storm. " Madam Hus had observed this to Jeanne earlier, leaning out the kitchen door and studying the western sky. "It always storms when it gets like this, and it's been almost two weeks without a drop of water."

Old Jalbert, with his gnarled hands and weathered face, who did most of the heavy work of cultivation agreed.

"It's sure to dry out again as soon as I get the garden started. Gray and cloudy and cold all spring--and then it does this! I've had to water my cabbages every day now. "

Cabbages--a staple here just as they were in France--not only made good soup, they could be stored or pickled for winter, a time when everyone hungered for whatever scrap they had.

"If you had agreed to marry Monsieur LeBlant, you could have stayed here near me and live in Quebec in a snug little house with servants of your own. Instead, you are crossing the river, going to live where the Iroquois and the English raid all the time, going to work like a *paysan* from dawn to dusk. I can't believe you would rather work like an ox and live in a place where any day you could be murdered in your bed. "

Agathe shifted restlessly. She'd been bleeding off and on and was now confined to bed by the midwife, a circumstance that hadn't improved her temper. Her big belly raised the sheet in an impressive fashion.

Jeanne couldn't help but be worried about her and about the size of her belly too. *Could she be carrying twins?* Privately she'd questioned the midwife. The constant leaking and bleeding was not a good sign!

The stout, sturdy midwife, Madam Philipot, mother of eight, agreed with Jeanne that twins were a strong possibility, but she had counseled, "I think it best not to alarm Madam de Couage or her husband. A woman who is soon to deliver--especially at her age--a first child must, above all, remain calm. "

She said she saw no reason to think that the business would not go well. "Her hips are broad enough--and, Madam Jeanne, I believe her time could be any day now. "

"As you say, dear Agathe, Monsieur LeBlant is a kind man, a gentleman with property, but he is far too old. "

"At least when Le Blant died, you'd be left with something. "

Jeanne wanted to remind Agathe that Monsieur Le Blant had grown sons in France as well as grandchildren who would inherit, but she bit her tongue. She understood that Agathe, uncomfortable, anxious, and understandably bored by confinement, simply wanted to argue.

"Now, my dear lady, don't let's quarrel. It upsets you in your--your--delicate condition. . . "

"Oh Jeanne! Don't you dare use that disgusting phrase! It's bad enough that Benoit insists on saying that!"

"Quarreling upsets me too, Madame. " Unfazed, Jeanne began to straighten Agathe's pillow. "To speak true, I am not in love with Monsieur Fleury, but he is hardworking and honest. He has a good stone house built already, all set on his own land because the Sieur values him and rewards his people. Even the Paysan who work the land there respect him. That is plenty for me. "

She spoke with as much firmness as she could muster.

Inside, however, her old rebellious self whispered that there was a man in her heart--a man "entirely unsuitable" and, therefore, exactly like her first husband...

"Now, my dear Madam de Couage, let me help you sit straighter. " Jeanne eased Agathe into a more upright position. "I will bring something tonic from the kitchen for you. Madam Hus has been making juice from the first cherries. "

"Tell her to be sure it is sweetened, please. "

Jeanne sighed as she left the room. Madam Hus would doubtless fuss about Agathe's need to give directions. That lady, Jeanne knew, often wished that Agathe and all her "notions" about cookery and housekeeping would sink to the bottom of the *La Grande Rivière* .

After all, Hus had had both kitchen and household as her private kingdom for years. She clearly wished she still had that privilege. In those good old days, she had been not only the chatelaine of the place but had also had the respect and attention of Monsieur de Couage, things she clearly missed.

"Do as you see fit, Madam Hus," had been the order of the day for a long time, but now that Agathe had come, it was no longer so.

Her master's marriage had reduced the older woman's status in the house, for these days, Monsieur expressed any wishes he had to Agathe. As a result, Madam Hus's orders came from that quarter.

Managing things in house and kitchen had grown far more complicated as the battle of wills between the two women continued. Agathe, certainly, had her own *idées fixes,* and as the undisputed mistress, she had the upper hand, a circumstance Madam Hus still choked upon.

Whenever leather-clad *Coureurs de bois* or soldiers from *Trois Rivières* arrived, Jeanne would manage to ask after Thibaut, but it appeared that no one, whether coming from the east or from the west, had seen him since last winter. Men who knew him suggested various reasons for his absence.

Perhaps he had returned to his father's house on the Saguenay, or perhaps he had gone to hunt the whales at Tadoussac, or maybe he'd gone farther, out to the islands beyond the Gulf of St. Lawrence to fish, which he had been known to do. Perhaps the commandant had asked him to do more scouting for the military as they continued to attempt to ward off the Iroquois who continually threatened their trade as well as the lives of the colonists on the Seigneuries.

Although she tried not to entertain the darkest thoughts, sometimes she'd lie awake in the night wondering if Thibaut had been killed. As time passed, Jeanne resigned herself to the idea that he was gone. Perhaps it was wisest to put the man out of her mind. It would be hard though, especially when she remembered his farewell, how he'd used the familiar, gazed at her with such emotion, and kissed her hand.

Sometimes, too, she wondered what it would be like to give herself to Fleury, an apparently decent man and one she could admire but for whom she felt no passion. She couldn't imagine it, really, but soon decided that it was best not to entertain those thoughts either. Worries about things not yet come to pass wouldn't help her anxieties or help her do what was universally acknowledged as "good sense. "

Besides, she discovered she missed the community she'd experienced in that raw, new village. She missed the women at whose sides she'd worked, missed the children, missed the sunrises and even the storms of rain over those hard-won fields.

Now, when she accompanied Agathe on a visit to the nuns, she prayed with renewed urgency. Sometimes she asked the Blessed Mother to protect her new community across the river. Sometimes she prayed for Thibaut hoping he had not died in some horrible manner at the hands of a brutal enemy. She remembered her promise to return to the Seigneury and prayed for the resolve to keep it.

August crawled in. Jeanne had prepared herself to sail to the other shore and enter marriage again, this time with the reserved M. Fleury. She'd secured passage on a trader's chaloupe that would travel that way, one that would be bringing supplies St. Marr had ordered sent to his property. Then all of that came to a halt. Agathe went into labor.

It came on early, as the midwife had expected, an event Jeanne had hoped to avoid. She feared for Agathe's safety, and feared that her newborn would not survive. It would have been easier to be elsewhere and only hear of the outcome later. Instead, she was here sharing the lady's travail.

In the end, she spent the following day and the morning of the next beside Agathe's bed alongside the midwife, witnessing, and attempting to assuage, the suffering that was woman's lot during labor. Now standing beside Agathe, she found herself in unwilling remembrance of the birthing tragedy she'd tried to prevent during last autumn's voyage. She prayed heartily that this labor would not end like that.

Agathe had been awake and walking since before dawn. At first, she'd been uncomplaining. When her husband awoke to find her pacing back and forth in the adjoining dressing room, he'd been certain at once that this was the onset of heralded birth. He was the one to call the maids for help and to have a messenger sent to the midwife.

Madam Philpot had matters in her own house to settle, so Jeanne and Lily had gone to help Agathe. They found the lady pacing, frowning, and occasionally pausing to lean on the table. She was pale but determined they should first arrange her hair.

"Well, here we are at your time of delivery, dear lady," Jeanne said. "Later, God and His Holy Mother willing, you shall hold your first dear child. "

"I am glad it has begun," Agathe said then forced her lips into a line, for another, stronger contraction came upon her. A slender white arm, emerging from the heavy sleeve of her gown, encircled her belly as she leaned forward and allowed a groan to escape.

"Come and sit for a little till it passes. " Jeanne moved a chair for her. "Then you can walk more if you wish. " She was almost surprised when Agathe followed her advice because the lady was usually quick to assert her own will even if it wasn't always sensible. This was the moment when Jeanne knew that the restlessness had begun to pass into genuine pain.

As they had feared, Agathe had been carrying twins. The first child, a boy, was born sixteen hours later as the sun went down. The second did not appear until the next day at sunrise. They were both small but survived their passage into the world. For her part their mother was utterly exhausted, unable to deliver the afterbirth.

The midwife had to assist, and it tore Jeanne's heart to see her benefactress so reduced by long suffering and fear.

The second baby was a daughter, smaller, and, like her weary mother, very tired. They were all overjoyed, when the baby, swinging upside down in the bloody hands of the midwife, her bent frog legs appearing barely sufficient to support her head, abruptly released a thin, gurgling shriek.

"Here, Madam Jeanne!" The midwife delivered the newborn maid into the swaddling wrap Jeanne held out. Feeling the warm, wet creature in her arms, she felt a surge of pity. Such a long, desperate journey this tiny being had already endured!

If she survives her first few years, she will have to face whatever this harsh new world has in store. If she lives long enough to bring forth her own babies, she too will suffer this same agony.

Jeanne and the midwife helped Agathe become accustomed to nursing, helped her endure the initial swelling of her small breasts and the sore nipples that tormented any new mother, especially a new mother who was nursing two. The twins were laid one across the other so they could nurse at the same time. It was difficult and awkward, and the babies were not always on the same schedule.

Agathe was exhausted, but she had help from her maids and assistance from a woman in milk who was brought to stay with them. That woman was also nursing her own new baby, so she too could give advice and encourage the new mother. The survival of both twins was more than anyone expected, however, in this circumstance, both babies had enough to eat and plenty of hands to tend them.

Jeanne could not imagine trying to handle this situation if Agathe was a poor woman without servants. *No wonder twins so often died!* It was a difficult and exhausting undertaking even with help.

Agathe took to motherhood with the same fierce determination she undertook any new project. To everyone's surprise, the girl, the smaller of the two, thrived along with her larger brother.

Privately Madam Hus rejoiced as the lady of the house was now far too preoccupied to "meddle" in household business. The twins' birth had allowed her to regain some of her old autonomy as well as valued personal time with her master.

Benoit de Couage was proud, but also surprised, to become the father of two. More than many husbands, he took an interest in how things were going in the nursery. He had the little ones baptized at once, something people rarely went to the trouble or expense to do here until a child had successfully reached the first birthday. The common exception to that rule would be, of course, if a child was dying and might need passage to heaven.

The children were named "Louis" after Benoit's father and "Marie-Claude" after Agathe's mother. Sometimes, though, the master of the house seemed a little impatient with his wife's new preoccupation. He clearly missed Agathe's attention because in business matters he'd found her to be a shrewd judge of character as well as a careful keeper of his ledgers.

One day, much to Jeanne's surprise, Luc Fleury came marching up from the waterside. When she arrived at the room where he waited, after being urgently summoned by one of the servants, she saw that his fair face was red--she hoped from the sun! He was wearing his best jacket, the one he'd worn at their first supper together. His fair beard was now neatly trimmed to show the square contours of his jaw.

No one had expected him, certainly not Jeanne, whom he'd demanded to "see immediately!" As soon as she entered the room, she could see from his manner that he was a man barely controlling his temper. Without preamble, he told her that she must either sign the marriage contract today and return with him to the seigneury by the next transport or he would leave tomorrow and she would hear from him no more!

"You are needed, Jeanne Dube. "

His voice was low, but she could tell that he was holding back strong emotion. *Anger? Fear?* She could not tell.

Before she could answer, he cried, "No, by Heaven! **I** need your answer, and I need it now! When you left us, I believed you would soon send a message asking me to join you here, and we would sign the marriage contract. Now, nearly two months have passed, and--by all the Saints--I will not wait any longer. Marry me and sail back with me! The harvest is already under way, and there is much to be done to prepare for winter. "

Surprised by his outburst, Jeanne stood amazed.

"Well Jeanne Dube do you agree?" In that instant it was clear that he not only needed her, he wanted her to be his wife.

"Yes, Luc Fleury, I agree to marry you. "

Jeanne came close and rested her hands on his chest. Fleury was mollified, but his breathing remained fast.

"We shall have the contract witnessed by Monsieur de Couage, and I shall return as your wife tomorrow. "

She was surprised again when he quietly captured one of her hands and raised it to his lips as if they were a noble lady and her gentleman, not merely pair of struggling *habitants* in a wilderness agreeing to a marriage founded upon necessity and mutual need. His manner seemed to bode well. She had seen his heart at last.

Chapter 6

As soon as they arrived at the dock, they were welcomed with a cheer that touched Jeanne's heart. She had been missed! Perhaps only by some in the Ville as another willing pair of hands but, nevertheless, a genuine welcome. She was surprised to find herself tearing up as she stepped onto the dock and again later when they were led to an *al fresco* feast that had been prepared for their return, everything set out on trestle tables beneath a maple tree.

The next day, as they worked by the fire, the normally taciturn Noelle confided that Fleury had been patient for a time, but his impatience and irritation had increased daily after the first three weeks had gone by with no news from her.

"I told him myself you would return, that you would not be afraid of our life here. Let me tell you! He lost his temper completely and roared at me 'to mind my own business,' and that you were free to do anything you liked and that he could care less one way or another,' but it was plain as his long nose that care, and cared very strongly, he did!"

The days passed in a swirl of harvest activities. Jeanne learned how to braid corn shucks to form a chain for storage, a trick the French settlers had learned from the Indians. The rest of the harvest was familiar. The community scythed wheat together, men and women, boys and girls. Any extra would be stored and traded for other things in Quebec.

After the wheat had dried a little in shocks, they hauled it in by cart, the oxen hard at work. The harvest went to an airy barn, which had been raised only a few years past. Threshing came next, another hard labor.

In the clouds of dust this raised, everyone had sore eyes and a permanently stuffy nose. Jeanne decided that farming was probably harder than any work she'd done in her life. Now she was sneezing and blowing her nose constantly as was almost everybody else.

In La Rochelle, I soon got used to my body and clothes stinking of fish, but this feeling of being continually half-sick is exhausting.

However, the rest of the community appeared to be in the same state of congestion and misery. For a few weeks, coughing, sneezing, short-tempers, and watery eyes were epidemic. Then, slowly, that complaint died away as the threshing came to an end.

Next they picked from the small orchard of apple and pear trees. The fruit would be washed, then cut and strung to dry from loft beams. Digging root vegetables and storing those in underground cellars followed. Some of that harvest could remain in the ground for a time before the hard freezes came. The sunchokes would be after that, followed by cutting and retting the last of the hemp.

Louise Renaud had explained to her that in the earliest days of the Seigneury, they'd had to do everything by hand, bringing the produce in on handcarts, because during the first year the oxen had not yet arrived. Even turning the soil in the spring had meant the entire small community needed to be out with shovels, hoes and digging sticks. Very little grain could be planted under those circumstances and every grain harvested had gone to feed the families here.

"We greeted those oxen like living saints when they arrived the next year! These two fellows we have are such good boys, both of 'em, just as gentle and willing as can be. "

The cattle on the farm--seven cows and the oxen--were all handsome animals but not as imposingly large as some farm cattle Jeanne had seen in France. The oxen were a rich, ruddy tan that shaded into black on their bellies, forequarters, legs, and hooves. The cows were the same, only smaller, pretty creatures with sweet faces. There was, of course, a bull, a living brown and black block terror of a beast who was kept in a large, heavily reinforced pen.

Both sexes of this breed carried small horns. The calves Jeanne had seen born in that summer had arrived as an all-over dun and cream. Now after just a few months, they were darkening, beginning to resemble their elders. The adults' bellies and udders were creamy off-white, much like the milk they gave. Jeanne, who enjoyed milking them, thought they were handsome cattle. When she said so, her husband replied in his usual factual manner.

"The Sieur, who is fond of cattle, studied the matter carefully. He chose these northerners because they are sure-footed and can handle our rough terrain and bad weather. They are also strong for their size. Beyond that, the cows give fine milk. "

There was kitchen work as well, preserving the last cabbages, shredding, then packing them in salt and vinegar to preserve. Beans, already dried, were still being shelled. More than once, Jeanne found herself running outside to carry in the drying trays to save the precious seeds from a sudden autumn shower. Crocks, as well as baskets woven by the Indians, were used for storage.

The Indian baskets were very beautiful. Belinha knew how to make them, and she had taught Louise, a woman who had Jeanne's desire to learn new things. Jeanne hoped to acquire the know-how, but there was too much else this autumn to occupy her. There were sunchokes and potatoes to harvest and clean. Wheat had to be transferred into sacks and large wooden barrels so that it could go to the just-completed mill, some distance away, to be ground.

Animals had to be taken to and from pasture and looked after, and the culling of the males among the young had begun. This meant blood and butchery and sausage making and smoking, salting and hanging strips to dry as well as tears from the more tender-hearted youngsters who had attached themselves to one of those pretty beasts now sent to die.

Jeanne had not been around much of this kind of work and was happy to be mostly excused from the bloodiest parts. She did wield a cleaver when it was time to cut the cleaned and skinned carcasses, in preparation for whatever preservation was intended.

The early months of her marriage passed in a blur. Jeanne was grateful for all the activity because it kept emotions she did not want to experience--about the past, as well as fears concerning this beautiful and terrifying new world--at bay.

Not only that, but it was strange to be someone's wife again. During the day, Fleury was somewhat formal. Some nights, when he wasn't too tired, he surprised her by being a lover in earnest. She had not expected that.

It made their intimate moments almost pleasurable, unlike her apprehensive imaginings. Her marital duties were no heavy chore.

Mostly that was a good thing, but sometimes Jeanne felt guilty that she did not feel the emotions she'd felt years ago in Pierre's embrace, that she could not match her new husband's desire. She simply did not feel for him the way he did for her. Maybe, she thought, that is to be expected in a second marriage especially as her choice had been so much driven by necessity.

There was not much time to indulge brooding, for she was, more and more, ever so tired, tired right to her bones. She barely noticed when the bright trees that had painted the hillsides a multitude of colors dropped their leaves.

The arrival of the winter was announced in days of harsh icy winds, gray rain, and one nasty freeze after another. Finally, the morning after a howling, frigid night, they awakened to snow--it looked as if a foot of it had swept in overnight. They had now entered the time of battling the long cold and the never-ending frozen precipitation.

Christmas came and went. She had a letter from Agathe, brought by the Sieur during one of his visits. He was mightily pleased that Jeanne had chosen to become one of "his people. " He brought a small keg of brandy as a present as well as the letter.

Curiosity about the contents was overcome by the hubbub. The big house was now busy and full with St. Marr, his aide, and a handful of soldiers. Once again, his wife had not come down from Quebec with him.

All the workers of the Ville came in to celebrate the holiday, and St. Marr had small gifts of script for everyone for it had been a good harvest. Jeanne was pleased she could delay opening the message until evening came and she and Fleury were in their own small stone house.

In the summer, she had noted how the houses were packed close together. Now, winter showed that this was practical. Soon the snow would be too high to dig through, and the less tunneling they had to do, the better. As they left the Sieur's home, she and her husband had been greeted by a bitter wind full of ice on their short, snowy walk. White walls arose on every side.

At the door, they were greeted by the newest apprentice who had been left behind to tend the fire and trim the candles. They'd stamped the snow from their feet on the stoop before entering. Jeanne noticed immediately that the boy appeared to have been frightened at being by himself. Hebert was twelve. He'd come from France in the last of the summer transports with a younger sister, who'd been kept to recover from the journey in Quebec. His anxiety, alone in this frightening place, understandable.

She smiled at the boy and then brought him a small glass of brandy, some of the last from their old supply.

"Before you sleep," she said as she handed it to him.

"Merci, Madam Fleury!"

Hebert was hollow-eyed and very thin. Clearly, the sea journey had been difficult for him as well as his sister. Not only Jeanne, but Noelle, the cook at the big house, had taken pity on him and had fed him well during his initial time at the big house.

"And who knows how well he ate in France?" She had lived among the poor in La Rochelle and recognized the boy's haunted look.

Fleury wanted Hebert to stay with them in their cabin this first winter. If he survived until next year, he would be housed in a cabin with other boy laborers.

Meanwhile, Hebert had downed his brandy. After a tug of gratitude at his forelock, he'd retreated up the ladder to a loft where his cot was set among storage. Soon, down to his shirt and with a cap on his boyish head, he would lie down on a straw mattress and pull up the covers.

Fleury carried some plans to their table and after moving his candle, he neatly laid them out for study. Jeanne settled into a chair where she could catch the firelight. She removed the letter from her skirt pocket, broke the seal, and began to read.

"Mon amie le plus aimable,

I hope you are well in the snow-bound wilderness with your new husband as happy at least as I remain with mine. Monsieur de Couage has been traveling west, and I am even now anxiously awaiting his return. As you may have heard, there is much fighting and theft of our goods along the trade routes. I shall remain very anxious until his safe return.

My babies are both well and growing, Praise our Blessed Mother Mary!

I am not as well as I might be; the harsh climate of this place as well as my recent travail appear to have cost me a good part of my customary strength and vitality. The children are becoming accustomed to a routine--at last! I am aided in every way by Lily and Marthe as well as by dear Madame Philpot, who comes often.

I must tell you of a new and welcome addition to our household. Madame Tullier had the ill-fortune to have a stillbirth quite soon after my delivery, but she has become an invaluable help to my daughter as well as to me. As her husband has been away at Trois-Rivieres, she is living here now and taking over nursing our little Marie-Claude, who began, as you may remember, somewhat small. Madame Tullier has become very attached to her over the past months, which gives me peace of mind. This allows me more time and strength to devote to Louis, who roars like a bull when he is hungry. Our little son grows bigger at my breast. He is quite the man and far more active and demanding than his sister.

The last months have been filled with many fears and accounts of terrible slaughters of our people and of our allies. I cannot bring myself to repeat news of these here. You will no doubt have heard for these tales of savagery must have reached all parts of New France by now. I shall spare myself the anguish of recounting all the ugly details.

I pray that this letter reaches you and that you are well and will be able to send an answer by the bearer or by another who may be coming to Quebec for supplies from St. Marr's Ville.

May The Blessed Mother and Her Holy Angels watch over you and keep you and yours safe,

> *je suis toujours ton amie,*
> *Agathe Martin de Couage*

Jeanne sat quietly by the fire holding the letter while her eyes took in the simple room around her--the pans hung beside the hearth, the crock suspended above the low fire, the still-bright wood of the mantel in this house that had been so recently completed.

Carefully, she turned the letter over thinking how difficult Agathe's life was going to be no matter how privileged her position in the colony. Jeanne was happy, certainly, that Agathe and her children had survived. Tonight, however, she was just so very, very tired. She would write a brief reply when she had time in the morning, so that St. Marr could carry it back when he departed again.

She glanced around the shadowy room. Night had come down hours before. Around the house, winter roared in what seemed a never-ending howl. Ice tapped and rattled against the walls.

"You have gone a thousand miles away, my dear. " Fleury's voice broke the silence. In a near-fatherly tone he continued. "Do you miss your life in Quebec?"

"No, my husband. There, I was of little use to anyone. It is better for the soul to be doing. "

"And here there is so very much to do!" Fleury broke into a rare smile. Jeanne felt a surge of warmth in her heart. She smiled back.

"However, just like young Hebert, Monsieur, I must sleep now. I am sorry, but I must. "

Fleury's smile faded, and his gray eyes darkened a little.

"Are you well, Madam? Of late, you have appeared much fatigued. "

"I know I have been slow to waken. Perhaps retiring earlier will surely cure it. "

She felt Fleury's eyes upon her as she retreated to their bed set against the far wall. To Jeanne, the bed appeared ever-so welcoming with the thick curtains pulled back to catch the warmth of the room.

Soon she would close herself inside and under the covers, face to the wall, fall into a deep sleep. Fleury's pen might occasionally scratch, but there was only the sporadic pop of the fire in the single room where they were safe from the wind and snow hissing and sighing outside.

The next morning, as usual, as if he had a clock in his head, Fleury awoke long before the light. He'd arise, pull on trousers, stamp into his boots, and call for the apprentice to come down if the boy hadn't leapt up at the sound of his master's stirring below. Jeanne always rose promptly too.

She tried to hurry while she pulled her dress over her head, wanting to make good on her promise of the night before. While she shrugged on her work apron, which functioned as an overall, her gorge suddenly rose and sent her racing across the room and straight out the door onto the frozen step. The shock of January pre-dawn air on her face and the cold snow upon her stocking feet calmed her for an instant. She ended, however, by being sick right there onto the icy mounds of snow by the door.

Fleury had followed her. When she had finished, he put one hand beneath her elbow while offering her a dishcloth with the other.

"I wondered if that might be the cause of your fatigue. "

When they were indoors, Fleury seated her and went to take a cursory glance at the pot hanging from its hook. The fire had just been returned to life, so he asked Hebert--now kneeling on the hearth--to swing it over the fire to heat before returning to where his wife leaned with her head in her hands.

"Well, well!" Fleury pulled up a chair beside her and laid a warm hand on Jeanne's knee.

"Why haven't you spoken?"

Jeanne shook her head but didn't answer. *She'd known. Of course she'd known!*

Still, the new life begun, in a world where she did what was sensible instead of heeding the call of her wild-goose heart, at times seemed too strange to be real.

This was, however, what was! She was married, her life inextricably entwined with that of this stolid, hard-working man. Now, as proof of the bond, she carried his child.

She'd felt the flutters quite clearly for the past few weeks when she lay down at night, but she had not been ready to share the news. She had not even been ready to admit it to herself.

Here was yet another step into the future even as her past dwindled away. She had cast her fate to the wind when she'd come aboard the Astree'. Now blown like a seed onto this wild ground, she'd found earth and begun to send down roots.

Winter was much like that of the year before with endless storms of snow, raw winds, and bitter, bitter cold. Jeanne endured her out-of-doors tasks as well as she could. She bundled up beforehand as much as she could and still accomplish all of the necessary tasks. How much to wear was difficult to gauge because the work was difficult, and she needed to bend while her hands and arms remained free.

Her mittens would clog with snow and turn into immovable blankets of ice as the heat from her hands melted it. Then, with time, it would swiftly freeze, and finally, against her fingers, it would turn into icy water. She'd have to shed them to keep using her fingers. This could not continue for too long under the frigid conditions that prevailed. When she'd arrive indoors, finally driven there by the inability to feel her fingers--or, in other circumstances--her toes. Afterward she'd sit by the fire, pulling off frozen boots and rubbing her burning, half-frozen flesh with fingers that also ached until the pins and needles pain resolved.

"You should not stay out so long, my dear," her husband would say. He would come to gather her icy hands into his, chafing "to move the blood. " Her fingers and feet stung and stabbed before they returned to life as if they'd been immersed in boiling water.

"You could get frostbitten, and trust me, that is not a fate you should tempt. You can lose a finger or a toe very easily in this kind of weather. "

In the kitchen of the big house, Belinha or Noelle did not mince words if she overstayed outside.

"Not only could you lose fingers or toes, but the gangrene can follow. "

"And then they cut and cauterize, but the infection will travel. Soon, Death cannot come fast enough. "

Jeanne understood this, but she stubbornly believed the constant fatigue must not defeat her. She had to measure up to life on this frontier.

Her attitude could not last. Fleury, who at first appeared impressed by her grim determination, began to caution her especially when February, the time when ice fell from leaden skies, arrived. Jeanne slept as soon as her head hit the pillow, utterly exhausted. Sometimes out of doors, she'd stumble, lose her balance, and fall into a snowbank while laboring forward with an armload of kindling as she made her way among the paths between sheds. These trails, ever filling in with snow, were now floored with ice.

Her pregnancy wasn't yet unwieldy, but Jeanne often felt as if she was carrying a passenger who sapped all her strength. Her days were spent in a kind of work-filled sleepwalk. Their little home was mostly tight and warm--the temperature outside considered--but unlike her last year in Quebec, the very real danger of the season was ever present lurking just beyond the walls of this wild place.

Jeanne was haunted by the knowledge of what a mortal threat winter was, far worse than any experience she had either in France or at the trading post. Sometimes, especially at night, she felt afraid when the wind howled for days. Even fetching wood from the nearby pile took all her strength. There were terrible icy mornings when they had to shovel snow temporarily inside the house in order to get out; every path they'd dug the day before had vanished. It was then she remembered the comforts of the trading post with longing.

After a series of gigantic snowstorms, they were cut off from their neighbors except by snowshoe. Shoveling short paths to reach the animal sheds now leaning against the chimney wall of their home or to reach the big house took entire, exhausting days of work beside her husband and his poor, skinny Hebert. Originally the distance between the homes in the settlement seemed but a few steps. Now they seemed frozen miles away. Sometimes they could hear voices--those of equally marooned neighbors snowshoeing or digging towards their storage sheds. At those times, *Bonjour!* shouted over the white drifts was their only form of contact.

She was too tired most of the time to think clearly about anything, neither unhappy nor happy, lost in numb survival, content to produce a pot of beans or some pan bread with which to fill their guts. This winter was terrifying in its fury and glorious in its hostile beauty. It was a twin of the last year in Quebec, but the danger of Nature in this isolated place was ever present. The moving drifts, like frozen dunes on every side, became a monster intent upon swallowing them, always snuffling about for a weak spot in their defenses, a place to penetrate the walls of their home.

One twilight beside the fire, after she'd cleaned the few dishes and moved the pot from which they'd been eating for days now to a place where it could continue to simmer, Jeanne had seated herself with a sigh of relief. She'd wrapped her shawl close around her shoulders and begun to doze. A little time later, Fleury, sitting beside her, laid a broad hand on her belly.

"This must be a boy. In fact, I am quite certain. "

Nearby the apprentice, wrapped in a blanket on the floor, stirred a little. He too was bone tired from the daily battle with winter.

Jeanne, nearly asleep in the ring of warmth by the fire, had opened her eyes.

"What did you say, Fleury?'

"You are carrying a boy child. Of this, I am convinced. "

"What makes you think that?"

This bit of whimsy was a surprise. Though half-asleep she roused sufficiently to manage a smile.

"My dear Therese was always especially tired before she carried a boy." His mention of the first wife was a rarity, but it pleased Jeanne to hear that her predecessor spoken of with so much affection.

"I don't think I am soon to give birth, Monsieur. " Jeanne raised her eyes to study him. The times when he showed a fanciful side were uncommon.

"I remember you thought June would be your time. However, I am sure you will give me a fine boy. "His face shone with pleasure at the thought. "I even have a name ready. "

Jeanne nodded. She had had a feeling Luc would want to name the first child of this union.

"And what have you decided? That is, if God wills I should deliver safely?"

Jeanne sent up a silent prayer to the Holy Mother. It was prudent to take nothing about her coming trial for granted. Agony was to be expected, but sometimes death was how childbirth ended.

"I imagine you will be pleased by my choice. Our son shall be called Jean-Baptiste for June is the time of the blessed saint's nativity. " He gathered her hand into his, so muscular and warm, tenderly pressing her fingers, "And that name will also be a salute to my brave wife, Jeanne. "

The Sieur visited. He brought bad news from Quebec. The colony was in yet more trouble. The Iroquois had raided along all trade routes as far as the enormous freshwater lakes that lay to the west. The Sieur brought Helene, Hebert's younger sister, in his retinue. Now that the girl had recovered her strength, she too must begin to work out her indenture.

Jeanne thought the poor girl appeared frail and wondered how much help she would be.

This land is cruel to the weak. I will probably end by having to nurse her back to health, poor little creature!

She had swiftly pushed the uncharitable thought aside for her heart went out to someone who, so young, had been sent so far away from her home. Instead, she clasped the girl's small cold hand in hers and smiled.

"I think for today Helene should sit by the fire, eat, and get all the way warm. Tomorrow," her gaze met the girl's gray eyes, "I shall show you your tasks. For today, however, I think, you must recover from that long journey in the cold. Then your brother and I will make a bed for you beside him in the loft."

Helene, still shivering, gazed at her new mistress with gratitude. Jeanne led her to a stool close by the fire.

"Sit now, little Mademoiselle, and get warm. You will be no help to me if you fall ill once more. "

Jeanne fetched a small bowl and ladled in liquid from the ever-simmering stock pot. Anxiously, Helene popped up to take it as if Jeanne should not have to take so much as a step.

"Did I not say sit?" Jeanne handed over the bowl, watching as Helene, eyes downcast, subsided onto the stool. "Time enough to serve! Sit while you can, my girl. "

Hebert, usually so solemn, had been elated to see his sister again. Helene proved to be a little taller than he was, but girls were often forward in their growth at this age. Jeanne guessed they must have been born close together.

She wondered briefly what family ill-fortune had sent mere children into such harsh and distant service then remembered that they had come from a northern farm. Hebert had once mentioned their father had taken a new wife. It was a story all too familiar to Jeanne only this tale had taken place among far poorer folk than her own.

Sheep dropped their young in darkness and snow followed by more snow and bitter wind. It would be almost three months later that spring came at last--and when it finally did, it arrived like an avalanche.

Life in the fields and forest burgeoned. The icy hide of those great drifts shrank away, revealing, at the muddy edges, green shoots poking through icy melt water. As the fields of white dwindled, the earth beneath emerged as a sea of mud.

This was followed by the greening of the forest floor. Soon, there were fiddleheads to steam and eat, everyone in the *Ville* hungry for something green. The work of farming began in a rush.

Her prediction was accurate. It was June, close to the Nativity of Saint John Baptiste, when Jeanne delivered. Wishing and fearing equally, life with the rolling, kicking, and drumming creature inside Jeanne came to an abrupt end. She was anxious, certainly, but ever so weary of carrying.

Labor commenced much as her earlier experience, which was just as she'd hoped. The first cramps woke her at dawn, but it wasn't much later than noon when she was delivered.

Her husband had gone early to his work, taking his apprentice with him. Jeanne asked Belinha not to send any message until the business was over. Noelle brought broth and water, but otherwise she remained at her own tasks in the big house kitchen. Summer was a busy time, and most were at work elsewhere either in the fields or the forest.

Jeanne came through well. Her baby did too although the child was not Luc's imagined son but a round, healthy daughter who squalled every bit as loudly as Michel had when he'd first come into the world.

"Well, well," Belinha said. "A maiden and not the man-child Fleury was expecting. I hope he will not be angry."

"He'd be a fool if he is," Jeanne said. "This girl and I have worked too hard these months--not to mention this morning--to put up with any prideful male nonsense."

Bolstered by pillows, she put her daughter to her breast hoping that there was some sustenance there. A colorless fluid began to leak straight away. It had taken two anxious days for her first milk to come after giving birth to Michel, and she hoped that, as the Dube women had assured her many years ago, things would move faster for this second child of her body.

"If Fleury agrees, I shall call her Mathilde after my dear mother who died many years ago. I was a disobedient daughter while she lived, and I wish to honor her memory."

"You must ask your mother's spirit to keep her in health," said her companion, whose religious notions were Catholic only on the surface. "Perhaps from your heaven your mother can protect this fine daughter."

"I hope so, my friend. I hope so."

Luc was not angry, but he was disappointed she could see as soon as he heard the news. Nevertheless, he smiled and heartily congratulated Jeanne for having come through her labor looking so strong and well. He'd bent to kiss his wife on the forehead and assured her that Mathilde was "perfect" for his new daughter.

"Well, well," he said as he gathered Mathilde into his arms, "Here is our pretty maid at last! She's big, too, I swear!" He rocked the baby in his arms gently, studying her and kissing her small waving fists. Jeanne loved Luc dearly at that moment.

How assured and tender he was with this new daughter!

The baby, whose gaze was astonishingly steady, regarded him. She was bald, and her eyes, like those of her father, were gray as ice. Perhaps, Jeanne thought, pink, bald Mathilde resembles Luc's other children.

Chapter 7

Thibaut worked daily on the chaloupe with his father and the new apprentice. The boy, Charles, was partly trained, his young fingers already leathery from unraveling rope for caulk, and he was by now handy with a skive. Simon Babin, with obvious pride, declared that "Charles learns fast. He has a natural understanding of the wood. "

Thibaut learned this youngster was Surette's son who had begun his training at Ile Royale in Port Toulouse, where once long ago, his own father had settled. Breton fishermen had been in those parts for a generation--sometimes two--and were among some of the first whites to settle in this land.

Many years ago Thibaut's father had sailed into Port Toulouse. He'd decided to give up traveling back and forth across the wide and stormy Atlantic and instead remain to fish and mend boats by these western waters. As a younger son, little awaited him in France upon his father's death.

Simon had been bound and determined to seek his fortune somewhere--anywhere. Even in this howling wilderness! That was the tale his father had told many times over the years while sitting by the fire.

Thibaut remembered a boy his father had had living here when he had first come to the cove. This half-brother had been sired by his father upon a Metis woman. The child of that union, Richard, was barely three years older than Thibaut.

Richard's mother had returned to live with her family at Tadoussac. Like Thibaut's mother in later days, she'd taken her son with her. She had died there during a sickly spring when pestilence ran wild along the river. As soon as the news reached him, Simon had gone to a nearby group of Mi'kmaq, one which still seasonally crossed the river to chase whales, and had asked for one of their girls, the woman who became Thibaut's mother. He was a man who had little interest in children until they had survived infancy and grown sufficiently to work with him.

At first, there was some rivalry between the two boys, but in the end, Thibaut formed a strong bond with his older half-brother. He remembered how frightened he'd been when he'd first come to live here with this strange man and his strange French ways. Simon often yelled at him in a language he didn't yet understand, and he used a rod for discipline. Richard--once they'd fought with each other and got that out of the way--had helped him to learn French and showed him how to "behave civilized."

Richard had drowned when his canoe was swept into a rock among the rapids in the fierce Saguenay. He must have struck his head and passed out because he was a strong swimmer.

That was another sad memory, the loss of his half-brother. Thibaut shook it off and got on with the day's work--but so much grief lingered in this place!

Their father had long ago explained to his boys that he'd learned to swim "the hard way," which meant that he'd nearly drowned after accidentally falling out of his fishing boat. Europeans, even the sailors among them, rarely knew how to swim, a circumstance the Indians of *Kitcikanii sipi* found utterly incomprehensible.

Thibaut remembered the old man making certain both his boys were competent in the water as well as upon it. During those childhood summers, a small band of Innu sometimes camped close by. Thibaut and Richard regularly swam and fished with their boys when they'd come down to their cove. In fact, it was from those same Innu that Thibaut's wife Silvie had come.

He kept fighting off all these old memories as he trimmed a board though it was hard not to feel his heart sink under the weight of remembered losses. He paused in his work and let out a long sigh. His gaze strayed from the wood down to the glint of the water beyond.

"Hey, Thibaut!" Paul Surette, the smith who sat nearby sharpening a file, smiled. "Ready to leave us already, you fella?"

"You know me well, M. Surette. When I am away, I miss this place and all you good people, but when I'm here, all I can think about is how to go sailing over the water or hunting in the forest again. "

"Breton and Mi'kmaq mated breed men who must ever be wandering. I'm always reminding your father that you are as restless he was when I first knew him. Last time though," Jacques said grinning through his beard, "he threatened to break a chair over my head. "

"What stopped him?"

"Bonne, of course! She said she had had to work too hard to get each and every one of those fine chairs into the house and that he better not even think of it. "

Paul laughed remembering the scene. Thibaut certainly could imagine it. The patient Metis woman Babin had finally taken to wife had a temper of her own--as well as a great deal of pride in every one of her hard-won household possessions. He smiled back at his companion who seemed determined to cheer him up.

Thibaut returned to the task at hand, but something was wrong. He stared at the wood, at first wondering if he was attacking it incorrectly. He'd learned, via hard cuffs from the old man, how to use those chisels to cut wood like soft cheese.

"Paul, either I have forgotten what I am at or this chisel is mighty dull!" He lifted the tool to better study it.

"Let me see. " Paul Surette came closer and lifted the tool from Thibaut's hands.

"Correct you are! Damn!" His weathered face folded into frustration. "The boss said he would take care yesterday before he left." He sighed and shook his head as he studied it. "Here, have mine for a while. Let me see to this. "

Afterwards, they settled into work. Paul took some time to check and sharpen other chisels wandering back and forth to the sharpening stone. Wood chisels had to be kept in prime condition to work properly.

A cedar board was being readied to incorporate into the *chaloupe*, which rested on the ribs of the jig. Thibaut found the smell comforting, not because of this place and the long days he'd spent training with his father, but because his mother's shelters had often used young cedar bows for the floors and to line the ground before their bedding had been laid down.

Whispering boughs of live trees above their shelter had been the music of his early years as his mother's band hunted deep in the forest during the hottest parts of the summer. The oil of the cedar mixed with animal fat was what his mother had rubbed into his skin to keep the flies away. That strong pungency was the scent of his forest childhood.

Cedar was also a fine wood for building boats. It was light, easy to shape and bend. The oils helped preserve the vessel from water rot. When those Mi'kmaq had camped nearby, his father had learned the secret of building ocean-going canoes. One of the old men knew how to make them, and this was a craft for which the Mi'kmaq were famous.

Thibaut remembered those days happily as he'd learned something of the long process beside his father, both under the tutelage of the elder, a weathered man whose old head held a treasure trove of sea-faring knowledge. His father had actually attempted a build of one of these large canoes back then. He'd been guided by the Mi'kmaw, a man who bore the proud name "He walks on water."

These canoes were long and rugged but took a great deal of time and care to assemble properly so that they would withstand salt water, and the strong currents and large waves of the ocean. As Thibaut had always had a desire to "walk on water" himself, he'd been on fire to learn.

The build, as he remembered, had been a long process. First, they extracted from the earth and then boiled spruce roots These were used to lace the canoe together and, in another process, render the glue to seal gaps. A boy, he had been set many of these arduous tasks, especially tedious stretches of digging and then tending the boiling roots, feeding the fire, and pulling lengths out with tongs for the Elder's inspection.

Thibaut found himself sometimes wishing that he'd had more practice with this wise teacher, a man who was far more patient than his father. He had a sense that learning such crafts would remain useful despite all the new tools and materials that were entering his world from the mysterious other side of the ocean. He--and his father-- had been hoping to continue to learn more.

When winter approached, the old master retreated into the southern forests with the rest of his band. Thibaut and his father had eagerly awaited spring and the customary return of that band, but a new pestilence ran, a wildfire rekindled, along the shores of *Kitcikanii sipi*. By summer, it was clear that the wise one and his band would not return.

After Thibaut returned home, it did not take long to repair the *chaloupe*. Relieved, he'd set out to Tadoussac to carry the news to the fisherman who wanted it.

About halfway to the fort, he met the fisherman, M. Gaulin, whom he remembered. The fisherman, who had two helpers with him, was ready to begin a tirade, but Thibaut cut him short by giving him the welcome news that the project had been completed.

"Well, at last! I've lost nearly half the season now. I've had to sail along with another man and have cut my profit in half. Your father and I shall have some hot words when I arrive, but I guess I can spare you all that, young fella. "

M. Gaulin had known Thibaut since his father had brought him home. The community of fishermen on the river was not large. Everyone knew everyone else. His father and Gaulin had even worked together years ago in Port Toulouse.

"I hope you are going to stay home now, son. Your father isn't getting any younger, damn him, but if he's going to go on pretending he's still *un charpentier naval,* you need to stay home and do the work for the old reprobate. "

Thibaut was relieved the encounter was civil. However, when Monsieur Gaulin assumed he would retrace his path beside them, he explained he had other business in Tadoussac, and he must continue on.

"Don't get distracted there and run off again! It's been good to see you alive and well, my boy. Watch your back with the army though, and don't let them talk you into hunting Iroquois with them. "

Thibaut smiled, nodded, and declared that he knew how to stay clear of the soldiers. A few more interchanges and they were all traveling their separate ways. Gaulin and his men headed north to Babin's cove, while Thibaut continued on his way to the fort.

When he arrived, he didn't enter the stockade but went straight down to the water's edge. He avoided, as much as he could, the ruined, gutted carcasses of the pretty little whales and the stink, blood, and smoking fires that surrounded the oil rendering. He scanned the shoreline. He hoped to find someone who might be sailing west toward Quebec and needed another hand.

Everyone seemed to be engaged in fishing, but he kept searching. Around sundown he spotted two men sitting by a campfire. As he drew closer, he thought he recognized the elder of the two. He approached, saluting them as he neared not wanting to seem threatening in the fading light.

"Camarades Marins! Puis-je vous rejoindre? Je m'appelle Thibaut Babin. "

"Babin? Babin, you say? Simon's boy?"

Thibaut entered the ring of firelight, doffing his cap to the greybeard.

"Yes, sir. Indeed I am. "

"Well, well, time flies. You were just a stripling when I last saw you. Come, come sit with us. Share the news. "

Ready to sit anyway, whatever this conversation brought, Thibaut joined them all while wracking his brain for the old fisherman's name.

Rateau? Raveau? Rivet?

He was fortunate, however, in that the younger one stood and said, "You aren't looking to go west are you? We are in need of a third to manage our boat. "

"I am heading for Quebec. "

"Ah, Rivet my friend! You have the devil's own luck! We've been sitting here with our cargo for the last three days, but the French ship for Quebec, which left about a week ago, has taken off all men available. "

"We ourselves are headed to *Ville Marie*. You are welcome to sail with us there, too, if you wish. "

"I thank you for the offer, Monsieur Rivet, for I am most anxious to head west, but only as far as Quebec. "

"Well," Rivet said smiling above his grizzled beard, "Perhaps you will discover that you must continue. We never know where we will end up once we take to the water! Eh? We shall be in that city for a few days while we unload, and you can make up your mind. "

"What happened to your third man?" Thibaut asked after he'd agreed.

"*Le salaud*? That useless scum? I caught him stealing! Poire here sent him off with a kick. "

He sailed toward Quebec, doing the work he knew so well aboard a *chaloupe*. He steered, trimmed the sail, and he kept watch, his eye out for would-be bandits. In fact, he'd had to take a shot at one of them. He'd missed his on-board targets, but luckily he'd managed to put a big hole in their longboat's bow at the waterline. That was sufficient to persuade those would-be assailants to turn back.

Even as he approached his destination, he had a sense of foreboding. He was tired after his last watch, completed during darkness, the most dangerous hours for attacks.

Now, the sun was out, and the breeze was fresh and brisk. He curled up near the bow and pulled his cap down over his eyes.

There wasn't a lot of room aboard because the ship was fully loaded with barrels and boxes. Sleep, necessarily in a fetal position between boxes, wasn't always easy. Thibaut was worn out, however, and the river was smooth, so there was only the persistent tacking back and forth as the little craft struggled upriver against the current.

He did sleep, dreamless at first, although sometimes he came near the surface hearing the voices of his shipmates or the sharp slap of the bow sail. Then, at last, he fell deeper.

He had reached Quebec and was hurrying up the slope to the trading post. The path seemed to stretch away endlessly before him and he was wandering among a sea of huts and cabins, all of which appeared to be empty.

At the door of one, Bonne sat on a stool at work with her drop spindle and a basket of wool. She called out to him.

"Thibaut! Where are you going? Your Papa is looking for you."

"I must find Jeanne," he'd said. "Then I will return. "

The trading post had been directly ahead when he'd started to walk, but now he couldn't find it no matter how high he climbed or how many huts he passed.

If only he could see a familiar face to ask the way! Where was everyone?

He awoke to the noisy luffing of the foresail and the curses of Rivet as he hauled on the bowline. Poire, now at the helm, had steered too close to windward. The heavily loaded vessel staggered against wind and current.

"Damn it, man! Watch what you're doing will you?"

Thibaut's body ached, especially his legs. He tried to stretch them a little before standing, remembering to remain bent over to avoid the boom. When he reached a place where he could straighten, he saw, from the shape of the next tall headland, that they were now approaching their destination.

It seemed to take forever to travel those last few miles and drop anchor in the shallows. Boys came out in rowboats offering them passage ashore. They would have to post their arrival -- who they were and where they were from -- with the military harbor master.

Rivet had seen how anxious to pursue his business here Thibaut was and allowed him to go ashore beside him. As they were rowed in, they could see a young man walking down the slope carrying a logbook under his arm.

"If any of my business partners happen to be here, I will need you to help us in moving our freight. "

"Certainly, Monsieur Rivet. I only wish to visit the trading post quickly. I can take a Notice of Arrival there for you. "

As he ascended the hill, the dream remained on his mind. He was pleased that so far everything seemed ordinary, the port, not particularly busy, but here and there were groups of people. The little shops and storage buildings were all present exactly as they had been before.

At the de Couage trading post, he found a man behind the counter he knew, Giroux, *Canadien* born as he was. While the broadside with the ship's name and cargo was posted among a few others on the public board at the bar, Giroux began to tell some long tale about the adventures of one of the *Coureurs de bois* they both knew. Thibaut found he could barely understand a word.

"Perhaps, Giroux, you can tell me if Madam Jeanne Dube is in the house today?"

Giroux, a proper front man, black-bearded with an impressively wide body and impressive forearms, shook his head.

"If you had any interest there, Babin, forget it. That comely lady is now over the river in St. Marr's Seigneury. I hear she signed a marriage contract with Monsieur

Fleury, a mason who has been building a mill. "

"Married?"

"Apparently, or de Couage would have never let her travel with him. "

Thibaut hoped his shock did not show, but it must have. Giroux, without another word, poured a small shot of brandy and solemnly placed it on the counter between them.

"Here, *ami errant*. On me."

Thibaut surprised himself by nodding, picking it up, and downing the burning fluid. With his father in mind, he rarely drank alcohol.

"Ah, never mind, Babin. Those Frenchmen always get the pretty ones. "

Thibaut did not linger. He put the glass down, thanked Giroux and returned to the waterside. He went back to work with Rivet and Poire after he intercepted them rowing in with a load of merchandise destined for Quebec buyers, one of whom was already pacing back and forth near the shore. This kept him busy, but his mind was occupied with the history of the winter past, the part before he'd gone with the soldiers.

He'd said too little, had not put himself forward. Jeanne was a clever woman, one who knew how to make her way, one who'd resolved herself to what life here would be, that he'd understood. Part of him was bitter, thankful that he'd said no more to her, for it would have hurt his pride to be rejected.

That was vanity, he knew. Another part of him, a deep-down inner part, felt sorrow.

About two weeks later, he arrived at the cove on the Saguenay again where he was greeted with anger from his father, whose feelings had been hurt. There were many accusations of disloyalty and dishonesty, the last of which he humbly accepted and apologized for. He promised all and sundry that he would not leave them again but would stay like a good son and support the family enterprise.

He kept that promise until the following spring soon after his father died of what Bonne called apoplexy. When Thibaut left, he said a proper farewell. His last view of the cove was of Bonne and Paul Surette, who had grown close over the winter in the course of his father's final illness, standing together alongside his half-grown sisters on the rocky shore. In New France, there were few widows that remained so for long. In this dangerous wilderness, women had to protect themselves and their children as best they could.

Chapter 8

Thibaut was weary of the endless fighting. He'd done too much of it, seen too much slaughter and cruelty.

For a time, after his father's death, hoping for a new life elsewhere, he'd left the Saguenay and had headed west along the old trade route up the Ottawa and onto the Great Lakes.

To his dismay, the land that had once held thriving Huron villages was now empty, the great stockades burned out, their gardens returning to tall grasses and scrub. Instead of the busy towns he remembered, there were only broken palisades and scattered bones. It appeared the Iroquois had utterly destroyed the people who had lived here.

The particulars he'd learned over time. After many waves of pestilence had come to break the Huron, the ever-warring Iroquois, in their quest to control the fur trade, had finished the job. Most survivors had fled, some to the south, others to the west.

Thibaut lived for the next year south of the lake with a wandering band of families, the remains of an Ojibwe clan, cousins of the

Huron, who'd once lived on *Mnidoo Mnis*, Island of the Great Spirit. This once-thriving, happy place was now barren, empty as it had been before Manitou had set the first people down there.

Thibaut had joined this group, following game, fishing or gathering wherever they could find in a ravaged land, avoiding the ever-encroaching white men and Iroquois war parties alike. He felt happy with these people and they accepted him. Here he soon found a new family, a young widow, Swallow-on-a-Reed, and her two boys.

He'd done what his father believed he'd beat out of him: returned to the life *sauvage*. He helped build canoes for the group and was beginning a small raft with a sail, for they'd planned to float down river to the Ohio in hopes of rejoining others like themselves who'd survived the holocaust.

Then came the dreadful day when he returned to camp after a few days away hunting to find only a smoking ruin, blood, and torn bodies. Among the dead he found his lovely Swallow-on-a-Reed and her sons. He could see that they'd fought to the last, refusing to be taken prisoner.

This latest loss nearly broke him. All he could see, as he howled into an ominous cloud-filled sky was a terrible, never-ending cycle of love and peace inevitably followed by violence, heart-rending loss, and despair. Meanwhile, the storm he'd returned to camp to avoid began to break with a mighty gust of wind and a full-force fall of rain. He dropped the deer he'd so proudly returned with and raced into the forest. All he knew was a red-hot desire for revenge.

He would follow the trail of these retreating monsters, left so carelessly behind, a last gesture of contempt for the people they'd slain, as if no one still lived to avenge them! He swore he would kill as many Iroquois as he could and then proudly die, the only refuge for a man so accursed.

He ran through the forest, only pausing to be certain of the tracks, rain pelting him, until he could see the bosom of *Ontari:io*, dark and white-capped beneath the wind. He could see the small figures of those he sought, moving slowly, a war party that felt perfectly safe as they walked into the tall-grass prairie that stretched toward the shore.

Then, as he rushed after them, at the empty crest of a hill, came an exploding body blow of light. Staggering, seeing nothing but shattering white, Thibaut was, in an instant, blinded, burned, stabbed to the heart.

***

When he came to, he was shaking and soaked, face down in a tangle of branches and leaves, face down among the ferns. For a moment, he thought he was dead and that this place, with its overwhelming scent of sulphur, crushed herbs, and wet wood, must be the beginning of whatever was to come

319

next. His head ached fiercely; he lay motionless and let the rain fall.

When he opened his eyes again, he was wracked with cold. His teeth chattered painfully. Memory returned, but when he tried to rouse himself, he couldn't.

"Be still, my friend. "

He could not tell who had spoken, but the tongue was Ojibwe.

Once more, darkness closed his eyes.

When he awoke next, he lay on his back. A crackling fire shone upon a dome of green branches. He smelled tobacco, rain, and the sweat of another man.

More sleep. Then, much later, the scent of cooking meat and a gleam of morning light. He found he could turn his head and was greeted by a view of his companion, kneeling by the fire.

It was a young Ojibwe from his band, another who had been away hunting. He would learn later that this youngster, Tall Boy, had returned to the ruined camp just as Thibaut had gone crashing into the forest. He'd followed the same trail Thibaut had followed, and had also been caught in the storm.

When Thibaut finally managed to rouse himself sufficiently to rise on one elbow, it appeared to be another morning. His whole body ached, particularly his chest.

After he'd gratefully drunk rainwater and eaten a little of the rabbit Tall Boy had snared, he'd said, "We have to return to the camp to honor our friends. "

"Not yet, " Tall Boy said. "You have been struck by the Thunderer. You still may die. So my Uncle has taught me. "

"What? Lightning? No. It was a tree limb, I think."

"I saw it happen. You bear the Thunderer's mark on your breast. "

Tall Boy had risen from his squat and went to pull aside one of the branches, letting in a sharp daylight that hurt Thibaut's eyes. Unsteadily, he used one hand to lift the worn hemp shirt he'd brought with him when he'd left Quebec.

Even through his tanned flesh, he saw the marks of The Power that had ended his chase. Spreading branches of red grew like a tree across his bosom, following the veins.

Had his heart's blood tried to leap from his body?

Stunned, head heavy again, Thibaut collapsed back onto the ground. His heart, like a trapped bird, fluttered against his ribs.

Two days later, Thibaut was able to walk, so they made their return. The circling birds and the tracks of scavengers large and small told them all they needed to know of what had happened to the bodies of their companions.

Tall Boy sank onto his heels and covered his eyes. Thibaut kept his feet, but he felt dizzy, sick.

It was too late to erect a platform for the dead. The creatures of Sky and Earth had already taken them.

They entered the clearing slowly. Not much of their friends' bodies remained. Corpses were strewn about, clothing torn to rags. After driving off the most aggressive of the birds, the vultures, they'd gathered whatever had once been human into a pile. Whatever gnawed skulls they found, they placed together, all turned to face West. Together, they'd prayed that the souls of their companions might yet find their way to the lodge of the beneficent Iouskeha Sun Face and his mother, Earth Woman, Aataentsic. They'd prayed that although their friends had died by violence, they might nevertheless be welcomed into the house of the dead. They'd wept as they'd asked for this favor, because dying in such a dreadful manner was said to condemn the souls to forever wander. They'd offered the last of their tobacco to the souls and to any angry spirits that might hover nearby.

After that was done, it was twilight. They left the gruesome scene of the massacre, then stripped and washed in the creek. They decided to sleep right there, by the water. It was not wise to linger longer in the area, but tonight neither man much cared what happened to them.

Chapter 9

Thibaut traveled beside a creek with a scattered detachment of soldiers, battle-hardened backwoodsmen, conducting a careful sweep through the ground. He'd become attached to a company from Montreal who'd been set to patrol along the southern shore of the river, an area filled with small farms which had been continually ravaged by Iroquois attacks.

War, never-ending war, my chosen path! Until an arrow, a blazing metal ball, a knife or a tomahawk ends me.

Thibaut had drifted back to *Kitcikanii sipi*, but no longer thought of much but killing. He dreamed of slaughtering every Iroquois he found--as well as any Dutchman or Englishman--he found in their company. However, what he most constantly and avidly sought was his own death.

Tall Boy had left him long ago to travel west in hopes of joining other refugees from the massacres. Thibaut knew he owed his life to the young man but there was little he could do anymore to protect or aid him. Tall Boy had his own destiny; he wanted to find a band and the warmth of belonging, which was exactly what Thibaut no longer dared to imagine.

Thibaut believed he was cursed, that anyone who stayed too long in his company was doomed to a violent death. He had failed so many, even his father, for he'd left both the old man's bones and his family obligations behind.

More likely, he'd at last decided, he was cursed for no reason at all, for this world appeared to be a place of endless cruelty, greed, and madness. He could find no solace in what little he knew of his father's faith.

If God was good, all seeing, and all powerful, then why did he allow such things to happen?

His mother's beliefs, which he also understood imperfectly, seemed to say that although this world had starvation, war, and cruelty, it also had moments of overflowing happiness and beauty that fell upon a parched soul like rain. There was Dark and there was Light. Punishment came for no reason—as did Blessing. It was man's fate to endure whatever came.

That night in a dream he saw an old blind man, eyes gray with mist, sitting beneath an ancient tree. He and the tree were brown, in some parts covered with bright green moss, as if his crossed legs were also a part of the great trunk against which he leaned.

Thibaut remembered a saying he'd learned from his mother: "*Honor age! Even an old blind man may guide you to a rainbow.*"

He badly needed to find that rainbow. Even while asleep, his heart ached.

"You walk among the shadows, young man."

The ancient one looked so frail, as if he might expire with his next breath, yet his voice, now that he'd spoken, came strongly enough.

Thibaut tried to answer, to explain, but nothing came. All that lay on his heart was despair, rage, and pain, each like a gigantic stone he'd swallowed. Finally he said, "No matter how many I kill, my women and their children, my friends--they are all dead! I remain alive, hollowed out, an empty gourd. "

"Look around, young man. There is sunlight and it shines within her."

The dream ended; he jerked awake, sitting upright among the sleeping forms of his companions. It was still dark, but in the branches overhead, Thibaut heard stirring, and the soft muttering and twittering of birds waking up. Such a sweet sound!

The next day the party with whom he traveled passed through an area that had been attacked earlier in the year. He no longer paid much attention to where he was except for the map he continually built in his mind of the territory he'd traversed. Whatever people he fought beside, he barely heard their voices. Inside the voice in his head mostly spoke either Huron or Ojibwe. He didn't associate with the Frenchmen in the patrol any more than he had to.

He remembered when the old folks in his childhood band had spoken of the "days before the from-over-the-waters," and how life then had balance, routine. The winter was for sheltering, hunting, and sometimes starving. Winter might bring war parties, young braves searching for glory, killing members of other tribes among the snows. These days, war was unceasing, a constant among his people as well as those terrible pestilences no one knew how to cure--not the people who had brought them nor the native people who now died from them by the hundreds.

The more he thought about it, the more he felt that it was the whites who had, with their trade goods, their new weapons, with their insatiable lust for furs, changed everything. That was terrible to believe for he was half white himself! Here was yet another reason to decide that his life had no value. The whites didn't want him, and at times, neither did the *sauvage* with whom he now preferred to live. He was now forever a wanderer, a stranger, doomed to fight until he died.

All these dark thoughts were occupying him when he suddenly saw her standing in a dancing patch of sunlight--a woman in a patched, stained dress, her exposed arms almost as brown as his. She was beneath a trailing confusion of supple willow branches, her dress hiked up to her knees because she stood in a pool in the small creek. She stood very still, which was why he hadn't seen her immediately.

Suddenly, in flash, she stooped to seine the water with a loosely woven basket. This tool he recognized for it was used for fishing by many tribes.

When she stood upright again, he heard a fish flapping in the basket. He watched while she turned and came out of the water holding the basket up as it drained. The struggle within sounded louder.

"Fish!" A small voice speaking French came from one of the trees. His attention moved to something else he had not seen, this a bundle hanging from a bough--a bundle with fat sturdy legs and arms and a child's round, fair ahead.

"Mama got another!"

The woman continued up the bank, her brown feet wet upon the gnarled roots of the overhanging tree.

"Hush," she said. "We must be quiet, or the fish will know we are hunting them. "

The child was kicking now and swinging. She was on a cradle board, but one she'd long ago outgrown, now cut to allow her chubby legs to dangle loose.

"I want to go down!"

"Soon, Mathilde. I must catch more. "

"No! Now! Please, Maman. "

"Shhhh. The *sauvage*, sweetheart. We mustn't let them hear us. "

Thibaut, who'd been creeping closer, froze in place, but it was too late. He saw the little girl's eyes fix on him and open wide.

"Mama!"

The woman whirled around letting the seine with its silver catch fall to the earth. Her right hand thrust itself into her skirt pocket. Thibaut knew what she saw: an armed man in buckskin, his face streaked with black.

Thibaut held out his hands, palms forward, and said, "Do not fear, Madam. " French felt strange on his tongue, and he pronounced the words with care. "I am from Ville Marie, a scout for their soldiers. "

The woman's face had paled, as fear overcame her tan. In that frozen instant, he recognized her.

"Madame Jeanne! Is that you?"

An astonished pause followed.

"Thibaut? M. Babin?"

"Yes, Madame Jeanne. It is Thibaut Babin. " He stepped closer and extended a hand.

"Oh, thank *Le Bon Dieu*!" He saw tears spring into her eyes. "I--I thought you were dead. "

In a soldier's reflex, he noted that she removed the hand from her pocket. Certainly, she had a knife hidden there, and she'd been readying herself to use it.

As he approached, he saw she trembled. To hide her fear and calm herself, she turned to soothe her sobbing child.

When the sobbing quieted, he stepped nearer. The little one, released from the cradleboard, swiftly buried her face in her mother's wet, stained skirts. Jeanne leaned down, continued to stroke the child.

"I thought you were Iroquois. "

"No, Jeanne. I hunt and kill those rattlesnakes every day of my life. "

He saw her suck in another deep breath still trying to quiet her racing heart.

She has seen terrible things. . .

"Come. I will take you to your *Ville.* "

The child, her face flushed and now streaked with tears, peeped at him then immediately turned away though not fast enough to prevent him from seeing the terror in her eyes. Thibaut bent to gather the fallen fish and pull up the stringer.

"You should not be out here alone. "

"I am good at catching fish, M. Babin, and these are for supper. Many from our ville are now dead, and there is not much time left to prepare for winter. We are either in the fields or out looking for food."

They began to walk. Thibaut found he had questions he dearly wished to ask.

Instead, he asked if any of their crops had been spared.

"Some, though much of it was burned. The Iroquois were driven off quickly because we were lucky. There were Huron hunters camped near us, and we had broken bread with them the night before. They were the ones who raised the alarm. Soldiers, on their way to their homes for the harvest, chanced to also be paddling by. They, too, came to our aid."

Jeanne stopped and faced him.

"It could have been worse, but. . . it was bad enough." Her dark eyes filled. Her child, now riding her hip, kept her face hidden from Thibaut's curious gaze.

He knew the look in Jeanne's eyes. She had stared into the abyss, into the same darkness he knew only too well.

When they arrived at the stockade and went inside, there was already a host of soldiers all wearing blue sashes. Some, weary, sat on stumps and others on the ground, leaning their heads against their weapons.

Jeanne saw Noelle and Belinha carrying out a heavy three-footed pot of whatever was available, probably turnip and pea soup. The new arrivals looked at it hopefully.

"Pardon, Madame, but I see there is food," Thibaut said.

"Please eat," Jeanne replied. "We always share what we have."

Soldiers were always hungry.

"I hope we will speak more, Madame, before we go on our way. "

"I am very happy to see you here and alive, old friend. I--I wish to talk, too, for where have you been these last years?"

"I was at Saguenay until my father died, then I went West. "

"For trade?"

"No. There is nothing but war everywhere. Today, I fight here, along *La Grande Riviere.* "

"I am sorry for it, but that is what our life is now. "

He nodded but did not leave. Instead, he stood studying her.

"Is your husband kind?"

"He was. He died just as May came in, in the first raid. "

Thibaut nodded slowly. His dark eyes regarded her in a way that showed not only sympathy, but understanding.

He looks like a skeleton.

"You are a widow now, just as you were when we first met. "

Jeanne nodded a "yes," at the same time remembering the story he'd told her about his own young family and how an Iroquois war party had murdered them.

"I am sorry to hear this. "

"Thank you, Babin. It is ever so good to see you again! I thought you had died, my friend. "

Thibaut looked at her in silence. Clearly, even beneath the black war paint, he felt some powerful emotion.

From the steps of a great stone house, a woman waved her arms and called. "Madame Jeanne! Did you catch any fish?"

Jeanne slowly turned away and walked toward the big stone house with her child and the small string of fish Thibaut had wordlessly handed to her. She tried to focus on what she had to do--clean the fish and help with supper. She wished she'd caught more, especially with this crowd of men inside the stockade.

As she settled Mathilde with one of the Renaud girls who'd been peeling turnips in the kitchen, emotions she'd been trying to fight against began to rise. Suddenly, she was blinking back tears.

Fleury--kind, generous, warm. . . He'd been murdered with two others who'd been at work cutting stone near the mill. All three who'd been early at work that day were now beneath the earth. They'd died in the pink light of a windy, chilly May dawn.

His death still didn't seem real. Everything had changed so fast, so unexpectedly. The later raid, in July, had done more damage to their crops and caused yet more deaths among the villagers. Those already in the fields who managed to run into the stockade had survived. Others had fled to the creek where they'd called for help to the men who'd happened to be paddling by.

Slowly, to steady her mind, Jeanne picked up a fillet knife and began to work on the fish she'd caught. At this task, she mustn't lose her concentration! She knew she needed to stay well and strong, and not to cut her fingers and risk infection from this devil of a knife.

The evening was spent in a flurry of cooking, serving, hasty eating, and cleaning up afterward. Mathilde was whiny and anxious, clinging to her mother's skirts like a mussel onto a rock.

Jeanne knew her daughter missed her father, his warm presence in her life. Luc had worked long, hard hours every day, but he'd always made time to hold and cosset his new daughter. He'd often eaten while holding Mathilde on his knee, all the while responding to her chatter and feeding her tidbits from his dish. His affection provided some evening relief to Jeanne, who was then able to eat a meal in peace.

After the clean-up from supper was completed, she'd caught sight of Thibaut among *les Indiens* seated around their own campfire. She had, after all, initially mistaken him for one of them. She wondered if he had now rejoined his mother's people. She'd hesitated to seek him out there.

Then as she'd been wondering what course to take, she had been distracted by a squabble among the children that had left Mathilde wailing. Afterward, she'd taken her daughter home where she'd discovered that the officer in charge of the soldiers had asked if he could quarter a pair of his men with her overnight.

Slender Helene had been bravely guarding the stoop, waiting for her mistress to return and make the decision.The beds in her stone house were as full as ever. Jeanne now shared it with her servant, Helene, as well as Mathilde. The loft was also crowded. A widowed woman, Madame Rose, had lost her husband and her eldest son in the July attack. Now, she and her three surviving children slept in the loft. Poor Hebert had died beside Luc, his master, back in May. Here was yet another grief their family shared.

Tonight, two soldiers slept in the house too, their feet toward the hearth, snoring like bears. When they'd entered, Jeanne had laid down the law about what was permitted in her house—no spitting on the floors or into the fire. They would have to get up and go out to urinate too. "Away from the door, please!"

Jeanne knew she would fall asleep despite the unusual noises in the house but found that at first she couldn't. The events of the day--and the fraught weeks past-- replayed themselves. In her mind, hoping to calm herself, she repeated prayers for the soul of her husband, a good man she had not loved as deeply as she believed a wife should.

Tonight, there were also disturbing thoughts about Thibaut and his sudden appearance in the *Ville*. For so long she'd believed him dead, and had resigned him to the past. Now, emotions she thought long buried--emotions that she knew should be loathsome to a widow who truly grieved, stirred, forcing their way upward from within the deep, hidden part of her mind in which she'd buried them. She'd tried to make them go away, but they wouldn't.

Thibaut! There he was again today, older, gaunt, and weathered like one of the Algonquian warriors. His brown eyes had given far more away than she'd seen in them before. When he'd recognized her, he'd looked like a man shaken out of a long, hard sleep to something--*miraculous*.

Mathilde and Helene were already asleep, and seeing them there so peaceful, Jeanne thought she should join them even if her mind was whirling. When she'd slid beneath the covers, the aches and pains of the day's labors let her know how much she needed to rest, to get warm, despite the turmoil in her heart.

The scent of her sleeping daughter, her lips slightly parted, breath coming and going evenly, her fair flesh, as well as the strong scent of the soap Helene had used to get her clean, was comforting. How she had embraced her and allowed the child's sleep to carry her off as well during the weeks after Luc had died!

She awoke, still in the dark, to the sound of one of the soldiers going out the door to make water. All the chaos of the day before came rushing back. Abruptly conscious, she waited until she heard the soldier return and settle himself in front of the fire again before she began to move, slowly making her way out of the bed and through the closed curtains.

The hearth fire had reduced to an ashy blue and red, embers crinkling. She could see the forms of the soldiers wrapped in their coats, heads resting against their packs. One snored, and the one who had risen, seemed, from his steady breathing, to have already fallen asleep again. It had been obvious how exhausted these men were.

When she reached the door, she slipped her feet into clogs, took her shawl from a hook, and went out as quietly as possible. Soon she was standing on the stoop in the chilly purple light just before dawn. It was nearly the end of September and already very cold before the sun rose.

The late stars still shone brightly, although trailing blue smoke of the campfires and chimneys drifted above in the silence.

Stars, stars, stars, sparkling like the ice that would soon envelope all living things...

In the spring of their first year together, Luc had set a long stone stoop for the house. Later, during the summer, he'd built a long wooden bench and set it there too. Jeanne and her husband had often sat here in quiet summer evenings after Mathilde was asleep.

Jeanne took a step or two along the cold stone before she sat. Memory stirred strong emotions. There was grief as well as fear about her uncertain future, but there was also warmth and a sharp shard of anticipation she hardly dared name.

Happiness! That was not something she'd felt often since long ago before her son had died. There had been days of happiness here, too, watching Mathilde grow and learn. Or, sometimes, with Fleury, whose regard and decency had warmed her, that had given her courage again, but so much of her marriage had been--and she'd always known it--gratitude to him for his care for her and for his kindness.

In France, she'd been served a full portion of contempt and disregard, but now she understood that she deserved far more. Here, in this untamed, dangerous place, she'd found people who looked upon her as a comrade, who smiled at her, who helped her. They were thankful for her, her hard work, her kindness, and her willingness to learn from everyone no matter how lowly their station.

The cold began to gnaw at her; for though she'd taken a shawl, she was only in a woollen shift. At supper, she'd looked in vain for Thibaut. After the clean-up was completed, she'd caught sight of him outside among *les Indiens* seated around their own campfire. She had, after all, initially mistaken him for one of them.

The sky was beautiful, but she was growing colder by the minute. After visiting the necessary, she crept back into the house and into her bed, the patch where she'd lain still warm. Closing her eyes, she began to recite the rosary, hoping to shut out all other thoughts.

She became conscious again as the light came up. She crept out from under the blankets, leaving Mathilde and Helene rolled away toward the wall together, still dreaming. Slipping across the room, past the still-snoring soldiers, she kicked into her clogs, grabbed a shawl, and went outside.

It was not yet full light, but the stars had faded. It wouldn't be long now until the sun rose. Standing on the stoop, she sighed, stretched, and noted the groan of the outer gate of the stockade as someone went out. She decided that she would go out too, walk down to the creek and see if the fyke net she'd set up yesterday contained any eels. This was a good time of year to catch them as they traveled by night.

I can walk down quickly, check, and then come back to help milk the cows.

So that's what she did, nodding to the sleepy soldiers leaning about the gate as she passed. A cow, one who had gotten loose from the pen, followed along. This animal wanted to get a drink in the morning first thing before she was milked and she was, unlike some of the others, quite fond of the company of people.

The cow ambled onward to lower her head to the water at the first level spot. Jeanne continued farther, finally heading down a steeper slope to the bank beneath the aspens, the place with all the trailing willows, to the pool in which she'd been fishing yesterday. The water was fairly deep after the heavy rain of a week ago although it had slowed and cleared now. Here, she leaned against a tree trunk to remove her clogs. Next, she unrolled her stockings, draping them over a branch.

She hiked up her skirt and, with an anticipatory shudder, waded slowly into the icy water to take a look at the fyke net. The bottom of the pool was full of silt. In places, the rocks were slippery beneath her feet, so she had to be careful.

Beyond the neutral shade beneath the trees, she saw the sun come up brightening everything. A gap in scattered clouds sent a shaft of light to illuminate the pool, transforming it into a shining mirror so bright she couldn't look into it. Despite her chilly feet and legs, she could feel the sun strike her with welcome warmth.

Instinctively, she raised her arms to it, drew a deep breath, and closed her eyes. For a moment, she could forget all her questions, fears, and sorrows, and just feel the light, chill breeze of morning all around.

"Madame Jeanne!"

The sound of his voice brought her back to herself. She turned and saw Thibaut, no more than a shadow beneath the trees. He stepped to the edge of the bank, appearing much diminished from the man she remembered. Now he wore only a ragged shirt and his buckskin trousers.

When he came into the light, she saw that the sad countenance of yesterday had brightened a little.

"*Bonjour*, M. Babin. I wanted to find you after supper, but you were at the campfire. . ."

"I hoped to find you this morning. M. Vallee said he'd seen a woman go this way. "

"I am very glad to see you again. " The net was forgotten, she turned and waded towards him. By the time she'd come close, he'd removed his moccasins and stepped into the water. He extended a hand to help her up.

"Please, sir, take a moment if you can, for we can speak privately. "

When they stood on the bank together, she braved asking the question that, for the last three years, she'd wanted to ask. The one that had troubled her ever since he'd departed that winter, leaving her at the trading post so full of hope and expectation.

"I don't know if it is fair to ask you after so much time, but all those years ago, I did hope you would return, M. Babin. I thought you would be in Quebec by spring, and I asked so many of those who knew you where they thought you might have gone, but no one knew what to tell me. "

There was a pause because she'd begun with so much, but at last, he replied.

"I went with the soldiers from *Trois Riviere* to hunt our enemies along *La Grande Riviere*. When they disbanded, we were within a few days of Tadoussac, my home place. I returned to my father's house, and there I found him failing, so I remained to help set things in order. "

"Summer came, M. Babin, but you did not return. Then, M. Fleury came to me with a proposal of marriage. I visited here and stayed for a time to understand what kind of life he offered. "

"And you remained as his wife. " Thibaut looked down. His expression was grave.

"I returned to Quebec, sir, where Madame de Couage had a difficult lying-in, and because of that, I remained with her for six weeks or more, but still you had not returned. Near the end of August, I signed the marriage contract with M. Fleury. I have been here ever since. "

All this poured out of her. She'd waited so long to explain herself even though it now seemed there was nothing, really, to explain.

He nodded, understanding. Had his long-ago slip into the familiar--that *tu*--into which she'd crazily written so much--been a simple mistake? She had sometimes thought so and had finally decided that as Thibaut had not returned, he had not meant it in the way she'd hoped. After all, simply wishing he loved her did not make it true!

"And now M. Fleury is dead and you have a little daughter. "

"Yes, my poor, brave husband has been dead for four months. I have Mathilde, and--and—work to do here. "

A long silence followed.

Jeanne, unable to bear that he still had not explained what he'd felt—if anything--said the first thing that came into her mind, all the while hoping he might say more.

"It is different to raise a girl. Mathilde is not at all like my Michel. "

Another long pause followed. She'd almost given up hope when Thibaut spoke once more. He did so deliberately, but what he said chilled her to the bone.

"I had sons, too. But they are dead now--all of them, dead. "

In the distance, they heard the desperate scream of a rabbit, a forlorn shriek as something, perhaps a hawk, seized upon it. It made them both look around.

"You told me about your boys, about your wife, and how they were lost when the Iroquois raiders came. I remember it well. Now--now—those same enemies have also killed my husband. "

From the look that washed across his face, Jeanne realized that her companion had suffered, too, but a newer, equally heart-breaking loss.

"I returned to Quebec, but the summer was nearly gone. " Thibaut began slowly, "You were here, across the river. A man I knew at the trading post said you'd married a Frenchman, so—so--I went home and stayed with my father until he died, near winter's end. After the ice broke, I traveled West, looking for friends I had once known among the Huron. "

"Did you find them?"

He did not answer, only shook his head and looked away, across the water. She knew that the man beside her was living on the edge, nearly overcome with his memories. When he suddenly turned away, as if to leave her, she sprang into action seizing his arm with every ounce of strength she possessed.

Do not let him go! Not again!

"Please, Thibaut--*mon ami*! Please tell me what has happened to you! I told you how I came to be here! Please, tell me where you have been-- for--for--I fear your heart has again been broken. "

They stood, now locked together, their breath coming fast.

"Ah, Jeanne! I am changed man from when you knew me. Vengeance is all that I now am, for I am a man who has killed and killed and who must go on killing until his own death finds him. Blood calls out for blood! That is the law of this land, and that is all there is now for me."

"But you were not so! You were a gentleman, kind and patient with me, a foolish, lonely woman, a stranger."

He did not try to pull away. Jeanne could hear her own heart, pounding in her throat. The early sunlight had vanished, suddenly obscured beneath a wave of clouds.

"As I said yesterday, the Huron and the Wendat towns are gone. Our enemy is everywhere. I--I was almost happy for a time with a band of Ojibwe and Huron who'd escaped the fury of the Iroquois. I lived with a widow who had two fine sons, but on a day when I was hunting, the Iroquois found them. They killed her, her children, and all my friends, all except for a single young warrior. Together we pursued our enemies, but I was...wounded. My companion saved me. Before the snow fell, he went away, south, to search for any who might remain of his tribe. I made my way back to *Rivière des Outaouais--Odawaa*--then down to *Kitcikanii sipi*. I have fought the Iroquois and their white allies almost every day since."

"Ah, M. Thibaut! What you have endured! *Quel mal t'a affligé.*"

He did not answer, only closed his eyes, seeming lost in anguish. She waited some time before attempting to engage him again, but she did not let go of his sleeve.

"I have heard stories from travelers and from our Huron friends, the few who still live with us here. Many have fled to Île d'Orléans. I know Quebec itself is in danger and that people from *Ville Marie* have been killed or captured by the Iroquois. "

"My hands—as you French say, my soul--is soiled, covered, with blood. How can I ever be clean?"

He sighed deeply. Then, very gently, he removed her hands from his sleeve and gathered them into his.

"I cannot be saved, Jeanne. I must die. "

"Thibaut! No! "

Her words changed nothing. He lowered his head, kissed her hands, then released her and started to walk away. The pain of losing him again came near to felling her. Instead of freezing, accepting her fate, she ran to capture his arm.

"Don't go! You are here--alive! You have returned—just as you said you would. "

She clung to him with all her might. She could not see his face, only hear the sharp intake of his breath, feel the stiffness suddenly leave in his body.

"Don't go! Stay!"

He turned to face her. In that instant, the sun flashed down again. It puddled light around them illuminating the golden grove beyond.

Suddenly, his face brightened. He felt as if endless darkness had lifted. Thibaut wore a faraway look as if he remembered something.

Then he drew her close, and very gently, he kissed her forehead. Afterward, they simply held onto one another, heart to heart. To Jeanne, it felt as if the embers of a long-banked fire now burned in a single, pure flame.

EPILOGUE

Sunrise sped toward her across the broad surface of the river. All around, a host of birds made a mighty chorus. The geese and pigeons were flying, too, fleeting dark clouds that sometimes nearly blotted out the light. Jeanne stood on a point, beneath aspens, looking east over the La Grande Rivière.

She drew a deep breath of crisp morning air. It would take time, even in late August, for it to warm. Her husband was down by the shore bathing as was his custom. She knew he'd raise his arms to the rising sun and give thanks for another day. She took another deep breath and did the same, something she'd done regularly since they'd been reunited.

So much had happened in those years. Over that first winter, he'd stayed with her, in St. Marr's Villette. At first, it was understood that he was a fighting man who'd stayed behind to help them through the winter. In time, everyone understood that Thibaut was Jeanne's new man. When the priests had come through, near The Feast of the Nativity, to baptize children and to bless such living arrangements, they were married according to Catholic custom.

When the following summer arrived, they'd paddled away together to begin their lives anew. Mathilde had stayed behind, with Belinha, as there was much to do before they had a home again. Here, at the place where the creek met the river, near the great marsh, they found the land St. Marr had allotted them. A few others were there already; a single Huron refugee family and another family of émigrés who'd already settled.

The first season, Thibaut hunted and fished to keep them fed. For that, the marsh was an excellent provider. He and Jeanne labored together to build a little cabin. Jeanne had even managed to dig a garden patch and planted seeds and tubers she'd brought, ones that Belinha had given her. They became acquainted with more distant neighbors, others who also lived along the shore.

As autumn painted the aspens in glowing yellow, Jeanne had gone up the creek with a trader to fetch Mathilde. They'd barely returned when she gave birth to a sturdy boy they'd named Honore.

Later that same autumn, Jeanne received a messenger from Quebec who'd brought her an unexpected bounty. With his customary prudence, Luc Fleury had set aside her dower portion to provide for her in case he'd died. Here was her father's final blessing, some of which went to Thibaut for tools to properly begin his boat-building trade. He and their nearest neighbor, Christian Bouquet, joined forces to work together.

The business had slowly established itself. On this very day, they would launch a large *chaloupe*. Nautically speaking, it was a longboat, one equipped with a sail as well as oars like many of the same design often carried on large, ocean-going vessels, one that could be disassembled until needed. This would deliver goods from St. Marr's Villette—wines made from the wild grapes and berries that grew in abundance here as well as wheat, a cask of ale, and baskets of apples and pears--to Quebec City.

Today's new craft would also carry Mathilde, now grown into a sturdy fair-haired maid. Her daughter had married a river trader earlier in the year, an older man who made his home at Quebec and

who had often done business with the
Seigneury.

Mathilde's husband, M. Gilles
Ouellet, had arrived a few weeks earlier
to trade and had brought his young wife
along for a visit with her family before the
storms of autumn set in. Today, Jeanne
would again bid her eldest farewell,
waving good-bye from the stony shore in
company with her husband and their
children, Honore, Martin, Henri, and Iris
Marie.

The first three were named for an
important person in their lives: Honore,
one of the aristocratic St. Marr's many
given names; Martin, for Agathe's family;
Henri for Jeanne's father; and Iris for the
glorious iris bleu, a wildflower that
covered the landscape in early summer.
This last was a tribute to Thibaut's
mother, whose name, in her tongue, was
that of this same beautiful flower. Jeanne
had lost a baby, another boy, born after Iris,
but knew she had been blessed by the five
healthy children she had.

Thibaut saw his wife standing on the rise
and knew that she too had been greeting the
sunrise. He raised an arm in greeting as he
approached, and she waved back. Even from
this distance, he could see her smile, the
blessed smile of the woman who had saved

him, had given him a reason to live again. A little higher up, stood his home, a cabin set upon stone.

Their first dwelling, framed by the aspen grove, had been burned in a raid, but they had all survived to rebuild alongside several soldiers from the Regiment de Carignan-Salieres who had elected to stay after their term of service and work the land. That had been another hard spring, what with the children, loss of their possessions, and a late snowstorm.

Jeanne had wept over losing her small wooden trunk and the items from her past they contained: the small Testament in French that had come from her Huguenot grandparents, a toy ship Pierre had carved for Michel as well as locks from the hair of her first family. There had also been letters from Agathe, her father and her brother Aubin.

Despite the loss of the book, Jeanne had managed to teach the children their letters and numbers, how to add and subtract, and how to write their names. St. Marr, who'd been sufficiently gracious to be Honore's godfather, had provided them with pious tracts and even several chapbooks meant to instruct children with tales of history and stories of saints, even with a ledger for Jeanne to familiarize her children with the practicality of bookkeeping.

They'd lived through everything—the winters, the lean times, the times of danger -

- because of Thibaut's forethought and planning for just such events, as well as his ingrained habits of vigilance. Though the terror of that raid was not something he often wished to remember, he knew on that occasion his planning had saved them.

Afterward they'd been grateful for the help they'd received from their neighbors, the Bouquets, and to the soldiers who, over the last few years, had lifted some of the pressure of constant defense from the shoulders of the *habitants*. One, who had settled near, a M. Cadou, a veteran who had been quick to come to their defense during the raid.

Cadou had this year acquired a French wife from among the first *filles du roi* transported by the King's decree to marry and create a proper colony such as the English and the Dutch had established. Jeanne had taken this young woman under her wing for, although she was pretty, she had come from a Paris orphanage and wasn't used to physical labor. Worse, she hadn't the least idea of how to do the hard, rough farm work the frontier required of a settler's wife.

When this tender creature had first arrived, he knew Jeanne often found her in tears, overwhelmed by her situation and an impatient husband. The young wife was already pregnant, however, and with winter coming on, her life would become even more difficult if she couldn't find her feet as a *habitant's* wife, especially if Cadou continued his usual practice of hunting during the snowy months. Jeanne thought they might end up having to take the young woman in to help her get through this first winter.

When Thibaut reached where Jeanne stood, he stretched out his hands to her. As their fingers touched, he felt the welcome of her warmth. Those hands were tougher now though the flesh was not as leathery as his were from boat building, wood cutting and the like, but they were her hands—*my beloved.*

"*Mon cher mari.* " She greeted him so every morning. He understood she'd been wondering whether she herself might be carrying a baby who would be born next year. A kind of youthful foolishness had overtaken them during one warm afternoon that had ended in a rendezvous among the golden aspens.

If this proved to be a girl, she'd said they should name her 'Mélèze,' for the aspens, with, of course, a proper Saint's name added for her baptism. That had made him smile. Such a sweet secret!

Hand in hand they began to walk to the house. It was something they did nearly every fine day until the change of seasons, when the snow, the darkness, and the accompanying frigid onslaught made it impossible. As they approached, they heard goats making a ruckus in the shed and the voices of Martin and Iris Marie attempting to quiet them a little before moving them to pasture.

Mathilde would be setting up their breakfast, bread, perhaps a little smoked fish and some small beer. Honore was already outside, busy splitting kindling. Honore was the second man of the house now working with his father and helping to tend the land. Thibaut was proud of his sons and hoped to see them all become independent and raise families of their own.

The geese interrupted his thoughts with their own commotion. The queen among them came strutting forward, rattling her wings warningly, until Thibaut spoke sternly to her. Geese, his wife said, were almost as good as dogs at raising an alarm. When she'd first said that, long ago when they'd acquired their first pair, it had made him smile, reminding him of his stepmother, Bonne, who'd also placed a high value on her geese.

Raiders still came and went, but for some years now, they'd managed to avoid trouble, as their house was well-concealed behind that grove of aspens. Thibaut had had to take arms once more, several times, since their marriage, but he had never gone traveling away from her except short trips when he'd sailed across the river to Quebec or Montreal during summer to trade or at St. Marr's behest.

When they came in, however, they saw that Mathilde had thought that on her last morning here, breakfast should be special.

She had laid out goat cheese that she and Jeanne had prepared earlier in the week, fresh, bright tasting, and creamy, as well as blackberry preserves made with some precious sugar from the trading post.

The land was full of berries although they had to be careful because bears liked them too. It always was a toss up whether the human pickers or the bears would gather the most although a shot from a gun usually scared the unpredictable beasts away.

Although this meal was only breakfast, everyone was happy to see Mathilde's choices. Jeanne's eldest was also pregnant for the first time, rounder than ever, her fair face pink from the week's sunshine and this morning's fire. She didn't complain of any of the discomforts that other women often did during those early months, and this made Jeanne happy and optimistic that all would go well for her daughter, especially when her time came.

A little later, when they were all seated around the table, hands washed, the light meal set before them, Jeanne, with her husband beside her and all her children gathered around, felt supremely happy. Everyone was gazing at her expectantly, so she recited the simple prayer she'd learned long ago:

Bénis-nous, oh Seigneur, et ces cadeaux que nous sommes sur le point de recevoir de ta générosité. (Bless us, Oh Lord, and these thy gifts which we are about to receive of thy generosity.)

Just those few words summed up their life together. Looking around the table, Jeanne fairly glowed with happiness.

The End

Bibliography

Dechene, Louise. Habitants and Merchants in Seventeenth Century Montreal, McGill-Queen's University Press,1992

Fischer, David Hackett. Champlain's Dream, Simon & Schuster, 2008

Desrochers, Suzanne. Bride of New France: A Novel, WW Norton & Company, 2012

Lacoursiere, Jacques, Philpot, Robin. A People's History of Quebec, Baraka Books, Septentrion, translation, 1932

Websites:

The Canadian Encyclopedia

Mi'kmaq Nation

Gouvernement du Québec, Profiles of the Nations

Dear Reader. Reviews mean everything to an author. They determine the placement of the book, and thus how many potential readers will see the book. I will be so grateful if you will take a minute of your time and return to the online store where you purchased your copy, and leave, even just a two-line review. It doesn't matter how long the reviews are, just the star rating and a quick comment will suffice.   Thank you so much, Juliet

358

"Not all who wander are lost." Juliet Waldron earned a B. A. in English Literature, but has worked at jobs ranging from artist's model and scrub tech to brokerage. Thirty years ago, after her children left home, she dropped out of 9-5 and began to write, hoping to create a genuine time travel experience for herself as well as for her readers. She loves her grandkids, kitties, long hikes, bicycles and gardens. She reads mostly non-fiction history and archeology. For over a decade, she's reviewed for The Historical Novel Society as well as presenting writers' workshops at two HNS conventions. When she was eleven, her mother took her to Nevis to see the island where her hero, Alexander Hamilton was born. Now, on 21st Century summer mini-adventures, she rides behind her husband of 60+ years on his "Bucket List" Hayabusa motorcycle.

Other Novels by Juliet Waldron

Alexander Hamilton and Elizabeth Seymour
Hamilton, A Master Passion

The American Revolution Series
Genesee
Angel's Flight

***

The Mozart Series
Nightingale
My Mozart
The Intimate Mozart

***

The Magic Series (paranormal, historical, fantasy/adventure)

Magic Colors, Red
Zauberkraft
Magic Colors, Green

***

Pennsylvania Romance
Hand-me-Down Bride
Butterfly Bride

Jay Lang grew up on the ocean, splitting her time between Read Island and Vancouver Island before moving to Vancouver to work as a TV, film and commercial actress. Eventually she left the industry for a quieter life on a live-a-board boat, where she worked as a clothing designer for rock bands. Five years later she moved to Abbotsford to attend university. There, she fell in love with creative writing and wrote five novel manuscripts in a year. She spends her days hiking and drawing inspiration for her writing from nature.

Jay Lang books also published by BWL Publishing

Hush
Shatter
Shiver
Storm
The Cove
Impulse
The Immoral
Deadly Ties
Run Baby Run
Snake Oil
The Flying Dutchman
One Take Jake
One Take Jake: Last Call